I slept badly that night, what slee *by what the barman had said abo* *The words being woven into a violent dream.*

A dream of the traveller who sought shelter at the snow house of Erdlaversissoq; and while he slept she pricked a hole in his belly and dragged out his intestines as a treat for her dogs. I never saw the face of the traveller, his head was turned away from the flickering yellow light of the stone lamp.

But when Erdlaversissoq turned, blood dripping from her long white hands, I caught a glimpse of her face. It was the face of Hannah Dawson.

GHOSTS OF GREENLAND

John Templeton Smith served as a fighter pilot in Royal Air Force and was active in theatres of operations including the UK, Canada, the Middle East, Africa and the Far East before embarking on an adventurous career as a civil and commercial pilot that took him around the world. In 1978 he set a world record for the fastest solo trans-Atlantic crossing between Newfoundland and the UK that was verified by the *Guinness Book of Records*. Templeton Smith was encouraged to write by his friend Desmond Bagley, resulting in his first novel, *Skytrap*. In the mid-1980s he moved to the USA and lectured in Creative Writing at Oklahoma City University. During vacations, he travelled around South America and the Pacific Rim, including to Viet Nam. These travels served as research for the John Winter Trilogy. John Templeton Smith currently lives in Gibraltar. Silvertail Books will publish seven of his books: *Skytrap*, *White Lie* (John Winter Book 1), *Saigon Express* (John Winter book 2), *Then a Soldier* (John Winter Book 3), *Ghosts of Greenland* (originally published as *Patterson's Volunteers*), *The Fifth Freedom* and *Rolling Thunder*.

GHOSTS OF GREENLAND

JOHN TEMPLETON SMITH

SILVERTAIL BOOKS • *London*

This book is dedicated to the memory of Clark 'Woody' Woodard –
Legendary American ferry pilot who logged 40,000 flight hours and was
on his 353th trans-Oceanic crossing when he went down in the vicinity of
the Azores on September 16, 1996.
It was a distinct and enduring privilege to have shared that 'little acre' of
God's sky with so fine a gentleman and friend.

Sometimes gentle, sometimes capricious, sometimes awful,
never the same for two moments together; almost human in its passions,
almost spiritual in its tenderness, almost divine in its infinity ...
John Ruskin – *THE SKY*

In then, and with some luck, right out
Of your Greenland; but I'll never doubt
Your original toughness, and your shout
Against going down
Easily:
    That learn.

And as for being a Christian,
Missing America, and not having beer ...
Well, we're all unsettled, Sir, and later
Sir,
    Perhaps.

Francis Berry – *GHOSTS OF GREENLAND*

Author's note

It is documented fact that during World War Two a squadron of US warplanes disappeared whilst overflying the desolate icy wastes of eastern Greenland. It is also recorded by the Greenland authorities that a lone American came to Greenland's east coast the first summer after that war to search for the missing aircraft. The same American, always alone, returned for fourteen consecutive summers.

It was during the fifteenth summer that he, like the quarry he had sought for so long, also disappeared.

PART ONE

She shouldn't have died! Not then at least. Not in this place. McKenzie had come forward yelling the oxygen system had failed. I had pushed him into the right seat, telling him to take control, then gone back into the cramped cabin. After five minutes of frantic manipulation I knew it wasn't going to work. I took her left hand anyway. Just one miracle, God! Just one tiny lousy miracle. But I was praying to the wrong God. My God was not hers, and probably never would be.

Quite suddenly eight years of life had been stilled. The fever-flushed cheeks of an hour earlier had taken on the appearance of yellowed wax, which tightened across her face, smoothing out the premature age lines of a childhood in the high arctic. At the corner of her mouth, a trickle of blood had dried in a mask of infinite sadness.

Damn you O'Shaughnessy! Damn your rotten, stinking hide. Not that O'Shaughnessy would worry. He would just sit and count the money. As long as he was paid for the charter he would be happy. It wouldn't matter that he had lied to me about the oxygen system. The one which I had previously reported as unserviceable. The one he had assured me was fixed before sending me off on the medevac flight to Longstaff Bluff.

I looked down at the frail child. Her head was angled towards the cabin window; eyes wide and staring at a sky she did not see. I closed them then forever and made my way wearily back to the flight deck.

McKenzie watched as I settled into the left seat and refastened my harness. He was waiting for an explanation. The young, fresh-faced kid with the shining new pilot's licence would want to know why I had taken him on this trip. Why I had made him witness the final, pitiful struggles of a sick little girl as she fought for air from a system where none existed. His hand moved to his left pocket and produced a packet of Lucky Strikes.

'No smoking in my aeroplanes,' I snarled. 'I'm not too concerned with the state of your lungs, but I am concerned with my gyro instruments … the nicotine clogs the filters.'

He gave me a look of pure hatred and stuffed the Luckies back into his pocket. 'What about her?' he said unhappily.

3

I readjusted the heading on the auto-pilot before answering. 'She's dead.'

'I know that,' he said scathingly. 'I meant why did the oxygen system fail?'

'Why do most things in aircraft fail at one time or another? This is a tired old aeroplane with more flying hours under her belt than you or I will ever have.' I could have told him the truth, of course. Told him that his penny-pinching boss O'Shaughnessy was responsible. Told him that aeroplanes die too. Sometimes in a matter of seconds. Other times, like people growing old, little by little. But he wouldn't want to hear that. He would rather believe that I had failed to check out the aircraft thoroughly before departing from Frobisher Bay. In one respect he was probably right. But there hadn't been the time. The flight, an emergency, had come up as I was going off duty. That I had to accept O'Shaughnessy's word on the medical life-support system to ensure we got back in daylight hours was not an excuse. Not in McKenzie's book at least.

He made no further attempt at conversation, but just sat, staring sullenly through the windscreen. I tried to remember being as young as that, in an endeavour to get through to him. But it was too far to go. Too far through a world of missed opportunities and distant faces of equally distant people. It stopped abruptly somewhere south of Hanoi; at a watercolour picture of yellow morning skies, rice paddies, mud-brown rivers and the bamboo jungle which threatened the gathering of palm-shaded huts. But then it always did!

I shrugged myself back into the present and selected the radio to company frequency. I wanted O'Shaughnessy to be around when I landed. I wanted an explanation. The sun was already sinking in the afternoon sky as the HF radio crackled into life. Below, and as far as the eye could see, the northerly wind was lifting the dry snow off the tundra in a thin white fog.

We arrived at Frobisher an hour later, drifting down towards the two-thousand-foot-high wall of blowing snow. It looked a bad one. Surface wind out of the north at over forty knots. Visibility half a mile, and dropping by the minute. Temperature: twenty-eight below freezing. The Twin Otter rocked uncomfortably as we were suddenly swallowed up by the white, swirling blizzard. Through unseen gaps in the pilot's door and the eye-level air vents, minute particles of glittering ice crystals invaded the cockpit. I ignored the stabbing pinpricks as the 'diamond dust' thawed on my face and concentrated on flying the instruments. Simply a matter of watching the altimeter gently unwind, down the frozen floor of sky.

McKenzie was waiting, head up, for a visual sighting of the runway lights; and I was waiting for McKenzie. Waiting, watching the instruments, and being plagued by the desolate thoughts which crawl out of the woodwork from time to time. Thoughts of descending into the side of a mountain. Thoughts that the radio beams I was following down could be hopelessly wrong. In theory it wasn't possible. In practice, pilots had died believing in that theory.

We had long since passed our decision height. That was the height where you could pour on the power and get to hell out of it without hitting anything, and divert to another airport with better weather. In this frozen treeless wilderness, we had neither. As the arctic saying goes: 'You're either good – or good'n dead.' My hands tightened convulsively on the control yoke as the Otter rolled and pitched violently in the gale-force winds. One hundred feet the altimeter said. One hundred feet and we would hit something. Come on McKenzie; the lights! Call out the lights.

As if reading my mind, he did; at that exact moment. I looked up and saw them instantly; I also saw the wavy lines of tarmac between the drifting snow. Dig a wheel into one of those drifts on touchdown and we would end up coal mining where no coal existed. I eased the Otter down to about five feet off the deck and held her there. Steady, steady. Power levers back ... further ... further. Come on you bitch, slow up. Wrong word to use to a lady. She slowed up with a vengeance, the stall warning bleating in sympathy with the wing's loss of lift. We dropped and hit hard. McKenzie did nothing to conceal the sneer on his lips; the one that said he could have done it a thousand times better. The one that said I was over the hill.

The ambulance was waiting at the side of the old hangar as I swung the Otter around into wind and chopped the engines. I heard the rear passenger door open even before the propellers had stopped windmilling. Then the sound of boots being kicked on the steps to free them of surplus snow. The footsteps followed, bringing the swirling, bitter cold of the arctic in their wake. I knew it was O'Shaughnessy even before he spoke.

'What the bloody hell's going on?' he yelled. Meaning what was so important that I had requested he be waiting for the aircraft.

I carried on removing my headset and unclipping the seat harness. When that was done, I turned to face him. 'Same question I was going to ask you,' I said.

'And what's that supposed to mean?' He stared at me with his one good eye.

'Outside,' I said quietly, 'a private word.' Then to McKenzie: 'Help the medics with the child ... and don't forget the tech log.' He looked distinctly unhappy; a subordinate who disliked taking orders. The half-hearted nod was as much as I would get. One or two years from now if he lasted that long, he might begin to understand the ways of the North.

Outside the ice crystals beat a clicking tattoo on the airframe. Inside, a sound belonging to all pilots, the post-flight whine of fading gyros. From the open rear door, a faint smell of kerosene and hot engines caught up in the wind and snow. I struggled into my parka and moved back down to the cabin, back to the child. My hand went instinctively to her forehead, rekindling painful memories. I had witnessed death before, but each time it was a new, unwanted experience. I would never get used to it.

I pulled the fur hood tightly around my face and went out into the gathering darkness and the penetrating arctic cold. Even now, after all these years, I could feel my face contorting against the icy blast, feel my eyelashes turning to miniature icicles, see the puffs of breath freezing instantly on the edge of the parka hood.

O'Shaughnessy was waiting under the Otter's high wing; parka hood off, red hair flying like a tattered flag in the wind. His face had that grey, unhealthy look, the result of too many sunless days. But it was the eyes you noticed. The right one was glass. Big, round and staring. Both were unusually green, both colder than an arctic winter. It was the face of bitterness, a face that had forgotten how to smile. Not that he had always been that way. Some of the old-timers reckoned it was the crash all those years ago. The crash which had robbed him of his pilot's licence. That's how O'Shaughnessy would have viewed it anyway. Not the loss of the eye, the loss of his licence. That the two were compatible was something O'Shaughnessy had never come to grips with. I had met grounded pilots before. Acrimonious, lonely people. Millionaires who had suddenly become paupers. Few ever adjusted.

'The girl,' I shouted above the wind. 'She's dead.'

'So?'

'What the hell do you mean "so"? The oxygen system, you told me it was fixed.'

'Is that all?' O'Shaughnessy said impatiently. 'She was just a Husky.'

'She was just a child, you bastard. A helpless eight-year-old child.'

O'Shaughnessy gave a cynical laugh. 'A child you say ... a child! No bloody Eskimo is ever a child, they're all born a million years old, you should know that.'

I took a step nearer. 'I know nothing of the sort. What I do know, however, is that a child is dead thanks to your negligence.'

'Don't push it, Spence, you know the story as well as I do. You know how it used to be with these people. Out there hunting the caribou; and when the herd moved on the Eskimo would follow ... except they'd leave the sick and elderly behind. They had to move quick, right? So they left the sick and elderly behind to sit and die in the snow. And now you're going on about some Husky kid who didn't make it.'

'You're living in the past, O'Shaughnessy. That's why we're here. We can get them to hospital. They don't need to die now ... not any more.'

'Pangs of conscience is it, Spence ... past catching up with you? You know, for a guy who wiped out about a hundred kids at the press of a button ...'

He didn't get any further. His left eye registered the mistake as I hit him. Only once, but that was enough to fold him in two like a worn-out rag doll. He slid silently to the ground, clutching his stomach.

'Biggest mistake,' he gasped, 'biggest mistake ... you ever made.' He sucked in a lungful of icy air and started coughing. 'I'll have you Spence ... if it's the last thing I ever do.'

I left him writhing in the snow and made my way towards the hangar. Beneath my feet each footstep sounded like gentle tapping on a sheet of polystyrene. Or the gentle tapping of a drummer as he waited for the firing squad. And after the long snarl of rifles, nothing. Nothing but the arctic silence.

I was in the terminal building early next morning when I saw him. I turned back towards the window and the cup of steaming black coffee. Not that he had to be looking for me, but ever since last night I had had time to think. It had only taken me an hour to pack a lifetime's worth of belongings, and less than that to give up on the boot-leather steak. I'd needed the usual couple of bottles of Labatt to wash down the dust caused by the central heating system. All the rooming houses in the North are the same. You can go outside and freeze to death, or stay inside and cough your way to an early grave.

After the two beers I'd placed a call to Big Pete LeFrance's outfit in Goose Bay. It seemed the season for pilots quitting. One of his had walked out that morning. That I'd been flying the arctic circle for seven years was the only qualification he wanted. The past, the one before that seven years, could remain dead and buried. All I had to do was catch the first flight to Goose.

Now, minutes away from that flight, I had seen Fullerton, which made me think that O'Shaughnessy had been having words. I was still staring through the window at a grimy picture of dawn creeping reluctantly out of a godless sky, when I heard the chair grate across the wooden floor.

8

'Morning Mr Spence, mind if I join you?' He made the word 'Mr' sound one step down from the gutter.

'Help yourself,' I replied.

'Hear you up and quit,' he continued, settling into the chair opposite me.

I looked at the little man with the gaunt face. At the ugly protruding frog eyes. Eyes which were permanently red-rimmed. Crusty with infection, or lack of sleep, or both. 'Seven-year itch,' I muttered.

'That long, eh!'

I said nothing as he pulled a cigarette from a crush-proof pack and lit it. He drew deeply before exhaling a thin stream of blue-grey smoke from the side of his mouth.

'Going south now, eh! Spend the ill-gotten gains on a bit of good living.' The frog-like face twisted into an ugly grin.

His south of course was Montreal or Vancouver. I saw no reason to disappoint him. 'Something like that,' I said at length.

He inspected his cigarette for a moment, then placed it casually in the corner of his mouth. Probably an affectation picked up from some gangster movie he had once seen. 'Hear you went up to Longstaff yesterday to pick up an Inuit!'

That was the latest government jargon. Eskimo, they had discovered, was a dirty word, coined by the Cree Indians centuries ago. It meant something akin to 'raw flesh eater'. The Canadian government had changed it to Inuit – the people – bringing niceness into the twentieth century. That they hadn't consulted the Eskimos was a moot point. It kept the paper-shuffling civil servants in Ottawa happy.

And you also heard she died when the oxygen system failed, I felt like adding. Felt like, but didn't. That was what he wanted. So I just nodded and went back to drinking my coffee.

Fullerton continued, 'TB case of course. Would have died sooner or later. But then if they will insist on living in those filthy, primitive conditions, eh!'

'The rights of an indigenous people. Besides, who's to say we're right.'

Fullerton eyed me steadily, the grin spreading back over his frog-like

9

features. 'Sounds too clever for me, Mr Spence. Something that old Mark Twain referred to as politicking. Now me, I'm just a simple inspector with the aviation department of the Department of Transport. Yes sir, nothing more, nothing less ... oxygen system okay on the Otter, was it?'

'All you've got to do is check the tech log,' I said harshly. 'All defects are recorded there.'

Fullerton said, 'Funny thing about tech logs and bush pilots. It's as though the two are incompatible.'

'And what's that supposed to mean?'

'Nothing in particular, Mr Spence ... unless you're about to tell me that you forgot to record something you should have.'

'As a matter of fact I never recorded anything; it was done by McKenzie.'

Fullerton's grin was back. 'But you were the commander on that flight, isn't that correct?'

I felt myself slipping into a trap. 'McKenzie's qualified as a commander.'

'On paper, Mr Spence. Only on paper. And yesterday he was occupying the right seat, isn't that so?'

'Yes.'

'So you should have signed the tech, log?'

'Yes.'

'But you didn't, did you?'

'No.'

Fullerton shook his head sadly. 'The Wright brothers ain't around any more, Mr Spence ... neither are Lindbergh and Will Rogers.' The red-rimmed eyes fixed on mine, making sure I understood. And the bottom line of that understanding was, 'These days we have rules – make sure you keep them.' Then crushing his cigarette out he pushed his chair back in one smooth, flowing movement. 'Have a nice flight down to Goose ... if I need you I'll know where to find you.' With that he was gone, threading his way through the growing knot of passengers for the Montreal flight.

How he knew about my flight to Goose Bay could have been nothing more than checking with the airline desk before coming up to the coffee shop. On the other hand I wouldn't have put it past the Department to engage in a little surreptitious phone tapping.

I was still sitting ten minutes later, watching the weather beyond the window getting progressively worse, when the American voice said: 'Captain Luke Spence?'

I half turned and found myself looking at a medium-tall overweight character with cropped white hair. Beneath the hair were a pink, well-scrubbed face, slate-grey eyes and at least three chins, the bottom one of which disappeared into the turned-up collar of a charcoal-grey cashmere overcoat. Expensive, but totally unsuitable for the arctic. Beneath the hem of his overcoat, the knife-edged creases of well-cut lighter grey trousers. The highly polished black leather shoes were as much out of place as the rest of him.

He peeled off a leather glove and extended a soft, flabby hand. 'Scarth,' he said in the same gravelly voice. 'Rollo Scarth. Thought it had to be you, they … er … said I should look out for a tall fair-haired guy.'

He was being polite of course. What they had probably said was, six feet tall, unkempt fair hair just about down to his shoulders – like a bloody woman, but don't say that because he's got a mean right – matching beard of course, just as untidy. And the wildest pair of blue eyes you ever saw. Don't say that either, his left hook's meaner than his right cross. The reason for the wild look in his eyes? Easy. He's gone bush. Too long in this place, and places like it.

I turned back to the window. 'So what can I do for you, Mr Scarth?'

'Rollo'll do fine,' he rasped, easing his substantial weight into the nearest chair. With that done he removed his other glove and rubbed his hands together to generate warmth. 'Hell of a place you've got here Captain, one hell of a place. Is it always this cold?'

'Most of the time.'

'Seems a stroke of luck I caught you,' he continued. 'Just got in on the Montreal flight, some guy said you were leaving this morning.'

11

I checked my watch. 'In about fifteen minutes if the Goose flight makes it on time.'

'Goose?'

'Goose Bay.'

'Ah yes, of course. In that case I'd better get straight to the point. I'm an aircraft dealer, amongst other things. Specialize in warbirds. Guess you know the score on that. Buy up old World War Two airplanes, get 'em rebuilt, then sell them off. To the Confederate Air Force in Texas, mostly. Good customers those Texans.'

'Sounds interesting,' I said.

'Hell, it's that all right. You know I just got a lead on a bunch of Japanese Zeros. I mean can you believe that? A group of intact Jap fighters standing virtually flight ready on a remote, overgrown Pacific airfield. Intriguing wouldn't you say? Planes parked in crumbling revetments, jungle vines over everything; gunbelts full. In fact everything as the Japs left it.'

'As I said, Mr Scarth, sounds interesting but if you're thinking of asking me to ferry one of them for you, forget it. Old aeroplanes have a nasty habit of coming apart; usually in the air.'

The fat, pink face creased into a smile. 'Nothing like that,' he ventured. 'Nothing like that at all. No, what I'm proposing is a joint partnership on a certain deal I have in mind. Could be worth a great deal of money to you.'

I tried not to look too surprised. Aviation is full of conmen with get-rich-quick schemes. 'Go on, I'm listening.'

Something like uncertainty caught for a moment in his grey eyes. Or perhaps it was just my imagination. 'Greenland,' he said softly. 'I want you to come to Greenland with me to find Patterson's Volunteers.'

There was a long moment of silence as I looked at Scarth in disbelief. How did he know about that? How could an aircraft dealer from civilization have heard about Patterson's Volunteers? That I knew the whole crazy story was one thing. But how did he?

It had happened a month previously when I'd flown a geologist from Goose Bay to Narsarsuaq. It was a sub-charter for Big Pete LeFrance's outfit. One of his planes had gone sick, and as I was in the area and positioning an empty aircraft back to Frobisher I had got the okay from O'Shaughnessy to do the run. That flight involved an overnight stop. One which, although I didn't know it at the time, was going to change a lot of things. My life included.

After a meal in the annexe building of the Arctic Hotel, I had wandered through to the bar. That was when I met Erik Palmarsson. Or perhaps it was the other way round. He met me. Palmarsson, it appeared, was the local meteorologist – when he was sober. And as booze in Greenland is rationed by the issue of monthly coupon cards, he was only sober when the coupons ran out.

The night I had stayed, however, he was in his element. Free drinks all the way. Not that I had to of course, but he had one of those friendly faces. The other reason, and perhaps the main one, was that if I bought him enough drinks it would eventually shut him up. He was a compulsive talker. By the time the torrent of words had slowed to a hesitant trickle I had become engrossed in the whole, disjointed story. Incredible! I would never be able to judge. Because just when he was poised on the reason for it all, his face turned deathly pale and he made a hurried exit through a back door.

His departure coincided with the arrival of two heavyweight types who looked like Greenlanders – flat, round faces, lank black greasy hair – but they spoke with heavy American accents. I soon found out they were the local police. I also found out that Palmarsson was black-listed and as such I should not have been supplying him with alcohol. They greeted my offhand remark – that I didn't know what the hell they were talking about – with a warning. They didn't want to see me here again … ever. The heavier of the two, the one with the coconut-crushing hands, made a point of flexing his fists. I got the message.

With that they frogmarched the cowering barman away and locked the bar. Through it all they had appeared in no particular hurry to pursue the wayward Palmarsson. It was only when I went outside to negotiate the fifty frozen yards to the hotel that I realized why. There was nowhere to run. Nowhere to hide. The airfield is trapped at the end of a long and winding fjord: at its eastern end an awesome glacier; elsewhere jagged white peaks. Beyond those peaks, thousands of square miles of the most devastating sight in the world. The ice desert! And even polar bears stayed away from that place.

I left at first light the following morning, sweating my way westbound down the snaking fjord. The cloud base was solid at 500 feet, which meant low-level stuff, dodging the icebergs and tracking the narrow ice corridor until I reached the open sea. After that, I let out a very tired and very old breath and started the long climb towards the sunshine.

The remnants of Palmarsson's story remained buzzing around in my head for the next few days. The story of how a squadron of P-51 (Mustang) aircraft had been returning to the USA at the end of the last war. Of how the sixteen aircraft had been caught up in the worst weather ever recorded over the icecap. And of how all sixteen had crashed in eastern Greenland, near to a place called Big Gunn. Winter had set in then with a vengeance, and no one had been out to search for the missing aircraft. By the following spring it was too late. The planes would have been buried beneath God knows how many feet of drifted snow.

How Erik Palmarsson knew of this was only a mystery to anyone unfamiliar with the arctic. The crashing aircraft had been observed by a small band of Eskimos. By their very nature, Eskimos are a hard, uncompromising people. Even now, in eastern Greenland, there are those who follow the old ways, the old traditions. Those of hunting and killing. They have little time for the white man. Therefore, even if a search party had ventured into that bleak Greenland outpost, and stumbled by chance across that band of Eskimos, they would have found nothing but immutable silence. The Eskimos would have looked at them in that detached, unsmiling way of theirs. A way ice-picked out of 5,000 years of surviving on the frozen roof of the world. Their eyes would have told the white man he was not welcome in this place.

But for Palmarsson, the stumbling drunk, the Dane with the friendly face, that had all changed when he had taken an Eskimo wife. The girl, who went by the name of Akalise, was the daughter of Ayayook the Elder. And Ayayook had been one of that small band of Eskimos who had borne witness to that long-ago disaster. Akalise had told Palmarsson the story during the first winter of their marriage.

Palmarsson had said that the squadron had been known as Patterson's Volunteers, Lieutenant Colonel George Patterson being the commanding officer of the squadron. He was leading his men back home when fate finally overtook them. But it had been more than that. More than a bunch of aircraft, and war-weary fighter jockeys returning home. It had to do with 'rogue U-boats' still operating in the North Atlantic, sinking allied shipping at will. All this, even though the war was officially over.

The Dane had lifted his whisky glass at that stage, swilled the contents around, and thrown it back with the expertise of a man who knew drink. There had been a twinkle in the brown eyes when he added, 'Did you ever read Greek mythology?'

'Once perhaps; a long time ago.'

'You know something my friend, Patterson could have been Jason. His pilots the Argonauts. Reincarnation of course ... you'd have to believe in reincarnation.'

His mind was obviously wandering, the whisky taking effect.

'What the hell are you getting at?'

Palmarsson had picked up his empty glass. His eyes pleading.

'Later ... what about Patterson?'

'King Aeetes, the Colchian King!' He had said it as though it was an everyday fact of life. As though everyone was at least on nodding terms with the mythical king. 'He put a terrible curse upon all who sailed in the *Argo*.'

He had lost me a long time ago. 'What's that got to do with Patterson and the missing squadron?'

The twinkle was still in the brown eyes, if anything it was brighter. 'Everything, my friend. Anything and everything. The curse you understand ... if they'd left the golden fleece ... would have been all right.'

15

I had followed that with an exasperated sigh. 'I don't follow.'

'It's easy,' he had crooked his little finger and beckoned me closer. 'Patterson! Patterson the Colonel was being used. Used ...' His voice had trailed away at that exact moment, the smiling face suddenly pale and haunted. That was the moment the police had arrived, and Palmarsson had scurried away like a frightened rabbit.

And that had been it. Except! Except for Lovatt. I had told Jack Lovatt about those planes. Not that much though, and definitely not about Jason and the Argonauts. That had been the drink ... perhaps it had all been the drink! After that Lovatt had gone on leave to New York.

I looked across the table at Scarth. 'Did Jack Lovatt tell you about those planes?'

Scarth scratched one of his chins. 'Yeah, that's the guy. Captain Lovatt. Met him on a helicopter hike into La Guardia. That's how I came by your name.'

'And you thought, on the evidence of some threadbare story, you'd drop by and see me, and then we'd head over to Greenland to find the missing planes. Is that about it?'

If he noticed the cynicism in my voice he didn't show it; instead he beamed expansively. 'That's about it, Captain.'

I stared at the fat man in disbelief. 'Have you ever been to Greenland, Mr Scarth?'

He shifted his weight into a more comfortable position. 'Well ... not exactly.'

'In that case I'd forget about it. To even survive out there comes under the heading of miracles. To actually find something – assuming of course it exists – which has been buried for over thirty years, makes looking for a needle in a haystack a game for two-year-olds.'

Scarth was thoughtful for a number of seconds. 'Be that as it may, I'd still like to go out there and take a look. I mean, no harm done if we come away empty-handed. And you'll still get paid of course.'

I could see he was hopelessly determined. It wouldn't matter what I said. Wouldn't matter if I told him that the arctic silence had driven men mad. Wouldn't matter if I told him about the penetrating cold

16

which would tighten like steel bands about his toes, face and fingers. Of how frostbite would eventually creep in when the agonizing pain stopped. And, when lulled into that strange belief that he had suddenly found warmth, removing his boots to find his toes turning black. When that eventually happened came the final fateful decision to take your hunting knife from your belt and amputate. If the stench of rotting flesh reached you first, you were too late. Gangrene would already have set in. After seven years I could handle it. I had eight toes to prove I could. The fat Scarth would never survive. He belonged to that other world; the world south of the tree line.

'Thanks for the offer,' I said. 'But the answer's no.'

He looked surprised. In his world money was everything, its purchasing power unending. 'Do you realize what kind of money we're talkin' here?'

'No, but that's not the point.'

'One World War Two Spitfire in flying condition is fetching somewhere in the region of half a million dollars. What price sixteen P-51s?'

'Assuming the story's true.'

'Well ... yes.'

'And assuming we find them.'

'Naturally.'

'And even if we found them, what sort of condition do you think they'd be in?'

'According to the engineers I've spoken to corrosion shouldn't be too bad considering ...'

I interrupted. 'To hell with that; what about compression?'

'Compression?'

'Yeah, compression. Look, where snow cover survives for a number of years it's transformed into ice, the snow at lower levels being melted by release of latent heat. The melted snow refreezes as ice.'

Scarth considered my reply for a moment and then said a little uncertainly, 'So what you're saying is that the aircraft would have been crushed beneath the ice.'

17

'Not necessarily; ever hear of snow transport?'

He shook his head. 'Not that I recall.'

'Okay, well it's a fancy name for movement of snow by the wind.'

'Go on,' Scarth replied impatiently.

'The wind over Greenland is predominantly easterly – at the surface that is. Of course depressions do travel north and penetrate the polar regions; then of course the wind is all over the place. However bearing in mind the former, strong horizontal winds would keep the snow cover to a minimum.'

'Reducing the risk of structural collapse, you mean ... what else?'

'Whaleback dunes! The wind would probably have transformed the loose snow around the aircraft into whaleback dunes which stretch in the direction of the wind.'

Scarth leaned across the table. 'So, all we have to do is find a bunch of these dunes and we have the planes ... right?'

I shrugged. 'Depends on where they went down. If they crashed into the mountain range on Greenland's east coast, forget it. On the other hand if they pulled off a forced landing up on the snowfield – the ice desert – there's a chance.' I checked myself. He almost had me believing it was possible.

'So you'll come?' There was excitement in his voice.

'Sorry Mr Scarth, but you're dealing in the wrong currency.'

He didn't understand. 'Okay, okay. So what do you want?'

'Forget it,' I said. 'Unless you have some private pact with God on granting life; as I said before, the mission's non-survivable.'

He hung on like a polar bear with its teeth into a seal cub. 'How about that guy Lovatt?'

'Jack you mean?'

'Yeah. Do you think he'd be interested?'

'Might have been once,' I replied. 'Didn't come back from New York.'

Scarth looked suitably puzzled. 'Quit his job you mean?'

'Amongst other things. Killed in an auto smash.'

'Sorry to hear that. Seemed a real nice guy.'

'Like a lot more I used to know,' I said absently.

'Vietnam?' It was said innocently enough. One of those everyday time bombs that everyday people drop.

I pushed my chair back. 'Time I checked in,' I said coldly. 'Hope you find what you're looking for, Mr Scarth.'

I left him sitting there, wondering where he had gone wrong.

The airline clerk gave me a sad smile and shook his head. 'No go I'm afraid. Got as far as Fort Chimo, picked up three Inuits and went back.'

'What's the met office giving?' I asked.

He shrugged. 'Not much better, I guess. You can give them a call if you like.' He slid the phone across the counter top.

'Five five three two?'

'Got it in one,' he said cheerfully. 'And there's a loose nurse on five five seven nine.'

'Ah. But you know what they say about nurses?'

He grinned and moved away to the next counter, and the waiting line of Montreal-bound passengers.

According to the airport meteorologist, it was in for the day. The Boeing 737 from Montreal had been lucky. He'd arrived before the winds had whipped up the snow into a total whiteout. Whether or not he would get out was all down to company weather minima and runway visual range. The self-respecting airlines with the big shiny jets operate that way – to the letter of the law. And with the Fullertons of this world skulking around hidden corners, that's how it has to be. With the cowboys – the small plane operators – it's a different story. To the Department they're the dregs of flying humanity, a mixture of yesterday aces and those who never got past the dream stage of big-jet flight decks. The Fullertons are still there, of course; looking, but not too hard. They let you bend the regulations, until the day you believe you can blatantly ignore them. That's the day they move in and pull your licence. Same game: different rules.

I was back at the shantytown hotel a couple of hours later, kicking my heels and trying to place a call to Goose Bay when the phone jangled

19

erratically into life. The operator with my open line! It wasn't, but at first it seemed something infinitely better. It was Big Pete LeFrance. He had heard that the Goose-Frobisher flight had only reached Fort Chimo before returning, which was just as well, he added. The job had gone. Just like that. No reason, no explanation. He hoped I'd find something soon. I sat staring at the phone in disbelief, until there was an impatient clicking noise and a lady with a harsh unfriendly voice asking me if the call was complete.

All I could think of was O'Shaughnessy. O'Shaughnessy and his parting threat. That he had invoked a kind of blackmail over me for five of the last seven years hadn't seemed so important at the time. I had needed the North more than it needed me. It had offered me anonymity; I had offered it respect. Now O'Shaughnessy was destroying it all. But if I was going down, he was going with me. I pulled on my cold-weather gear and phoned the trading post for a taxi. No one walks anywhere by choice – not even half a mile. My eight toes were living proof of that.

The operations office was deserted, the only sound the muted hiss of the company radio beyond the long counter top. The despatcher had obviously taken an early lunch, which was just as well. We would be undisturbed. I unzipped my parka, shook off the remains of melting snow and made my way to the door at the far side of the room.

He was there of course, hunched over his cluttered desk, sifting through papers – unpaid bills at a guess – and doubtless wondering which Peter was going to be robbed this month to pay which Paul.

He looked up as I entered the room, his left eye registering emptiness, surprise and anger, in that order. 'What the hell do you want?' he yelled, leaping to his feet.

'Words,' I said angrily. 'Now shut up, sit down and listen.'

His good eye darted around the room, then beyond me to the deserted operations office. He was trapped and he knew it.

'Sit,' I said more quietly. 'I've never hit a man sitting down ... not yet anyway.'

He sat. 'I don't have to listen to you, Spence. You don't work for me any more, remember. In fact you should think yourself lucky I didn't file an assault charge with the RCMP.'

'When I've finished, O'Shaughnessy, you can call in every Mountie in the Northwest Territory. And while you're doing that I'll be calling Fullerton at the DoT.'

His eyebrows arched. 'What the hell's Fullerton got to do with this?'

I said, 'Quite a lot at a guess. But just for starters how does "closing you down" sound?'

'Closing me down?' he laughed cynically. 'Closing me down. You're crazier than I thought, Spence. Do you think that Fullerton would listen to the likes of you?'

'Okay, let's try Big Pete LeFrance. What exactly did you say to him?'

'What the hell's that supposed to mean?'

'It means that last night he offered me a job down in Goose; then this morning he phoned to say it had gone.'

The laugh was back. 'And you think I was responsible?'

'I don't think. I know. And bearing in mind that one inescapable fact, I want you to tell me what you said to him.'

The grey face hardened. 'Look you Anglo-American sonofabitch, I've spoken to no one. And if LeFrance says I have he's a bloody liar.'

'You're the liar,' I said menacingly. 'I've known you too long to be convinced otherwise.'

'For the last time Spence, I know nothing about it. Now I suggest you get to hell out of my office before you regret it.'

I didn't move. He wasn't getting off that easily. 'Five years ago,' I said. 'Remember? After that clapped-out Beaver of yours packed up on me.'

'Sure I remember. And if you hadn't gone the scenic route and stuck to your flight plan the search planes would have picked you up, instead of you having to walk fifty miles back.'

'I'm not talking about misplaced heroics. I'm talking about what happened when I got back half dead.'

'Oh that,' he sneered. 'So you were delirious. So you talked about Vietnam. What you seem to forget is that you came here seven years ago with a clean licence and a neat, pat little story about flying with the

21

Royal Air Force in England. I hired you on the strength of that, not on what I later found out to be the truth.'

'But you capitalized on it, didn't you? You made sure I knew you knew. All that sharp pencilling of duty hours. Always logging ten minutes less each flight so the planes would go longer between checks. Never logging defects that would ground the aircraft.'

'Look,' he snapped irritably, 'you know the score up here as well as I do. In fact as an ex-jailbird you should have thought yourself lucky I kept you on all these years ... you're your own worst enemy Spence, do you realize that? And now that you haven't got a job it's no use whining to me about it.'

I moved across to the desk. 'You're missing the point, O'Shaughnessy. What I'm saying is that you queered my pitch with LeFrance, so by way of recompense – just to keep the books balanced, you understand – I'm going to pull the undercarriage up on this entire operation.'

The anger drained slowly from his face. 'You're forgetting one thing,' he said in desperation. 'You start blabbing to Fullerton and it'll be your licence as well.'

'I've already thought about that,' I said, reaching for the telephone. 'But then there's always South America. Another country, another licence.'

I dialled the number and waited, until a shrill female voice said, 'Department of Transport, can I help you?'

'Inspector Fullerton, aviation department.'

'The inspector's out to lunch right now, can I take a message?'

'Yes, could you ask him to call in at the Northern Wings operations office when he returns. Tell him it's urgent.' I heard the voice ask who was calling as I replaced the receiver. Fullerton would find out soon enough.

'For Christ's sake,' O'Shaughnessy pleaded. 'Let's talk about this. I mean, once you involve those bastards ...' He stopped as a garbled voice drifted through from the outer office. I spun round. There was no one there. That was when I realized it must have been the radio. The radio! Which meant somebody was flying. Surely to God nobody could be trying to get in on a day like this!

22

O'Shaughnessy was halfway towards the door before I realized; I followed him to the despatcher's counter. Then the voice was back.

'Northern Wings Frobisher this is Papa Tango ... how do you read?' I didn't recognize the voice at first. O'Shaughnessy acknowledged and waited for a reply.

'Papa Tango reading you fives also ... overhead at five thousand ... can't get back in.' There was a long crackly carrier-wave pause. The pilot's thumb still holding the transmit button down. I could almost hear him thinking. Then: 'I'm running short of fuel, Mr O'Shaughnessy ... I'm running short of fuel.' That was when I knew. Recognized the thin, frightened voice. The voice of young McKenzie.

I reached across the desk and grabbed O'Shaughnessy by the throat. 'Who's with him?'

'He's by himself,' O'Shaughnessy croaked.

'You sent him off solo; are you crazy?'

'It was okay first thing.'

'In a pig's eye it was. If you'd checked the met report you'd have seen it was going out. Besides which, you mad bastard, he's not experienced enough to handle the Otter by himself.'

O'Shaughnessy struggled to get free, but I gripped him even tighter. He said, 'He's got enough hours.'

'Sure he's got enough hours. Enough hours at some sunny little flight school in Florida flying single-engined spamcans; but that hardly equips him for this type of operation, does it?' I shook him until his teeth rattled. 'Does it?'

'He's ... he's flown enough with you.'

'He needs another winter with me before I'd be satisfied,' I snarled.

We were still arguing when the door banged open and Linda Mitchell waltzed in. She stopped in mid-stride, the smile fading instantly from her lips. That was when I realized I was still half strangling O'Shaughnessy. I pushed him away and turned to her. 'Get on the phone to the hangar. Tell them to pull out the first plane they can get their hands on.'

There was indecision written all over her face as she looked beyond me to O'Shaughnessy. 'Is that... is that all right, Mr O'Shaughnessy?'

'Don't bother asking him,' I said angrily, 'just do it.'

She moved cautiously around the counter to the bank of telephones. O'Shaughnessy, composure returning, moved to stop her.

'I wouldn't,' I warned. 'Remember what I said about Fullerton?'

He paused. 'You take one of my planes, Spence, and I'll have you up on a theft charge.' He meant it.

'So what happens to McKenzie? Leave him up there until the tanks run dry ... then what?'

'He shouldn't have tried to make it back ... I'll talk to him. He'll get in.'

'Is that Jamie you're talking about?' Linda said in a small voice.

I turned to her. 'Jamie?' Then I remembered his first name was James. 'Yes, He's overhead, short of fuel. Now get on to the hangar.' Her bottom lip quivered as she did so.

O'Shaughnessy was watching me, a mixture of confusion and hatred in his left eye. 'What are you going to do?'

'What the hell do you think I'm going to do? Go up there and get him down.'

The radio crackled into life. 'Northern Wings this is Papa Tango ... fuel state critical... can you advise ...' It was a call from the depths of his soul. The place where fear lives and breeds. And sometimes breaks free. It was free now, inside McKenzie. Eating his innards; sending burning bile up his throat. Soon he would lose control of his bladder; then he would sit dumbstruck in a spreading pool of urine. The screaming would begin when the fuel ran out and the engines died. But by then it would be too late.

'Find out what his exact fuel state is,' I said sharply. 'And when you've done that I want to know the tops of this weather. Tell him to circle over the beacon with a thousand-foot separation between him and the tops. And one other thing. Get him to switch box two to 123.5 and listen out. Got it?' O'Shaughnessy nodded dumbly and picked up the hand mike. I turned back to Linda as she replaced the telephone receiver.

'What are you going to do?' she asked shakily.

'Get him down before he has no choice.'

'But the weather!' She turned to the window. Beyond the snow-spattered glass the visibility was practically zero.

'What did the engineers say?'

'They're pulling Lima Foxtrot out. They asked if they should preheat the engines; I said yes. Was that right?'

'Good girl, that was fine.'

There was a flicker of a smile. 'He will be all right won't he ... Jamie?' Unexpectedly her face crumpled in despair, tears welling up in her large brown eyes.

That was when it clicked. Linda Mitchell, the young daughter of the Northern Wings chief engineer, was in love with the equally young McKenzie. Surely I couldn't be that old? I couldn't have missed the symptoms, not when I saw them both on most days. No, Spence, not that old; you were never that young, that's all.

I reached out and rumpled her hair. 'Sure, he'll be all right; just between you and me he's the best young pilot I've ever flown with. Don't tell him that though, wouldn't want him to get big-headed about it, would we?'

She shook her head with the affectionate obedience of a small girl.

O'Shaughnessy was lighting a cigarette with shaking hands when I turned back to face him. 'No more than twenty minutes to dry tanks, he reckons,' he said. Then more bitterly; 'I meant what I said about taking one of my planes.'

I looked at him in disbelief. 'For a once upon a time pilot O'Shaughnessy, you disappoint me. But then I guess you were about as third rate as you are now.' That hurt more than any threats of violence ever would. I had desecrated the one thing he had left. The memory of once belonging to a now distant sky.

I slipped and slithered on the ice, my body leaning forward at an impossible-seeming angle against the wind. At that moment I had my doubts. With over ten thousand flying hours in all the hellholes of the world, this was one trip I would never have made by choice. From the airmanship point of view – that ethical code of conduct, for the most part unwritten – it was a no-go situation. But then I and the book of rules never had got on that well together.

The Otter was half out of the hangar, the ground heater pipes linked up to her engines like long snaking vacuum-cleaner tubes. Where the hot air escaped from the engine cowlings, great clouds of vapour were scattered like wraiths on the moaning wind. It was a mirror image – the other side of hell.

I grabbed the first mechanic I saw by the shoulder. 'Is she ready?' I yelled.

His eyes registered some kind of understanding as he pulled the parka from his mouth. 'You're not flying in this are you?'

'What's wrong with it?' I screamed, waving an arm towards the whiteout of sky. 'Any silly bugger can do it when the sun's shining.'

He thought about that for a moment then grinned, his sharp yellow teeth the only colour in a face which seemed more dead than alive. 'You're all bloody mad,' he conceded, 'every last one of you.' With that, he thrust his hands deep into his pockets and shuffled away.

The snowplough led the way to the threshold of runway 36, spuming out snow in a cascading uphill waterfall. I taxied into position and ran quickly through the pre-take-off checks. Finally I flipped the radio transmit switch.

'Lima Foxtrot ready to go.'

There was a brittle silence, then: 'Lima Foxtrot you're cleared to take off at pilot's discretion. Be advised visibility recorded at less than a quarter of a mile.' I mouthed a silent curse. In other words they were not approving my take-off. On the contrary, they would file a violation with the Department of Transport the moment my wheels left the ground.

I advanced the power levers smoothly forward and checked the auto-feather ARM light was on. 'Lima Foxtrot rolling.' No one answered, which made me think they were already writing out their report.

I was still trying to maintain runway heading on the directional gyro when the Otter leapt clumsily into the air and started a violent, bone-jarring ascent through the blizzard. Things eased off as I approached 4,000 feet. Grey, imperceptibly changing to lighter grey. Lighter grey transforming to an eye-aching white. Then we were out, exploding silently into the endless blue of space. The spine-jolting turbulence ended as suddenly as it had begun; all that remained was the diamond dust shining peacefully in the sunlight.

I leaned forward in my seat and started a slow methodical scan of the upper sky. Over the beacon, over the beacon, over the ... got him. I pulled the aircraft's nose up and homed in on the silver and blue wings above. 'Papa Tango this is Lima Fox on 123.5, do you read?'

The wings twitched in the sunlight. 'Reading you fives Lima Fox.' The voice was shaky.

'Okay McKenzie, this is Spence. What's the problem?'

There was a long nerve-tingling silence. He was thinking. Racking his brains. Wondering what the hell I was doing in this place. Wondering how the hard-bitten bastard who was an impossible taskmaster and a perpetual thorn in his side had suddenly appeared out of nowhere to taunt and chide. At that very moment I was the last person he wanted. He said, 'Weather's out ... can't get in.'

'What weather?' I said curtly.

'What do you mean "what weather"? I just shot an approach and didn't see a thing.'

'What you mean, McKenzie, is that you're not the pilot you thought you were, isn't that it?'

The wings snapped level as if in anger. 'It's nothing to do with that,' he replied testily. 'No one could land in that.'

'Except me kid, but then I go back a long way. One thing I remember though; we had your sort even then.'

'What do you mean, "my sort"?'

'It means the sort who can hack it when the pressure's off, but fall apart when the going gets rough. Yeah, I must have seen a hundred like you in my time. Tenth raters, every last one.'

'It won't work, Spence. Don't think you can rile me into making another approach. It's impossible.'

I pressed the transmit button and laughed. 'Course it's impossible. That's what I said to Linda, well not that exactly; more the "pilots are born not made" line.'

'That's a damned lie, Spence. A dirty damned lie.' At that very moment I had him. Now he wasn't thinking about aeroplanes and turbulence and low fuel. Now he was thinking about a young lady. The rest of the would could brand him as a coward and he wouldn't give a damn. But Linda Mitchell, that was something else.

'It's the truth, kid, and you know it. Anyway it's easy enough to check up, all you've got to do is select company frequency and give her a call. She's down there.'

He was silent. For twenty seconds I sat a few feet off his port wing and waited. Then he was back, voice firm and positive. 'What's the visibility now?'

'Good enough,' I smiled. 'Now listen carefully, this is what we're going to do.'

I briefed him quickly on the ILS let down. With approach flap set at ten degrees he would maintain 85 knots indicated airspeed all the way down. I would be his number two, flying tight formation on his left wing tip. That he had never flown formation lead before could prove disastrous, as my only reference would be his left wing tip. Everything that wing tip did I would follow. If his flying was anything less than one hundred per cent accurate we would both end up very dead.

'Eighty-five knots. Commencing descent, now.'

I tucked in behind the voice, my right hand jockeying the power levers until I had a steady ten-foot separation – wing to wing. 'Don't forget, McKenzie, keep your head inside the cockpit, I want those ILS needles in the perfect cross, as if they were glued together.'

He didn't answer, but I knew he had got the message. He was now pouring every drop of concentration into deadly accurate instrument flying. At the end of it all, it was an apparently straightforward matter of keeping two needles perfectly crossed in the centre of the dial. The instrument landing system – two needles! The vertical one, the localizer needle, kept you on the centre line of the runway. The horizontal, the glide-slope needle, kept you sliding down an invisible electronic banister to touchdown. On a calm and peaceful day with no wind drift it's like falling off a log backwards. Today, with the lower sky an angry whiteout of swirling snow, where only the blind could feel at home, it was going to take the ultimate flying skill. 'When you can,' I said, 'give me a readout as briefed.'

He didn't wait; he came back immediately. His voice was still firm. Firm and clean and young. Unsullied as yet by the years he hadn't lived. 'Speed steady eighty-five, rate of descent five hundred feet a minute, passing four thousand three hundred feet ... established localizer and glide slope.'

'Good, now stay with it. Don't look up at any stage of the descent. I'll give you the word on that. The bumps will start any second now.' I checked my feet were hard on the rudder pedals and took a firm hold on the control yoke. This was it! The big moment. And I'd been worrying that he had never flown formation lead before; when the hell did I last fly in formation?

A fifteen-year-old flashback leapt out of my subconscious, and for one almost glorious moment I was back at the controls of a real aeroplane. An F-4 Phantom. Following Harry Marlin down through the warm tropical rain into Udorn, Thailand. Harry had taken a direct hit in his afterburner section as we were departing Thud Ridge. The 85-mm shell had initiated a torcher, but when Harry switched off his afterburner the fire went out. I stayed with him as wing man all the way home. Then we were jinking down that dark, rain-sodden sky, down towards a glistening concrete highway. At first I thought we'd made it, Harry and I. But then his undercarriage collapsed as he touched. The machine slewed violently sideways before commencing a series of cartwheels down the shining wet runway. It exploded in that heart-stopping moment. Like some vast yellow flower – blossoming death across the fragile beauty of the east. Suddenly and unexpectedly Harry Marlin, the placid veteran of another long-forgotten war, and an advocate of the eastern philosophy that all things are impermanent, had been taken over by the most impermanent of them all — life.

McKenzie's Otter twitched left and then right as we hit the turbulence. The brilliant light started to fade as the snow clouds pressed darkly in. I eased up a few more inches and wished I had a spare hand to wipe away the sweat which was already running towards my eyes. Just fly the needles, McKenzie, forget everything else. Pretend you're sitting in a flight simulator with some crusty old flying instructor sitting outside twiddling the knobs, and feeding in turbulence just for the hell of it.

The sky was darkening more by now, the blowing snow rushing against the windscreen with a roaring hiss. I refocused my eyes to a new point on his wing, my right hand cradling the power levers. He dropped sharply. I snapped the control column forward and then back. 'Bloody hell,' I shouted. 'Bloody, bloody, bloody hell.' My voice echoed briefly inside my head before the sound of engines and rushing snow returned. The tension remained.

'Passing three thousand, eighty-five knots, rate of descent five hundred. Fully established.' There was a growing confidence in his voice. I wanted to tell him he was doing fine, but there was still a long way to go.

The world exploded in that passing second. One moment he was there, leading me down. The next, he dropped like a stone, his extra speed carrying him deeper into the whiteout. He was gone. I slammed the power levers closed and transferred to instruments. Speed back ... back. Eighty knots. Good. Hold it.

'McKenzie, position report!'

'Hit ... hit a bad patch. Sorry. Speed steady now, eighty-five knots. On the centre line but low.'

I banked the Otter rapidly to the left. 'Get on the glide slope as quick as you can. Advise when you're there.' I straightened up the Otter. The localizer needle said I was slightly left of the centre line. Hopefully I had sufficient separation to prevent me chopping his tail off. Of course what I should have done was shout 'abort', with him breaking right and me breaking left. Then, a quick climb back to the sunshine, reform, and start all over again. Yes, that's what I should have done. But as McKenzie's engines were all but running on fumes, seconds were vital.

McKenzie's voice crackled in my headphones. 'Have it now, fully established. Speed eighty-five, rate of descent five hundred feet a minute.'

The moment of truth! Suicidal maybe. I pushed the nose down and banked gently right. The speed flickered through 85 knots. I pegged it stone dead at 90 as I slipped beneath the glide slope. Now I was back on the centre line, but lower than McKenzie. Happily I should drift down until his tail section appeared in the windscreen. Happily!

'Are you still there?' McKenzie again. A slight edge to his voice.

'Course I'm bloody here,' I lied. 'You're leading me down, remember?'

The cold sweat was running into my beard. I ran my tongue nervously across my lips, tasting the sharp tang of salt. How far away was he? How bloody far? I tried to work out the distance interval over one minute. He'd probably accelerated momentarily to about 95 knots. I had reduced to 80. Come on, Spence, think ... think. One minute at fifteen knots, say a quarter of a mile at most. Now I was closing up at five knots ... that would take me three minutes. Too long! We were descending through 2,000 feet. In four minutes we would be on the ground; either way.

I eased on the power until the airspeed indicator gave me a steady 100. My brain gave up on the mental calculations. Instead my eyes swept rapidly up and across the screen at each scan of the blind flying instruments. The Otter yawed and lurched, pitched and rolled, in an attempt to get away from me, but I had the measure of it. It was playing to the wrong audience. The altimeter slipped through 1,000 feet. Then McKenzie was back. 'One thousand feet, eighty-five knots, rate of descent five hundred. Still established.' For a moment he reminded me of someone else.

The turbulence increased, suddenly and dramatically. I blinked and shook my head in a futile attempt to get rid of the sweat which was slowly blinding me. Then it hit me! Turbulence ... turbulence! It was his bloody slipstream. I looked up, snatching the power levers back. A moment later and we would have merged into one final ear-shattering collision. The ghostly apparition of his tail practically bounced off my windscreen. I trod energetically on the left rudder and tweaked on the power. I was back. Miraculously I was back on station. Locked on to his left wing tip. The knot of fear strangling my gut eased ever so slightly.

'Height read-out, McKenzie?'

'Passing six hundred feet.'

'Good ... bloody good. Maintain ILS all the way, I'll let you know when I see the lights.'

'Four hundred feet, can you see anything?' His voice was beginning to crack. 'We're not going to make it, Spence ... I can't hold it.'

'Shut up,' I yelled. 'We're almost there.'

Somewhere beyond his left wing tip there should be lights. But somewhere could be anywhere; if we were anything more than a few degrees off course we would never see them.

'Approaching one hundred ... approaching one hundred feet. Spence ... Spence!'

'Steady kid, as you go through one hundred feet reduce rate of descent. Tell me when you're doing it.' The knot of fear was winding up again, sending searing pain through my stomach.

'Easing the nose up ... Now!'

'Head up,' I commanded. 'Head up. Lights ... left of your nose.'

His wings rocked then dipped as he picked up the runway. I dropped in behind him, driving the wheels on to the ground and snapping the levers into reverse. We were down. Thank you, God. Not much for a life, for two lives ... but it was all I could offer. I looked down the runway, but he had already disappeared into the blowing snow. I'd told him to keep rolling on touchdown, and he'd remembered.

I brought the Otter to a standstill and sat for a long, long moment, drinking in the heady wine of survival. The unbelievable joy of being simply alive. I pressed the transmit button as the snow turned once more to warm oriental rain and watched as the crash trucks followed the damaged Phantom. 'We did it, Harry ... Jesus Christ, we did it.'

There was a brief silence. One that could have lasted fifteen years. 'Spence? Are you down?'

'I'm down,' I said tiredly.

'You ... you called me Harry!'

I shook my head as the pictures faded. No Phantom, no crash trucks, no warm oriental rain ... no Harry. No bloody Harry! I screwed up my eyes and willed the picture back. Willed the dream over. But there was no dream, just the killing whiteout of snow rushing across disillusioned retinas.

The voice came back. The bewildered voice of young McKenzie. 'Spence ... you called me Harry!'

'By way of a compliment,' I said. 'Now I'm turning and taxiing back. Follow me, but slowly. We don't want to break anything at this stage of the game, do we?'

'No problem,' he replied confidently. I switched to tower frequency and told them we were down. They didn't seem too impressed, which was about what I had expected.

The Otter's engines died in unison. Two aircraft, four engines. I flipped off the last of the switches and hauled my legs out from under the instrument panel. Outside the February afternoon was already drawing towards premature night. I had just secured the passenger door when I saw Linda Mitchell. She was half running, half stumbling towards the other Otter and the slim McKenzie who was standing near the tail. The hero returned. I struggled towards them, the snow cutting into my bare face.

McKenzie released his hold on Linda and turned to face me. In his eyes there was a look of pride. 'Well,' he shouted above the scream of wind, 'how did I do?'

'What do you mean, how did you do? One piece of advice, McKenzie. In this game you're on Easy Street for ninety five per cent of the time. You still get paid of course, even though it's a job a trained monkey could do. Now the other five per cent, that's different. On those days you earn your money. Today was one of those days. Nothing more, nothing less.' He looked crestfallen. He had wanted to hear something

33

different. Something about pilots being minor gods; heroes every last one. What I had offered was the unpalatable truth. 'One other thing,' I added. 'If you'd been with me in Nam, you'd have been okay.' With that I turned on my heel, leaving the two young lovers wrapped in each other's arms.

O'Shaughnessy was waiting outside the door leading to the operations office. He wasn't alone. He was flanked by Fullerton and the uniformed figure of Jack Davidson. I sensed trouble before anyone spoke.

'Well!' O'Shaughnessy glowered at Davidson. 'What are you waiting for? Arrest him.'

Sergeant Jack Davidson, the local Mountie, hesitated. He had known me all the years I had been in the Northwest. Had taught me just about every last trick in the survival book. How to fish through the ice; how to trap ptarmigan; how to skin a seal. How to handle dogs. The fan hitch; the tandem hitch. Using a thirty-five-foot-long braided sealskin whip. We went back a long way, Jack and I. Now he stood with uncertainty in his eyes; a big dark man; his black beard flecked with grey, frozen white around his mouth and nostrils where moisture lasted for less than a second. He was a strong silent type, the stuff some Hollywood actors portray to an admiring public. The difference between the two was that Jack was for real.

I said to O'Shaughnessy, 'You seem to have forgotten something!'

'I've forgotten nothing, Spence. I know your type; you'll keep your mouth closed.'

He was right, of course. I wouldn't turn him in to Fullerton. But not for the reasons he supposed. There was young McKenzie, Linda Mitchell, her father, and a lot more people who relied on O'Shaughnessy's two-bit company for a livelihood. 'Next time,' I said quietly. 'And believe me there'll be a next time.'

Jack Davidson was looking confused when he said, 'Sorry Spence, I'm going to have to take you in.'

'What's the charge, Jack?'

The confusion changed to embarrassment. 'Theft,' he said simply.

34

'Lead the way then.'

O'Shaughnessy said, 'Aren't you going to put the cuffs on him? He is a criminal, after all.'

Davidson spun round and for a fleeting second I saw anger burning in his black eyes. 'Criminal be damned,' he growled. 'He's a bloody hero.'

O'Shaughnessy managed one of his cynical little laughs and left it at that. Davidson turned back to me. 'Come on then, Spence.'

'Before you go officer, a word with Mr Spence.' It was Fullerton. I'd forgotten all about him, but then he was that kind of person. Eminently forgettable. I turned and waited.

'The flight you just made,' he said casually. 'You realize of course it was illegal. The visibility was way outside the operating minima set down in the Northern Wings operations manual, and you ... er ... are no longer employed by that company.'

'Extenuating circumstances,' I replied.

'Always the man with the words eh, Mr Spence ... always the man.' He placed the inevitable cigarette carefully in the corner of his mouth. 'Only this time they're the wrong words. You see I'm sure you are as aware as I am that the Air Navigation Order does not consider foolhardy stunts as extenuating circumstances.' There was a kind of satisfaction in his eyes when he added, 'And bearing that in mind your licence is hereby revoked pending a departmental hearing.'

I shivered involuntarily. Not so much at the shock of losing my licence. More at the cold and tiredness which had crept into my very bones. The flight had drained me more than I had realized. All I wanted at this moment was somewhere warm. Somewhere out of the wind. A place to rest. 'Is that it?' I said.

'That's it Mr Spence ... pity you never made that flight to Goose, eh?' He turned and followed the smiling O'Shaughnessy into the operations office. I walked with Jack Davidson to the waiting car, realizing it was the first time in seven years that I had seen O'Shaughnessy look anything like happy.

For the second time in my life I found myself in a jail cell. Only difference was, this was a civil jug; the other had belonged to the military. Apart from that I had the consolation of knowing that Jack Davidson was firmly on my side. He was convinced that any jury, when faced with the evidence, would find me not guilty. I was less optimistic.

It was evening. Davidson's wife had brought in some home-made shepherd's pie. Jack and I had eaten in silence, then he had produced a couple of bottles of Labatt.

'Strictly against regulations,' he said in his quiet Canadian accent.

'I'll drink to that.' I raised my bottle.

'Not much of a one for rules are you, Spence!'

I half smiled. 'No,' I replied cynically. 'But then I've seen some of the clowns who make them.'

Davidson took a swig and wiped his mouth with the back of his hand. 'Speaking of ineptitude ... which I assume you are.'

'If you're being polite, you mean.'

His eyes twinkled. 'Part of the job,' he said. 'The Yukon was a long time ago.'

'Everything was a long time ago, Jack; the best movies, the prettiest girls ... anyway you were saying.'

'Something that might interest you,' he remarked, 'as you were a friend of Jack Lovatt's.'

'What's that?'

'Received the official accident report yesterday, from the New York police department. Do you know how he died?'

'Car smash I was told.'

Davidson ran the cool bottle across his forehead before replying. 'It was that all right, but they said he had lost control of the car while driving on icy roads. No other vehicles were involved. Don't you find that strange?'

I stopped drinking and looked at Davidson with renewed interest. 'Strange? No! I'd say bloody impossible.'

'My words exactly. A snowmobile champion for the last three years, winning every race he entered. Plus the fact he spent all his time driving

36

on packed ice, like the rest of us. Maybe not the same distances, but,' his voice trailed off.

'Have you told them that? The New York police, I mean.'

'What's the point, he's dead whichever way you look at it.'

'Yeah, I guess so ... what do you reckon though?'

'Well ... I would have said foul play, but for that there would have had to have been a motive. He wasn't robbed. And as far as I'm aware he didn't have any enemies. Not that sort, at least.'

'You're forgetting O'Shaughnessy,' I said thoughtfully.

Davidson looked surprised. 'O'Shaughnessy? I thought they just didn't see eye to eye.'

'Not many people do ... no, it wasn't that. You remember that freight contract O'Shaughnessy lost about six months back?'

'To Pete LeFrance's outfit, you mean?'

'Yes. Well, O'Shaughnessy figured Lovatt had passed on his figures for the tender — bit of industrial espionage if you like. So of course Big Pete undercut O'Shaughnessy and ended up with all the work.'

Davidson was thoughtful for a moment. Then he said, 'So what was Jack Lovatt getting out of it?'

'At a guess I'd say a better-paid job than he had here. His contract with Northern Wings would have ended this summer.'

'So how does O'Shaughnessy engineer a fatal accident in New York ... bearing in mind he hasn't been south of the tree line for God knows how many years?'

I sat back in my chair and smiled. 'You tell me, Jack. You're the policeman.'

We carried on the post mortem, with the aid of a few beers, until lights out. That was when Jack got to his feet full of apologies. The lights-out rule, and the one which said he had to lock the cell door for the night, were unbreakable. It could cost him his job if one of his superiors decided to do a spot check. I waved the apology aside, but it did little to ease the dull emptiness I felt as the door clanged shut.

At eight o'clock the following morning I had a visitor. He was still dressed for the city; still twice too heavy for his height; and still a pedlar of exotic dreams. He had waited until Jack Davidson had left the cell before he put forward the proposition. The same one he had put forward the previous day.

'I'll say one thing for you Mr Scarth, you don't give in that easily.'

'Mark of success,' he replied in his gravelly voice. 'Well?'

'Circumstances have changed since we met yesterday, or hadn't you heard?'

He waved his pink, fat hands in the air. 'Sure I heard. I also heard you saved a young kid's life.'

'That as it may, I'm here until there's a trial.'

'Not necessarily,' he said quietly. 'I've persuaded Mr O'Shaughnessy to drop the charges.'

The silence was electric. 'You've what?'

'I've persuaded ...'

'Yeah. I heard you first time. You've persuaded O'Shaughnessy to drop the charges. How the hell did you manage that?'

'Everyone has their price, Captain Spence.' The cold grey eyes fixed on me for a moment. 'It's just that some people take longer than others to realize and accept it.' He put his right hand to his forehead and ran the palm down the left side of his face. He had done that before, at our first meeting. I hadn't paid much attention to it then, but now I realized it was some kind of nervous reaction. As though he was brushing away a cobweb that had settled on his face. I had known guys in Nam with fighter pilot's 'twitch' – an unconscious, nervous, muscular contraction usually in the vicinity of the eyes. It was, amongst other things, a result of undue stress. I wondered what stress Scarth was under.

'Well? What about it?'

'Even if I agreed,' I said, 'there is something else. I've lost my licence.'

'That would be your Canadian licence, I take it?'

'If you say so.'

'But you have an American one as well?'

'As a matter of fact I do, but ...'

38

'No problem then,' he interjected. 'I'll get hold of an American-registered airplane for the trip. Now regarding financial remuneration, I guess you'd like to discuss that?'

Overweight he may have been, but his mind was pure quicksilver. It might also have been a little mad. But then he was offering me a job. And the job was still in the North. 'We can talk about the money later, 'I said. 'First off I'd like to get out of this place.'

He brushed away another cobweb. 'Good. There's a flight leaving for Montreal in forty-five minutes. I took the liberty of booking a couple of seats ... under the circumstances I didn't figure you'd want to hang around.'

I started pulling on my parka. 'Under the circumstances I think you got it about right,' I replied. 'I'll need to locate my baggage though; checked it in for the Goose flight yesterday.'

Scarth smiled briefly. 'No need,' he said, 'I already did that. It should be loaded on the Boeing by now.'

'Did you ever consider I would turn you down?'

'No,' he murmured as we left the cell. 'Can't say I did.'

Gander airport was practically deserted as I made my way to the terminal building. Above the entrance, caught in an endless ripple of wind, a flagpole rope tonged mournfully. Below that, a large sign with the red maple leaf of Canada and the inscription TOPS GANDER. Trans Oceanic Plane Stop. Once maybe, I thought, and if they ever brought back the relatively short-range piston-engined airliners it would be again. In the meantime, the sign sat patiently, viewing the vast, sprawling emptiness of one of the largest airports in the world, and on clear days the white contrails of big jets painting their way westbound to New York, or eastbound to London.

The coffee shop was as quiet as the rest of the place. Long tables stretching endlessly away from the chromium-plated barrier at the serve-yourself counter. I helped myself to a ham sandwich and a cup of coffee, paid the under-worked cashier, and picked out a chair midway down the first row of tables.

It had been two weeks since I left Frobisher. Scarth and I had stopped over in Montreal for two days, and whilst I had been purchasing what I could in the way of survival gear for our trip to Big Gunn, Scarth had been busy locating a suitable aircraft for the operation. He eventually came up with a single engined de Havilland Beaver. The plane was based in Gander and was fitted with hydraulic skis. Still on the credit side it had a zero-hour overhauled engine and was on the American register. On the debit side it was twenty-five years old; and was the same type that had fallen out of the sky with me five years earlier.

The following day Scarth went on to New York to arrange the bank transfer. I caught the first available flight to Gander to inspect the aeroplane. When he got the okay from me he would wire the money. That okay took eight days. Eight days of niggling radio problems, oil leaks, hydraulic snags, and a thousand and one other minor faults which all added up to a tired old aeroplane. And whichever way you looked at it, the '$8,000 US dollars Scarth had paid for the Beaver was about twice too much. She was an over-painted old hag, and had been with too many men over the years to be worth that sort of money. But as Scarth had said, when I aired my disapproval during a long-distance telephone call, it was his money. He also said the Beaver was becoming something of a vintage aircraft – a collector's item – and the price would continue to go up. I didn't believe a word of it. But then I was biased.

Now, today, the last day of February, Scarth was arriving from New York. Following a day or two of planning, arctic survival briefings and hopefully fair weather, we would depart for Greenland.

I finished my coffee and checked the time. Midday. I had been working at the hangar since seven, doing those last-minute checks every pilot does before entrusting his life to a single engine over 1,500 miles of icy North Atlantic and the desolate snowfields of Greenland. Last-minute checks like fuel-flow readings on the ferry-tank system, ski hydraulics working, engine runs to check the magnetos, cabin heater, a third compass swing in as many days. Right down to pulling the wheels off to make sure some dumb engineer hadn't packed the bearings with grease. In the arctic you fly with dry wheel bearings. Grease freezes and locks the wheels. It may cost a few more dollars in replacement parts but at least you don't end up on your back with a broken neck.

As Scarth wasn't due in until three o'clock I decided to make my way back to the Albatross Hotel for a shower and a beer. I hadn't reached the door when the three ferry pilots walked in. Their battered flight bags told you that. You didn't need to look into their eyes to see the strange loneliness of solo ocean fliers. I sidestepped them and was halfway through the door when a voice said hesitantly, 'Is that you, Spence?'

I stopped and turned, and found myself looking at Lincoln Kullman. Alternatively known as Linc or 'Killer Man' – dependent upon whether he was on the ground, or 'greening up' an F-4 as he entered the battle zone at 24,000 feet. But it wasn't the Killer Man I had known. This one was older, greyer, one of yesterday's tomorrows. The slightly built youth, ill used by time, had become an old man.

I moved slowly towards him. 'Linc?'

His dark eyes smiled tiredly. 'Older but no wiser,' he said, as if reading my thoughts. 'Just another aviation junkie who can't kick the habit.' He half turned to the other two. 'Catch up with you guys later.' They moved off towards the food counter.

'Long time,' I said, holding out my hand.

'And then some,' he replied. 'What's with the beard and the hair? Don't tell me, you're getting back at good old Uncle Sam and his indoctrination programme!'

'Forget the "good" label and you're not far out ... anyway who are you flying for?'

'Myself. Ferrying stuff... out to Europe mostly. Lucky you caught me though, this is the last one.'

'Then what?'

'Something else that's lucky ... let's grab a coffee. I'll tell you all about it.'

He outlined the last ten years in as many minutes. How he had started ferrying for a company based at Wiley Post airport in

Oklahoma; then after the first year how he had gone freelance. Now, he was about to complete his one hundredth solo Atlantic crossing. Not that he had to do it; he already had the money he needed. No, this one was for old time's sake. And after delivering the twin-engined Piper to London, he was catching the first flight to Miami. From there, down the Florida Keys to Key West. To a Cessna 185 floatplane and the new company he and his wife had started.

The tanned face creased into a half-remembered smile. 'Money for old rope,' he was saying. 'We take the tourists on adventure flights out into the Gulf of Mexico. Fishing, scuba diving, that sort of thing.'

'Sounds a good deal!'

'Good!' he exclaimed. 'It's great.' He stirred his coffee for the tenth time. 'So what are you doing these days?'

'Not a lot. Just finished a seven-year contract up in the Northwest Territories. Got myself a job flying a Beaver at the moment. Temporary, but something else will turn up.'

'Why don't you come down to Florida? We could always do with a second airplane as a backup. You'd get a share of the company, naturally.'

I smiled at his enthusiasm. 'Sounds too rich for me, Linc.'

'Too rich be damned. You just said you've been flying out of the Northwest Territories for the past seven years; you must have saved a fortune!'

He caught the hesitation in my eyes.

'Don't tell me you've worked your butt off all these years and blown it all?'

'Not exactly,' I replied, swilling the coffee dregs around the bottom of my cup. 'Call it an investment.'

He let out a sigh of relief. 'Had me worried for a moment there. So what's the problem? Not what happened back in Nam, is it?'

'No,' I said quietly. 'It's not that.'

'Well?'

'Thanks, but no thanks. Anyway I've got a job, taking the Beaver to Greenland.'

'But as you said it's only temporary. You could always head down to the Keys after you've finished up in Greenland.'

'Maybe. I'll think about it.' I pushed back my chair. 'Where are you staying?'

'Albatross.'

'I'm heading that way now, want a lift?'

'Catch up with you later, I've got to take the ship out and do a compass swing first. It's still a big ocean at the speeds we fly.'

I left him sitting there, staring tired-eyed into his coffee. But it was more than coffee he saw. It was swaying palms, white beaches, and endless sunlit days. The ultimate dream.

Scarth arrived at three o'clock. He was still the best-dressed man in the North as he elbowed his way through the minor throng of disembarking passengers. He was also the only man accompanied by an attractive, long-legged blonde. Before they reached me I had taken in the early-thirties face pinched by the cold, and had decided that if she smiled she would look beautiful. The full-length silver fox fur draped casually across her shoulders framed a fashionable French-blue ski-outfit and knee-length suede boots. Totally impractical, but then wealth has that effect on some people.

'There you are,' Scarth called out. 'Figure we must be about set for the big journey?'

'More or less,' I replied, my eyes still on the captivating blonde.

Scarth said, 'Like you to meet Hannah Dawson, my secretary.' Then turning to her, 'Hannah, this is Captain Luke Spence.'

She flashed me a brilliant smile. And she was beautiful. 'I've heard a lot about you, Captain Spence,' she said as I took her hand.

For once in my life I was tongue-tied; lost for words. Or the right words at least. I'd obviously been out of that kind of circulation for far too long. I felt my face go hot with embarrassment as I nodded dumbly.

Scarth clapped his gloved hands together. 'Good! Introductions over, might I suggest we find our luggage and move on to the hotel ... I take it they're better than in Frobisher?'

43

'Where we're going, Rollo, even Frobisher hotels will seem like the last word in luxury.'

'Hear that Hannah, sense of humour as well. As I told you, we'll all get on fine together.'

Scarth caught the questioning look on my face. 'Forgot to mention it before,' he said casually. 'Hannah's coming along with us.'

My head jerked up rapidly. 'To Greenland?'

'Where else?' he said. There was a smile at the corner of his lips.

'Impossible!'

The smile slipped. 'What do you mean, impossible?'

'What the hell do you think I mean? It's not exactly a Sunday-afternoon church social we're going on. It's Greenland. The hardest place on God's earth. Even the Greenlanders only have an average life span of thirty-four years, and they're born and raised in the place.'

Scarth gave me a hard, penetrating look. 'We're not going for a lifetime, Spence. We'll make out.'

'And who takes care of Miss Dawson here, while I'm amputating one or two of your fingers, because you left your mittens off too long?'

'Let's not get too dramatic, I can look after myself. Besides Hannah has a pilot's licence.'

I let out a small laugh. 'And that's supposed to make her immune to cold, is it?'

Scarth's face was fit to explode when Hannah intervened. 'Like Rollo,' she said confidently, 'I can take care of myself.' The captivating smile was back, attempting to lure me to mute acceptance.

'I doubt that very much, Miss Dawson. Have you ever been in a sixty-below blizzard?'

The smile was still there. If anything it was wider and more friendly. 'No, Captain, but I'm sure I will survive in your capable hands.'

'I wish it were that simple,' I replied. 'But if anything goes wrong out there, it's all over. Even for me to survive, with all my experience of the North, will need the assistance of the odd miracle or two. To pull Rollo out at the same time ... and now you. No way! It's impossible.'

'Nothing's impossible,' Scarth growled. 'And let's not forget, if it hadn't been for me you'd still be rotting in that jail cell up in Frobisher.'

'Okay, so I owe you a favour. And that favour, unless you've already forgotten, was to take you to Greenland to search for a bunch of missing aircraft. Nothing's changed in that respect, but I'm not about to accept the added responsibility of another passenger.'

Scarth's right hand went to his forehead and brushed away an imaginary cobweb from the left side of his face. His eyes looked hunted. 'She's not just a passenger,' he said. 'She's also a pilot. What happens if you get injured?'

He had a point, of course. Damn the man; he had thought this out very carefully. I played my last card. 'Even if I accept that, there is the payload problem to consider.'

'I'm listening,' Scarth fired back.

'Basically any aeroplane will only lift so much. So bearing that in mind,' we take on another passenger and extra baggage. Problem now is, something has to go. And the only disposable something we have is fuel. Get rid of any amount of that and you're reducing range. All you then need is a fifty-knot headwind – where the met. forecaster reckoned none existed – and you end up short of your destination in the only glider Mr de Havilland ever built ... get the picture?'

'I've already thought of that,' Scarth replied confidently. 'We alter the routing. Instead of direct to Big Gunn, we go via Goose Bay and Narsarsuaq.'

He almost had his homework right. Almost, but not quite. The routing was perfect. But whereas Goose had a plentiful supply of avgas; Narsarsuaq hadn't. I'd found that out on my last trip there in the Twin Otter. The Otter being a jet-prop aircraft meant it ran on kerosene, and they had plenty of that. But the high-octane petrol required for piston-engined aircraft was a different story. I said, 'There's no avgas in Narsarsuaq.'

'What do you mean, no avgas! There has to be.'

'It's shipped up every summer. Obviously they didn't take enough last year. Anyway what little they have left is ear-marked for emergency use only.'

Scarth said, 'What constitutes an emergency?'

I thought for a moment. 'Overflying aircraft being ferried between Iceland and Canada running into strong headwinds and deciding he's not going to make destination with what fuel he's got on board.'

'Okay, so we declare an emergency.'

'Bad airmanship,' I said. 'Any pilot who does that hasn't planned his flight correctly.'

'Horse shit!' exploded Scarth. 'You're just looking for excuses.'

'No,' I said quietly. 'Not excuses; call it plain old professional pride. A lot of things I may be, but a bad pilot isn't one of them.'

Scarth let out an exasperated sigh and stormed off to the baggage reclaim area.

Hannah Dawson said sweetly, 'First round to you, Captain Spence.'

I turned and looked into the appealing blue eyes. 'Forget the captain tag,' I said. 'The Air Force belonged to another lifetime.'

'So what do people call you this time around?'

'If they're being polite ... Spence.'

'And if they're not?'

'Not repeatable in front of a lady,'

The ready smile was back in an instant. 'What gives you the idea I'm a lady?' Her voice was no more than a provocative whisper.

'I think we'd better go and find your boss. I've got a car waiting outside.'

'You didn't answer my question,' she said, falling into step beside me.

'No need, Miss Dawson. You answered it for me.'

She didn't say another word all the way back to the hotel. Come to that, neither did Scarth.

I was in the bar later, drinking in the silence with a cool bottle of Labatt, when the Killer Man walked in.

'Bad habit!' he said, settling on to the next stool.

'What's that?'

'Drinking by yourself.'

I grinned. 'What are you having?'

'I would have said the usual, but you wouldn't remember that, would you?'

'Kentucky Painkiller! Right!'

The Killer Man rocked back on his stool. 'And there was I thinking you were getting old.'

'Only on the outside,' I replied, beckoning the barman. 'When you leaving?'

'Tomorrow sunset, if the weather holds.'

The barman slid the bourbon across to the Killer Man. 'To a safe trip,' I said, raising my glass. 'And may all your winds be a hundred knots on the tail.'

'Once maybe,' he said, lifting his glass. 'So tell me about this Greenland trip.'

'Not much to tell,' I said guardedly. 'Rich New Yorker wants to visit real Eskimo country. Amateur anthropologist ... you know the sort of thing.'

'Yeah, I suppose I do. Come to think of it I suppose you're a bit of an expert on the arctic after all these years.'

'Seasoned perhaps. Expert! ... I have a feeling the real Northerners would dispute that.'

The Killer Man grinned and took a packet of cigarettes from his pocket. 'Still use these?'

I shook my head. 'No thanks. Packed it in five years ago.'

'Wish I could,' he said absently. 'I guess it's all down to will power in the end. Right?'

'Something like that,' I said. It wasn't, of course. It was down to crashing on the white open tundra and trying to survive. And at the end of it all, realizing that the body could not be reliant on artificial stimulants. Nicotine, like alcohol, reduces mental and physical efficiency. Out there that is all you have.

'Another drink then?'

'Beer. Thanks.'

He waved a finger at the barman and ordered a large bourbon for himself and a beer for me.

47

'So,' he said, when the drinks had arrived, 'my toast, I believe. How about to all the warriors we left behind? May heaven be full of Phantoms but no missiles.' He laughed. 'Not forgetting of course an endless supply of bourbon.'

The glass was halfway to his lips when it stopped dead. Hannah Dawson had swept into the bar. Her eyes rested on me as she came towards us. The fashionable blue ski-outfit had been replaced by a red cashmere jumper, a predominantly red tartan skirt, and knee-length, tight-fitting red leather boots. The effect was totally devastating.

'Stag night?' she said to me. 'Or can ladies join in?'

I introduced her to Linc and pulled up another stool. I said, 'What do lady pilots drink these days?'

Before she could answer Linc said admiringly, 'A pilot as well!'

She treated him to one of her winning smiles. Compliments, it seemed, did not go unrewarded. 'Well I think so, and the FAA issued me with a licence which gives me the impression that they think so; but Spence, it seems, has other ideas.'

Linc laughed. 'He's not that bad really ... once you get to know him.'

'Provided you can hang around for a geological ice age or two, you mean!'

Linc turned to me. 'She's got you taped, pal, and you know what they say? The first time's usually the last.'

I looked at Hannah. 'Well?'

'Is that a proposal, or are you still asking me what I'd like to drink?'

'The drink I can probably afford. Chains I need like a mid-air collision.'

'In that case I'll have a beer please.'

I ordered the beer and another round for Linc and myself.

'So,' Linc was saying to Hannah. 'What are you flying around these parts?'

'Oh nothing ... I was hoping for a flight with the illustrious Captain Spence, but it seems he has other ideas.'

The Killer Man smiled knowingly. 'The secret is, don't give in. Somewhere beyond that ravaged exterior he's as soft as a kid's teddy bear.'

She said, 'You believe that?'

'Sure I believe it ... you know what he did once in Danang? There was this crippled kid ...'

'Leave it out, Linc. We don't talk about those things any more.'

He caught the look in my eye. 'No, maybe not,' he replied, and knocked back the remains of his Kentucky Painkiller. There was a heavy silence before he added, 'Well, if you'll excuse me I'd better be turning in; there's a long day and a long night ahead of me.'

'Maybe catch you at the field tomorrow,' I said.

'Sure you will ... if not, remember what I said about the Keys. Be like the old days, wouldn't it?'

'Yeah, guess it would,' I smiled. 'Take it easy.'

'And you pal, Greenland's a pretty wild place especially in the winter ... but then I guess you know all about that.' He raised his hand in a farewell gesture. ''Night Hannah.'

She slipped down from the stool. 'Time I turned in as well. You can escort me to my room, Linc.' The Killer Man was positively beaming as Hannah turned back to me. 'Goodnight, Captain.'

I half raised my left hand and watched them go: the beautiful platinum blonde who had aroused more passion in me than she could ever realize, and the ghost from a long-ago past. The ghost who had stirred up a hornet's nest of memories and with it a lot of bitterness and pain. I turned to the overweight, grey-haired barman and ordered another beer.

'Nice looker!' he said wistfully, glancing at the now empty doorway.

I caught the drift instantly. 'The ones to look out for,' I replied.

He smiled. It was one of those reflective 'if only' smiles. Then he said, 'You're not from these parts, I guess!'

'Frobisher.'

'Yeah, I kinda figured it was that aways. Spent some time in that area myself, up on the DEW line with the Air Force. Bad-medicine place ... you know, all I ever remember is that ball of yellow sun shining through the ice crystals and never giving off an ounce of heat. Either that or those northers dropping the temperature to sixty or more below. Those

49

times you could even hear the aurora crackle in the night sky. Yes sir, real bad medicine ... only fit for Eskimos and polar bears and that's a fact.' He went back to polishing a row of already sparkling glasses. 'She ... the dame,' he continued, 'she kinda reminded me of someone. Ever hear that Eskimos yarn about a woman called Erdlaversissoq?'

'The "entrails robber", you mean?'

'Yeah! That's the one. Crazy story that. Of course that's all it was ... a story. But they reckoned the Erdlaversissoq dame had the golden-white hair of the sun, the blue eyes of the sea, and was dressed in red ... fires of hell, or something. As I said ... crazy story!'

I finished my beer and slid the empty glass over the bar. 'Not to them,' I said, getting to my feet. 'Night.'

'Yeah,' he said absently. 'Have a good one.'

I slept badly that night, what sleep I did manage being plagued by what the barman had said. The words being woven into a violent dream. A dream of the traveller who sought shelter at the snow house of Erdlaversissoq; and while he slept she pricked a hole in his belly and dragged out his intestines as a treat for her dogs. I never saw the face of the traveller, his head was turned away from the flickering yellow light of the stone lamp. But when Erdlaversissoq turned, blood dripping from her long white hands, I caught a glimpse of her face. It was the face of Hannah Dawson.

I was out at the airport early the next morning. Six o'clock early. It was still dark, and bitterly cold. About minus five at a guess; but it was that damp Newfoundland cold; the sort that creeps insidiously through your cold-weather clothing ... all the way to the bone. I had left a note at the hotel desk for Scarth, telling him to come out to the Eastern Provincial Airways hangar as soon as he could.

I opened the heavy metal access door and went into the dimly lit hangar. It was heated, but as always around those Godless dawn hours even heated hangars had a feeling of the grave. The early shift was already on duty, working on their gleaming Boeing 737s. I made my way towards the red-and-yellow-painted Beaver, which was tucked away in a darkened corner. She looked even older in that sort of company. A museum piece without a museum. But at least she was an airworthy aeroplane – a tool of the trade. My trade. And whichever way I viewed Scarth's proposition, he had me cold. With no job, no money, and fast running out of ideas; I knew, as I had known since his arrival yesterday, that Hannah Dawson would be coming along. That circle of thinking brought me back to the load-sheet quandary. With the internal ferry tanks I had fitted, and the subsequent increased fuel uplift, our take-off weight was already ten per cent over manufacturer's stipulated all-up weight of 4,820 pounds. And that critical overweight condition only included Scarth and myself. Now if we had been sitting in Iceland with the prospect of the relatively short hop across the Denmark Strait it would have been different …

The anomaly struck me with the intensity of a lightning flash. The obvious, the overlooked! The idea that we were probably chasing moonbeams before we had even begun. I found the Jeppesen charts behind the pilot's seat. Having selected those I needed, I closed the aircraft door and made my way to the other side of the hangar, and one of the better-lit offices.

My guesstimate wasn't far out. Keflavik, Iceland, to Bluie West One was in the region of 650 nautical miles. Bluie West One was the wartime designation for Narsarsuaq, and it seemed more than likely that Patterson's Volunteers would have routed that way. That they went down a long way short of their destination, and well to the north of their intended track, seemed to somehow contradict Erik Palmarsson's story. Confirming my suspicions was easier than I could have hoped.

I found Silent Sam Mason three offices down from where I had been sitting. One of the mechanics on the hangar floor had pointed me his way. 'See Silent Sam,' he'd said. 'Anything he don't know ain't worth knowing.'

S. W. Mason, Chief Engineer, as the sign said on the door, was puffing quietly on his pipe, and working his way through endless piles of paperwork. As his nickname suggested he was not given much to words – not until I mentioned P51's that is – then he stopped shuffling the papers and looked at me with renewed interest.

'Range of the P-51 you say! The old Mustang, uh?' He scratched his bald head and thought for a moment. 'Course you could have asked me how long's a piece of string? They knocked out a lot of different marks, you know.'

'What about American 8th Air Force based in England around 1945?' I asked hopefully.

The pipe went back between his yellowed teeth. 'Now you're talking. Yeah, could have been the 4th Fighter Group ... they were based in England. Place called Debden. Ever hear of it?'

'Not offhand.'

'No matter. Now let's see; if memory serves me right they were operating the P51D. Range wise, can't be too sure. I was just a fixer, not a fly-boy. But they were long-legged sons of bitches ... know what I mean?'

I nodded, and he scratched his head some more.

He said, 'Ball-park figures only, but I'd guess they had a range of over two thousand miles. Used to escort the bombers on the daylight raids over Germany.'

'What kind of speed would that have been at?'

'Oh, pretty slow. The B-17s loaded up with bombs would be knocking on around two hundred and thirty ... two forty miles an hour; so the P-51 jockeys would have those Packard Merlin engines throttled right back. Mind you, if they had to mix it with enemy fighters and go to throttle bent that would screw up the range figure.'

'But if you were ferrying one you'd get over two thousand miles?'

Silent Sam smiled. 'And then some. Can't remember the fuel capacity, but I do recall they fitted an extra tank behind the pilot's seat. Used to have radio gear in there at one time. Then of course you had the underwing drop tanks instead of bombs ... yessir, with all that I guess she'd just about fly for ever.'

I returned to the Beaver, dug out the tool kit and went to work removing the cowlings. Reconditioned engine or not, you could never be sure. And if anything's going to go, it usually does in the first fifty hours. I started by removing the spark plugs. By the time Scarth arrived at nine o'clock I had already done half a day's work.

'So this is the baby,' he rasped. 'Not bad, not bad at all.' He ran a gloved hand down the leading edge of the starboard wing strut. His eyes moved ahead, stopping at the de-cowled Pratt and Whitney engine. 'Problems?'

'No, just checking and double checking. Careful pilots live longer.' I finished refitting the oil filter and looked up. In a better frame of mind I might even have laughed. Scarth was dressed in cold-weather kit, the added bulk of which gave the word obesity a new meaning.

'About Hannah ...' he started.

'Stand by on that. More important matters to talk over; the first of which is that coffee machine over there.'

Having purchased two cups of steaming black coffee, and handed one to Scarth, I led him through to the deserted mechanics' rest area. It was a dirty, untidy little room, with oil-stained chairs, discarded plastic cups, the musky scent of hydraulic fluid and the faint garlicky smell of metal and leather. The walls were liberally covered with seductive females in varying stages of undress. Scarth gave a cursory glance at the over-large breasts and sank heavily into a chair. He removed his gloves, unzipped his parka and produced a fat cigar. I waited while he stoked it up and blew a long stream of blue smoke at the ceiling. 'Now,' he said. 'You were saying something about important matters!'

I ran quickly over the P51's range figures, and how it seemed highly unlikely that Patterson's Volunteers could have crashed as a result of fuel starvation.

Scarth eyed me steadily for a moment. 'Did this guy Palmarsson specifically indicate that they'd run out of gas?'

'Not that I remember.'

'So! Supposing it was something else!'

'Not possible. One, maybe two could have suffered engine failure. But we're talking sixteen aircraft. And if sixteen aircraft go down at the same time it can only be for one of two reasons ... correction, one of three reasons.'

'Which are?'

'Number one, they all run out of gas at exactly the same moment. Which is highly unlikely. Fuel burn-off figures would vary, pilot technique on fuel management for one thing; not forgetting that some of the engines could have been high-time and therefore less efficient. So looking at the flying-to-dry-tanks deal, you'd have sixteen aircraft strung out over a hell of a distance.

'Which brings us to the second reason, which like the first is a nonstarter. The squadron gets hopelessly lost and decides to put down while they have engine power.'

Scarth gritted the cigar between his teeth. 'What's wrong with that idea?'

'Well in either case if they had a fuel range of two thousand miles or so and they ran into problems after the first five hundred miles, all they had to do was turn back east, to Iceland.'

'You're sure they would have gone through Iceland?'

'Positive. Coming west-about from England you're bucking headwinds all the way. So they would have staged through Keflavik.'

'You said three reasons! What was the third?'

'The formation leader is too low as he approaches the east coast of Greenland and simply flies into the side of a mountain. Easy to do in a whiteout, or partial whiteout condition. As the rest of the guys are all playing follow my leader, and providing the formation was tight, the result could have been a series of rapid explosions. Of course that's just as crazy as the other two. The P51 had a supercharged Packard Merlin engine, which means it would have needed to operate above twenty thousand feet to obtain best fuel economy.'

Scarth shrugged and looked up at the heavily breasted nudes. He didn't appear overly concerned that I had found a hole the size of Gander airport in Palmarsson's story. 'What would you have done?' he questioned. 'Assuming you'd been leading that squadron.'

'A lot of praying at a guess.' Then noting the seriousness in his eyes,

54

I added, 'Hard to say, without knowing more details. All I do know for certain is that if a formation of planes gets lost and then goes to critical fuel state, the first priority is to get down. And as Greenland is not particularly well endowed with airfields, that would leave the ice desert for a forced landing site.' I paused, long enough to picture that unenviable scene. 'But even assuming you survived the landing, there is still the long walk. In my book you're dead either way.'

Scarth puffed thoughtfully on his cigar. 'Looks difficult?'

'Chasing wild geese always is.'

We sat in silence for a few minutes. Scarth chewing his cigar and occasionally brushing the left side of his face. Me, drinking my coffee and inspecting the tarty ladies on the wall.

'About Hannah,' Scarth said suddenly. 'I want her along.'

'So we're still going?'

'I've come too far not to. Besides, you're getting well paid for this.'

'I am?' I said in mock surprise. 'You never did tell me the exact amount.'

'Plenty of time for that.'

'Not if you want to get the show on the road by tomorrow,' I replied.

'And Hannah?'

'Depends on the price ... your game, remember. And as we'll have to stage through Narsarsuaq ...'

'What do you want?' Scarth said guardedly.

'What are you offering?'

'Depends if we find the planes.'

'And if we don't?' I said.

'I take it you have something in mind?'

'As a matter of fact I do.' I put forward the proposition, which had formulated in my mind that very morning while I had been working on the Beaver's engine.

Scarth hardly gave me time to finish before he said, 'I don't work that way, Spence. What's wrong with hard cash?'

'Old Eskimo tradition,' I said. 'Trade furs and pelts for supplies. Money's no good in the North.'

'You're talking horse shit again ... anyway what happens if we don't find them?'

'You lose,' I said quietly. 'You lose.'

'No go,' he barked. 'It's hard cash or nothing. And then payment depends on results.'

I leaned back in my chair and smiled. 'You seem to forget it's you who wants to go to Greenland. Me, I can probably live without it. Might give me a few sleepless nights, of course, but I figure I'll get over it.'

Scarth mulled it over. I could see his eyes shuttling back and forth; hear his brain working on the angles. Was he going to lose? Or could he win both ways! There was a look of almost sinister satisfaction on his face when he said, 'You drive a hard bargain, Spence. And here was me thinking you were just another two-bit pilot. Know something else, if you'd 'a been an airplane dealer you'd have been a millionaire a long time ago.' He stubbed out his cigar and hauled his body weight into a standing position. 'I'll find a lawyer and have the papers drawn up right away. You can sign them later at the hotel.'

I sat for a long while after he had gone. Alone, except for a hundred naked ladies who leered at me from every conceivable angle. I should have felt pleased about the deal. At the very least, pleased. But I had a sneaking suspicion Scarth had somehow won the day. He had accepted my terms far too easily.

I was in the main terminal shortly after noon, having spent the remainder of the morning in the local town picking up extra emergency supplies for the new and unwanted addition to the party. The cafeteria was deserted as usual. I ordered steak and eggs, helped myself to a coffee from the polished chromium dispenser and found my usual chair midway down the first row of tables. Linc Kullman walked in five minutes later.

'You seem to be taking a liking to this place,' he said cheerfully, putting down his tray on the opposite side of the table.

'Not for much longer.'

'You're leaving, then!'

56

'Looks that way. You?'

He consulted his watch. 'In about two hours. Low-pressure system winding up west of St John's, want to make sure I'm ahead of it. We don't fly up with the angels any more, do we?'

I ignored the last remark. 'What's it like up around Greenland?'

'According to the latest satellite chart clear as a bell. What about Hannah? Is she going with you?'

'Could be. Why?'

'No reason; she's a nice lady, that's all.'

'Used to getting her own way, I would have said.'

The Killer Man grinned. 'You're right there. And that's something I'm going to miss when I get back to Florida ... no night stops in faraway places ... no willing young ladies. And you know something else, I can remember the time you would have at least put up a fight; but not any more, uh?'

'No Linc, not any more ... truth is she's not my type.' I said it but didn't believe a word. The sudden pang of jealousy told me that. It was totally unfounded of course. I'd only met Hannah Dawson the previous day. And where I had come from the Hannah Dawsons of this world were noticeable by their absence. Beautiful women don't go to the North. Just polar bears, flat-faced Eskimos, and men with a past to hide ... or a future they didn't have the courage to face.

The Killer Man looked at me, made as if to speak, then changed his mind. We finished our meal in silence.

Suddenly it was time to go. There had been no more mention of Key West and the seaplane company. No more offers to join in that idyllic dream. Not that I had expected it, of course. One plane one pilot would be the only way to make such a venture work. All I was short of was the plane. And if it hadn't been for my big investment there probably would have been one.

I followed the Killer Man through to the international departure lounge. The feeling came too, the uncomfortable feeling, which hadn't been there yesterday. The Killer Man tried to straighten it out as we parted.

'Look Spence … about Hannah …'

'Forget it,' I said. 'Whatever it is forget it.' There was sadness in his eyes when I added, 'Keep your feet dry, pal; as you said last night, it's a big ocean.'

I watched him go then. The slightly built youth with the dark brown eyes. The youth who didn't exist any more. The youth who had died along with a younger Luke Spence, consumed by too many battles in the deep unending blue of the stratosphere. And as with any war, the spoils were nothing more than a few spent and tarnished shells.

I was back at the hotel later, padding barefoot around my room, enjoying the spartan furnishings and cheap threadbare carpet beneath my feet. Soon the warmth would be gone and the hardships would begin. My packing was nearly complete. Essential items only, any excess weight would have to be jettisoned. In the corner of the room the television was playing softly to itself.

For the first time in two weeks I felt totally relaxed, totally happy. Tomorrow I would be back in the sky doing the only job I knew how; enjoying the endless freedom of space. The enormity of the Greenland search was still distant enough to be ignored. At least for a few more hours.

The word 'airport' followed by 'crash' stopped me midway between the open holdall and the bathroom. I turned towards the television and moved silently in on the newsreader. The report, or at least what I caught of it, was brief. 'Light twin-engine aircraft crashed on take-off from Gander airport less than thirty minutes ago. No further details yet available.'

I went to the bedside table and picked up my watch. Three minutes past five. Beyond the window the Newfoundland sky was turning to night. Couldn't have been the Killer Man, for Christ's sake. It couldn't have been! He was planning to leave at three o'clock. Except I was a pilot, and as any professional who makes a living from the flying game knows, planned departure times and actual departure times come adrift nine times out of ten.

I sat on the edge of the bed and willed myself to pick up the phone. Then I dialled the airport. In my mind the picture of Hannah Dawson came flooding back. Her long white hands were dripping with blood.

It took me a few minutes to get through to Flight Planning, and another few minutes before I spoke to someone who vaguely remembered me as the pilot of the Beaver who had dropped in frequently over the past two weeks to check on Notams for the Northwest Territories and Greenland. It appeared that three aircraft were due to leave that afternoon. The first one, a Piper Navajo, had crashed shortly after take-off from runway 04. The pilot had survived it seemed, but had suffered severe burns.

'Could you tell me the name of the pilot?'

The voice on the other end of the line pondered the question for a moment. 'Well ... I don't really know if I can release on that sort of information at this time ...'

'Okay, okay ... was it a guy by the name of Kullman? Lincoln Kullman!'

There was a moment's pause, then: 'Yes ... that's him.'

I felt my blood run suddenly cold. Felt the sudden dizziness starting in the head, working down to the neck. Felt the familiar aching emptiness in my stomach. A feeling even Nam had failed to temper.

'Where is he now?' I said shakily.

'At the General Hospital.'

'What about the other two planes that were going out with him?'

'Cancelled. The pilots are down at the hospital right now ... I guess he's a buddy of yours, right?'

'Yeah, something like that. Anyway, thanks for the information.' I put the phone back into its cradle, somehow unable to take my eyes away from it. It was all a bad dream. A lousy rotten stinking bad dream. Not the Killer Man. Not the bloody Killer Man. The voice screamed around in my head. The screaming stopped as the realization sunk in. Then the shocked whisper took over. He was too good a pilot for that to have happened. He'd been around too long. Too long or for ever; whichever way, it wasn't long enough. What was it we used to say all those years ago – 'every mission ages you ten years'. Every mission ... every time you zapped a MIG high over Banana Valley ... every time you got back ... or you didn't. And for the ones that didn't, at least they had died believing they had grown old. Any other way would have been indecent. Kids with a hundred years in their eyes – the happy warriors from Stateside. Four missions was all it ever took. Of course what we all forgot was the survivors. The kids who had sold their youth for a mess of pottage – or a few hundred hours' fast jet time in the stratosphere. Old men came back. Young bodies full of decaying old men. And now they've got you, Linc ... on the last big mission before going home.

The banging on the door brought me to my senses. 'It's open,' I yelled.

Hannah Dawson rushed in; face pale and distraught. 'Did you hear the news?'

'Yeah ... I heard it.'

'Linc,' she cried. 'Linc was leaving this afternoon.'

I looked at her; watched the blue eyes searching my face. Then I picked up my shirt and started to put it on.

'Was it him?' she said more quietly.

'Yes.'

Her hand went to her lips as she sank down on to the end of the bed. 'Is ... is he ... ?'

'Dead ... no.' What the hell was I talking about? Of course he was dead. Even if the burned body survived it wouldn't be Linc Kullman. It would be a skin-grafted creature full of ugliness. Some sad, sorry monster hiding in a dark corner for ever.

'Well! What happened?'

'Apparently got burnt; that's all I know. I'm going down to the hospital now.' I stood up and tucked my shirt into my trousers.

'I'll come with you.'

'You'll stay here,' I said firmly. 'You've done enough already;'

She leapt to her feet, anger flashing through her blue eyes. 'What do you mean, I've done enough already?'

I pulled on a thick, oiled-wool sweater.

'Well!' she shrieked.

'Well what?'

'You said I've done enough already. What exactly is that supposed to mean?'

'It means, Miss Dawson, he's a happily married man. He's also the best friend I ever had. Loose women are excluded from those kind of circles.'

She moved in quickly. Her right hand whipping out, catching me a stinging blow on the left side of the face. 'You ... you bastard. You rotten warped-minded bastard.' Her hands came up; talon-like nails searching for my face. I grabbed her roughly by the wrists and flung her down on the bed.

My voice was full of quiet anger when I said, 'We look after our own, Hannah Dawson ... something you may find hard to understand, but that's the way it is.' I grabbed my parka and went towards the open doorway. 'Tell Scarth I'll be back in an hour or so to sign those papers.' I didn't wait for a reply.

The hospital was much the same as any other. Long well lit corridors; polished linoleum floors and the overbearing smell of ether and medication. The nurses moved about quickly and efficiently, their footsteps, in their white low-heeled shoes, neat and economical. I found the reception desk in a small alcove, and was asked the usual question. Was I immediate family? No, but I was a friend. The polite smile, and if I would wait, she would speak to one of the doctors.

I went over to the waiting area, a few uncomfortable chairs arranged neatly alongside a coffee machine. Two flying-jacketed types were sitting there, staring morosely into their coffee cups.

I said, 'Were you the guys going out with Linc?'

The first of the two, an angular-faced individual, looked up and surveyed me. 'Yeah, we were.' His accent was Midwest. Cowboy country.

I held out my hand. 'Spence,' I said. 'Old friend of his.'

He took my hand in a firm handshake. 'Yeah, remember you from the airport yesterday. Bob Young ... this here's Al Stepanovitch ... don't worry about the name, he's on our side really.'

Stepanovitch raised a hand and threw a tired salute. 'How's it going?'

I pulled up a chair. 'Any idea how bad he is?'

Young fixed me with a steady gaze. 'Pretty bad, I'd say. Burns to head and hands, both legs broken ... that's as much as we know.'

'What about his wife?' I said.

'Called her a short while ago,' Young replied. 'She's leaving right away. Should be here sometime tomorrow morning.'

'What went wrong? Any ideas?'

Stepanovitch, still staring into his coffee cup, said, 'Must have lost one of the motors on take-off. Shit ... I tell you, we're all crazy, you know that! Crazy men. We get paid a thousand bucks and an airline ticket home, and for what? I'll tell you. The FAA gives us a written dispensation to overload the aircraft by ten per cent and we dumb motherfuckers go and fill up the cabin with fuel tanks; which leaves us sitting on the top of a bloody great bomb. All you need then is for one of the motors to up and leave town and what have you got? I'll tell you that as well ... you've got a one-way ticket to the local marble orchard.' His voice was emotional when he added, 'Linc would have been better off there.'

I looked at Stepanovitch, and then at Young. They appeared to be late thirties, early forties. Old hands in a dangerous game. And when the game claimed one of their elite band; they were understandably angry. But they were men. Real men. As much as the aces of the race car circuit, the wall of death riders, or soldiers going off to war. Only difference was they did their job under a cloak of total anonymity. There was no public acclaim, no winner's laurels, no medals. They went unseen, unnoticed, flying aircraft dangerously overloaded, aircraft that were designed to fly on one engine – should the other quit – with one proviso. And that proviso was that the total all-up weight was not exceeded. The irony was in the fact that they had to be overloaded to have sufficient fuel, and therefore range, to cross the ocean.

I left half an hour later having been told by a sympathetic woman doctor that the Killer Man was in a critical condition. His entire head had suffered third-degree burns. Now it was down to six-hourly morphine injections to combat the pain, and the intramuscular tetracycline four-hourly against infection. She hadn't told me about the treatment, of course; I knew that from my Vietnam days. I doubted it would have changed that much. What I also knew, although she hadn't mentioned that either, was that it would be something in the order of two weeks before they could even touch him. If he survived that long!

Young and Stepanovitch were still sitting sad-eyed by the coffee machine as I started the long walk down the neon-lit corridor.

I found Scarth in the bar at the Albatross. He was in conversation with a seedy-looking individual who was wearing over-large horn-rimmed spectacles. Hannah Dawson was nowhere to be seen.

Scarth looked up as I approached the table. 'Just the man,' he exclaimed. 'Got the papers all ready to sign.' I pulled out a chair and sat down.

'Mr Piquet's the lawyer who drew them up,' Scarth continued. 'He'll witness the signatures.'

I gave the seedy-looking Mr Piquet a brief nod. He didn't look much like a lawyer to me. But then, my rambling six-foot bulk, complete with shoulder-length hair and untidy beard, wouldn't have me marked out as a pilot.

The lawyer passed me a cheap plastic ballpoint. 'Three copies altogether,' he piped in a thin, effeminate voice. I picked up the first copy, which consisted of a number of sheets stapled together.

'Seems a lot for such a straightforward transaction,' I said.

Scarth smiled thinly. 'That's Mr Piquet's department. The first page outlines the deal. The ... er ... rest is what you might term legal claptrap.' Piquet winced noticeably. Perhaps he was a lawyer after all.

I glanced quickly over the first page, my mind straying to other things. Things like overweight aircraft crashing. 'Where do I sign?' I said to the lawyer.

'That would be right here,' he said, reaching over and turning to the last page. 'On the dotted line,'

I should have read the document in its entirety of course, but I was suddenly past caring. I signed. The lawyer slid the other two copies before me and I signed those also.

'What say we have a drink on that?' Scarth said as I folded my copy and put it into my pocket.

'Some other time,' I said, getting to my feet. 'By the way, did Hannah tell you about the crash?'

'Did mention something,' he said matter of factly.

'Good, because we won't be leaving in the morning now.'

'Why the hell not?' Scarth said gruffly.

'The guy in the bent aeroplane was a friend of mine; his wife's arriving in the morning from Florida and I just want to make sure everything's okay.'

Scarth's eyes narrowed. 'Look Spence, you're working for me now. Sure I'm sorry the guy's had an accident, but I'm running out of time.'

'They've been there for over thirty years,' I said tiredly. 'Another day isn't going to hurt.'

'Except every day is costing me money.'

'One day,' I repeated. 'And besides we need to go over one or two planning details yet.'

There was thunder written all over Scarth's face; but with his tame lawyer sitting at his side he managed to keep it controlled.

I went back to my room, pausing briefly outside Hannah's doorway. But it was too early for words; we were at each other's throats now, and only time would ease the anger. Apart from that I had had quite enough for one day.

Jacqueline Kullman was nothing like I had expected. She was petite, with long, black raven hair and a flawless complexion tanned to a golden brown. Her eyes were dark, almost black until you saw them in the daylight, then you found they were the deepest indigo blue.

She had arrived at the hospital early that morning after completing a marathon overnight journey which had included changing flights four times. Her face showed the weariness now, as I took her back to the hotel in a taxi.

64

'I'll be leaving First thing in the morning,' I said. 'Be up in Greenland for a couple of months. If there's anything I can do before ...'

She put a hand gently on my arm. 'Thank you Spence, I'll manage.'

'Money!' I said clumsily. 'Will you be all right?'

She gave me a wistful smile. 'I'll be all right. Careful folks we Kullmans; not that Linc was always that way. But since he started ferrying he said we needed to carry a lot of heavy insurance...' her voice broke and her eyes filled with tears.

I took her hand in mine. It was small and fragile and very, very cold. 'What will you do now ... about the seaplane company, I mean?'

She forced the tears back and put on a brave face. 'I'll run it myself... for Linc.' Her voice became as fragile as a summer breeze rustling through the trees when she added, 'And you know something, it will work. It will be the success we always planned it to be ... except that isn't what's important any more; what is important is that the price of dreams is too high.'

After a while I said, 'What will you do for pilots?'

'Oh I guess I'll find somebody ... there's an outfit up at Grassy Key who operate seaplanes, they might have somebody spare.' She turned and looked at me. 'What are you doing after you return from Greenland?'

'Hadn't really thought about it.'

'I don't suppose you would consider working for me?'

I half smiled to myself, remembering the offer from Linc. Now she was offering me his job. The left seat of his seaplane. 'I'm sure there are plenty of experienced pilots in Florida, Jacqueline.'

'Experienced perhaps, but you and Linc went back a long way. He talked about you a lot, you know ... said you used to save his life every other day during the war.'

I let out a small broken laugh. 'Don't you believe a word of it. It was strictly the other way around.'

She smiled. A brief sad smile. 'Well ... will you? I'm sure Linc would have wanted it this way.'

'I've been away a long time Jacqueline ... you see there was a lot of trouble ...'

She didn't let me finish. 'I know all about that. Linc told me. He also said you were innocent. Anyway that's in the past; and as for you having been away a long while ... perhaps it's time you came home.'

I said, 'Maybe. I'll think about it ... is that all right?'

'That's fine,' she said. 'Will you call me either way ... after you get back?'

'If you want me to.'

'Do you have our ... my number in Key West?'

'No.'

She opened her handbag and produced a business card. 'Don't be a stranger, Spence ... not now.'

'I won't,' I promised.

She sat back in her seat then and closed her eyes. Closing out the real world; running to the memory of Lincoln Kullman – pilot. Lincoln Kullman who had died minutes before she arrived at his bedside.

The afternoon was spent with Scarth and a subdued Hannah Dawson, running over basic arctic survival techniques. At first Scarth had shown little interest, reasoning that as I would be along, what was the point of it all? When I countered with should we crash, and I be killed, he started listening in earnest. I touched on everything I thought was vital to a forced-landing situation. Draining the engine oil as soon as possible after the crash. The oil would soon solidify, giving fuel for a fire and cooking. How to find fresh water if we went down near the Greenland coast. Ice a year or two old rarely has any noticeable saltiness, while ice two or three years old is generally fresher than the average river or spring water. Old sea ice can be distinguished from the current year's ice by its rounded corners and bluish colour, in contrast to the rougher sea ice which has a milky-grey colour.

What to do in the event of hypothermia. The treatment consists of returning the body temperature to normal. This is achieved by putting the affected person in a sleeping bag, making sure their buttocks, shoulders and feet are well insulated. The patient should then be warmed by placing heated rocks, wrapped in material, near various parts of the body. If the number of heated units is limited you place them as far as they will go in the following order: pit of stomach, small of back, armpits, back of the neck, wrists and between the thighs. Stimulation with hot drinks also helps if the patient is conscious. Avoid the use of alcohol as it opens the blood vessels at the surface of the skin, allowing body heat to be lost more rapidly.

After that I had moved on to frostbite; then using wet tea leaves in a cloth as a cure for snow blindness; fire and smoke signals, light signals and so on. Right down to building a snow house and making various kinds of deadfall traps to catch wild game.

Of course it wasn't enough. Any three-hour discussion on surviving in the arctic can never be that. And as Hannah Dawson hadn't heard or said a word since I had told her about the Killer Man's death, and as Scarth's physical shape was totally against him, if they lost me for any reason they were both dead.

Scarth said, 'Can you run that frostbite deal past me again? Seems to me that's the first problem we'd have.'

'There's a lot to it,' I said. 'I'll run through the preventive measures again … we can go over the symptoms and treatment on the flight out in the morning. Basically, to avoid frostbite there are nine points to remember. One, keep wrinkling your face to ensure stiff patches do not form. At the same time watch your hands for white patches. Two, watch each other's faces and ears for the same white patches. Three, don't handle metal with your bare hands. Four, avoid tight clothing which will reduce circulation and increase risk of frostbite.' I continued, listing the remaining five points. At the end of it Scarth looked as confused as ever. Hannah still hadn't heard a word.

'That's about it then,' I concluded. 'We can discuss the flight routing over dinner tonight.'

'What time are we planning to leave?' Scarth enquired.

I said, 'Four thirty in the morning; that's from the hotel. Should be airborne about five thirty. There is one minor problem which had slipped my mind, however; keep your fluid intake down tonight and in the morning, unless you've got a six-or-more-hour bladder.'

Scarth said, 'Ferry pilots I've used in the past always carried bottles for that contingency.'

'Great,' I said lightly. 'What about Miss Dawson ... different equipment.'

Hannah Dawson coloured ever so slightly, being taken off guard by the remark. Then her eyes glinted gun-metal blue: 'Don't worry about me,' she said icily. 'I can take care of myself.'

'I doubt that, Miss Dawson, but if you think you'd like to try the first thing you've got to do is forget about Kullman. He never existed.'

There were tears in her eyes as she said angrily, 'You're a hard-hearted bastard, Luke Spence ... just because ...'

'Don't flatter yourself, lady. Just because nothing. Kullman knew the risks. He paid the price, that's all.' I turned to Scarth. 'If you want me I'll be in the bar.'

PART TWO

We landed at Narsarsuaq early the following afternoon, clambering stiff-legged from the Beaver and stamping up and down in the freeze-dried snow in an attempt to get the circulation going again. Hannah Dawson noticed it first as I thought she might. She stood near the Beaver's propeller, her ears straining, motioning to Scarth to stop flailing his arms.

'What the hell ...' he started.

'Shhh!' she replied, raising her mittened hand to her mouth. Then turning to me she said, 'What is it? There's something wrong.'

I looked slowly around the deserted airstrip to the gathering of huts and prefabricated concrete buildings, then back along the sweep of white soaring mountains. 'Nothing's wrong,' I said quietly. 'Except for the sound – or rather the lack of sound. What you hear is the arctic silence.'

She smiled in astonishment. 'It's amazing! There are no birds ... nothing!'

'In the summer,' I said. 'You get ravens and arctic skua then.'

'Do they sing?'

'Not much, more of a shriek.'

Scarth had moved back to the aircraft and was hauling baggage out of the rear locker. 'How much of this stuff do we need?' he asked gruffly.

'Just our overnight kit. Providing of course we can get the fuel.'

'Leave that to me. I'll sort it out ... even if I have to drill for the damn stuff myself.'

A lightweight truck bounced across the snow and skidded to a halt by the aircraft's nose. The Eskimo driver slid down from the cab and walked slowly towards us, his toes pointing inwards in the 'kamik-walk of the mountains'. I greeted him in Inuktitut and asked if we could put the Beaver in the hangar for the night. It was not for him to say, he replied. I would need to see the station manager of Greenland Air.

'You speak Eskimo pretty well,' Scarth remarked as we climbed into the truck.

'Not so difficult. As the guys up in Frobisher used to say, it's like English backwards with the vowels taken out ... only problem is, if you're on the receiving end you get a shower as well.'

The Greenland Air operations shack was practically deserted, their helicopters that did the passenger and freight shuttle to the west-coast settlements having finished for the day. The station manager, an ugly man with a permanent sniff, was however happy to do business when Scarth produced a bundle of American dollars. He would take care of the fuel and the hangarage, he said. No problems.

'You may speak their lingo,' Scarth said as we walked out of the door. 'But this stuff,' he patted his inside pocket, 'this stuff is international.'

We re-boarded the truck and started the bumpy drive towards the Arctic Hotel. I tapped the Eskimo on the shoulder and asked him to stop at the weather station; then turning back to Scarth, said, 'We'll get off at the building up ahead on the right; there's someone I want you to meet. Hannah can take the bags on to the hotel and check us in.'

Scarth nodded. 'Got that, Hannah?'

She gave me a disapproving look before she said she had.

'I take it this is the guy Palmarsson!' Scarth said, jerking a hand at the door of the weather station.

I waited until the truck's engine revved up and pulled away. 'You've got it. Erik Palmarsson.' I reached out and grabbed Scarth's shoulder as his hand fell on the door handle. 'Before you go in, I've been thinking.'

Scarth pulled his fur-lined hood tightly around his fat face. 'Couldn't we do that inside? Damned sight warmer.'

'We could take him with us,' I said.

'What? Palmarsson?'

'Yes! Palmarsson. We could take him with us – to Big Gunn.'

'What's the point?'

'His father-in-law is the Eskimo Ayayook ... if he's still alive, that is. We might be able to get a better fix on the location. Those dollars of yours won't be any good over there. Different kind of Eskimo.'

'And you reckon the old man would confide in Palmarsson?'

'It's possible.'

Scarth removed his right mitten and rubbed his eyes. 'Yeah, could be worth a try. How do we persuade him to come along though?'

'Give him our *rationeringsark* ... our drink coupons. You'll be issued with those at the hotel. You could also give him a few spare American dollars; black market supply!'

Scarth hurriedly pulled his mitten back on. 'Jesus! Doesn't take long, does it?'

'What's that?'

'Goddam cold. How long did I have that glove off? Thirty seconds ... a minute?'

'Wait until it gets really cold,' I said, reaching forward and opening the outer door.

We banged the loose snow from our boots and went through into the dimly lit corridor. It was still the first door on the left, as it probably had been since the Second World War when the Americans had erected the building as a temporary wooden unit.

Palmarsson was leaning over a synoptic chart as we entered the room, drawing in isobars with an unsteady hand. He stopped and looked up, the sun spokes around his eyes wrinkling into a friendly smile.

'Ah, Captain Spence. Welcome ... welcome.' He transferred the pencil to his left hand. His right hand was trembling as I took it in greeting. Too long without a drink.

'Erik, want you to meet a business associate of mine. Rollo Scarth.'

Palmarsson held out his hand to Scarth. 'I am pleased to meet you, Mr Scarth.'

'Just plain Rollo'll do fine,' Scarth said magnanimously.

Palmarsson smiled and turned to me. 'So you are back. You stay for the night I think,'

'That's about it. We're leaving for Big Gunn first thing in the morning,'

The warm smile disappeared instantly. 'Big Gunn? You are going to Big Gunn?'

'That's right. Rollo's an aircraft dealer from New York. Wants to try to find the missing aircraft ... the ones you told me about, remember, Patterson's Volunteers.'

Palmarsson stepped back unsteadily, in his eyes a look of betrayal. 'I think it is not possible, Captain. It was a very long time ago. No, I think it is indeed not possible. Also it is very dangerous country.'

Scarth unzipped his parka and sank wearily into the chair by the teleprinter.

'We wondered,' I started. 'We wondered if you would come with us!'

'Come with you? I do not understand.'

'To Big Gunn. We'd like you to come with us to Big Gunn.'

Palmarsson's lips moved briefly, silently. Then the words came with a slow, staccato precision. 'To Big Gunn! It is also impossible. My job, you understand. It is here. I cannot leave.'

Scarth intervened. 'Could you give us an exact location on the missing planes then?'

Palmarsson went back to his synoptic chart; to the refuge of something he knew and understood. In that at least we were much the same. I had spent most of my life with aeroplanes; to the point where I could talk to a sick engine and make it better. Erik was no different. Except his understanding was with pressure systems; isobars, isotherms. Katabatic and anabatic winds; decoding station circles; making out terminal area forecasts. He probably talked to the elements the same way I talked to aircraft. And like me he might have found it was easier than dealing with people.

Scarth coughed. 'Well, Erik. What d'you say?'

Palmarsson looked up nervously. 'I know not where these aeroplanes are, Mr Scarth. If they are there at all.'

'I pay well,' Scarth continued. 'How does a year's supply of whisky sound?'

It sounded good. Too good. You could see from the changed expression on Palmarsson's face. Whatever his reasons for not wanting to part with any more information had been, they evaporated magically in that thousandth part of a second. Making at least a thousand good reasons why Erik Palmarsson would have made a lousy poker player. 'You ... you will give me that?'

'If you can tell me the exact location ... yes.'

74

His reply was instantaneous. His liquid brown eyes alive with the fever. The fever that too much whisky brings. 'I will speak with my wife later this day. It is her father who knows of this. I will see you later. Tonight!'

I said, 'Where? The hotel?'

He shook his head. 'No, it is not good. The police ... I am not, how you say, forbidden in this place.'

'Allowed,' I corrected.

'Yes, so. I am not allowed in this place. No, we will meet here at eight o'clock. Twenty hundred hours. This is possible?'

I nodded. 'It's possible.'

'There will be no lights, but the door it is open.'

'Thank you Erik, we will see you later.' I found myself talking back in his brand of stilted English.

'You make sure,' he said shakily, as we were leaving. 'You make sure no one follows you.'

'Don't worry,' I said. 'We'll make sure.'

'One hell of a frightened guy, I'd say,' Scarth remarked as we walked down the unmade road to the hotel.

'He's had a few run-ins with the police, or at least that's the impression I got on my last visit here. Probably blacklisted at every watering hole in the arctic.'

'Wasn't that so much. It was when you mentioned Big Gunn; he seemed to go on the defensive straight away.'

'Yeah, he did, didn't he; can't understand why, though.' I glanced sideways at Scarth. 'Any ideas?'

The slate-grey eyes levelled at me. 'No,' he said emphatically. 'Not a one.'

I turned my face back towards the north. The wind was getting up; the sharp, cold wind I knew. But it was more than that. It was the smell of snow out of a clear blue sky.

'We won't be going tomorrow,' I said, watching my breath condense in puffy little clouds.

'What's that?' Scarth wheezed.

'We won't be going tomorrow ... snow coming in from the north.'

Scarth looked at me in disbelief. 'Now how in hell's name do you know that?'

'Wind ... smell ... stick around for seven years, you'll get the idea.'

'You know something Spence, you're a comedian.'

'You're wrong, Rollo. Now if you'd said mad, I might have agreed with you. That's something else you get for your seven years.'

'And you're asking me to stick around ... as I said, you're a comedian.'

'Okay, I'm a comedian ... and today's joke is we ain't going tomorrow.'

Scarth didn't even laugh.

By seven o'clock that evening, we had had a meal at the annexe building of the hotel and were now sitting in Scarth's room going over the details of the final leg to Big Gunn.

'By the way,' I said, 'I'd make sure you both have a good shower before we finally depart. It'll be the last you have for a long time.'

Hannah said, 'How do we go about washing ... when we get to the east coast, that is?'

'Easy, we don't. We all sit around and smell to high heaven. But don't worry, you'll get used to it.' She wrinkled up her nose in mock disgust.

'What about latrines?' Scarth questioned.

I looked up with interest. I didn't know a great deal about Scarth, but he was adding to my meagre dossier all the time. The word 'latrine' is strictly a military one. One which indicated at some time or other Scarth had served in one of the armed forces. As I had his age pinned down to late fifties, that could have meant Korea, or even the latter part of the Second World War. I said, 'Should be okay at the Kulusuk airstrip; once we move up to the ice desert we dig our own. Downwind of course.'

Hannah Dawson pulled another face. Slowly but surely the stark reality of the situation was sinking in. And when it finally hits bedrock, I thought, you'll pray to God you had never heard of Greenland.

Scarth leaned forward in his chair and started pulling his boots on. 'Is that bar still open next door?'

'Should be,' I said.

'Good! In that happy event I'm going to get myself a very large bourbon and some supplies for the journey.' He stood up and stamped his feet. 'Can't say I'll be sorry to get rid of these things,' he said, looking disdainfully at his snow boots. 'Ah, what the hell!' He picked up his parka from the bed. 'You coming?' he said, turning to me.

'No thanks. I'll meet you over at the weather station at eight. Might be better if we go separately.'

'How do you figure that?'

'Police patrols up around the airfield. If you're stopped you can say you're out for an after-dinner walk. They'll think you're mad, of course … just say you are a visiting pilot; first time here. I'll wait till ten after eight; if they haven't escorted you back by then I'll see you over there.'

'And if they have?'

'If they have, they'll be here with you at the hotel, which means I'll have a clear run.'

Scarth gave a suitable scowl. 'To hear you talk anyone would think we were in a police state.'

I smiled. 'But we are, Rollo … or didn't I mention it?'

Scarth turned to Hannah. 'Come on, Hannah, let's go and drink to those airplanes we're about to find.'

She smiled prettily and followed him out of the door.

At precisely eight minutes past eight I was huddled tightly against the wall at the east side of the hotel watching the airfield road for any sign of headlights. The wind was bitingly cold now, screaming out of the north like a wild banshee. The smell of snow was nearer.

I checked the luminous dial on my watch: 8.10. Scarth must have made it okay. I moved out quickly across the snow, avoiding the hotel access road. Old Eskimo hunting tip – never stay on the game trail, all wild animals watch their back trails. The Greenland police, the two I had met on my last visit at least, slotted comfortably into the wild-animal category.

I reached the weather station about five minutes later, having

77

curved my way round in a wide arc. The door was open, banging in the wind. I took a last look up at the black and starless heaven, gave a momentary shudder, and slipped quietly into the building. No lights, Palmarsson had said. I felt my way through the inner door and then along the wall to his office. My hand fell on the door handle at the first attempt.

'Erik ... Rollo!' The whisper echoed softly back. I took the flashlight from my pocket and snicked it on. The narrow beam swept quickly around the room. It was empty. I cursed to myself and went back to the corridor, then switching off the torch I moved further into the darkened building, all the time listening. But there was nothing, the place was deserted.

The dull thud, somewhere ahead, rooted me to the spot. I pressed myself hard against the wall, ears pricked, heart thumping. Thud! There it was again! I willed my body slowly and silently along the wall, reaching out with my left hand, feeling my way ... inch by careful inch.

Ten painfully slow footsteps later the wall ended, the corridor opening out. It was then my eyes locked on to the vague outline. As it moved I felt a chill whirlpool of wind brush against my face. The wooden thud of an open door banging in the wind followed. I let out a long and shaky breath and scanned the area with my torch. The open door was one of a pair, and must at one time have served as the main entrance to the building. Perhaps it still did! From this area the corridors branched off in three different directions. On one of the walls was a large varnished board with the legend 'Operational Movements'. It looked distinctly 1940s vintage. Something else my fellow countrymen had left behind in their rush to go home.

What made me go out through the double doors I don't know. Perhaps it was easier than finding my way back down that darkened dusty corridor. Or perhaps it was some long forgotten fear of old, dark buildings – a childhood fear of ghosts! Whatever it was I went out into the cold night, securing the door behind me.

From what I could make out in the strange night-light of snow, the ground fell away fairly steeply from that side of the building. In the distance was the thin ethereal sound of water slapping gently against icebergs. The fjord.

I moved cautiously down the outside of the building, towards the end, which housed Palmarsson's office. From there I could get back to the hotel the way I came. I couldn't have been more than halfway down the wooden structure when I stumbled over the rock. Except it wasn't a rock! I realized that when I fell across it. It was soft, pliable ... living! I recoiled instinctively, scrambling to my feet.

The flashlight beam fell on the hip, or what had once been a hip. Now it was a red crater, as if it had exploded out of itself, splattering red on the white snow beneath. I moved the beam from the congealed mass of blood, feeling the hot bile rise in my throat as I did so. Then the shaft of yellow light fell upon the upturned face; rime and clots of snow ground into the hair. Below that, the half-opened eyes showed only white; the nostrils flared. The once smiling face was wiped clean of everything but a snarl. A frozen snarl with animal, angry teeth. It was as if the long-clenched jaws had tightened down beyond some ultimate cog and savagely locked into their own torn lips in one final silent scream.

I fell back against the building, the torch beam still playing on the face of Erik Palmarsson. 'My God,' I said quietly. 'You poor, sad, unlucky bastard.' I started to move then. Started, then stopped. The torch was still on, and less than two feet from Palmarsson's body lay the murder weapon: black and bloody, tendrils of flesh still clinging to it. It was a hand-held harpoon; the type Eskimos use for sealing or even whaling. Razor sharp with long pointed barbs. It would have ripped Palmarsson's innards to shreds.

My mind was in a turmoil as I moved away; the only sound the rising and falling moan of wind coupled with my footsteps. Footsteps which creaked across the dry carpet of snow. Why? Why Palmarsson? And where was Scarth? I reached the end of the building still in a daze. At the limit of my vision the white lights of the Arctic Hotel flickered welcomingly through the blowing snow. I started to run. Once I had crossed the unmade airport road I could follow my old trail back. Once

I had crossed ... I was less than halfway when I heard the engine, and no more than three footsteps further on when the headlights blazed through the thin curtain of lifted snow.

I made the snow bank which bordered the road as the vehicle's brakes squealed to a stop; the sound of slamming doors carried downwind like rifle shots. The shouting voices followed as I slithered down the other side of the bank and started to run again. Up ahead were the buildings which housed the Greenland Air personnel. In through the front, and out – hopefully through the back. Then a ninety-degree turn to the right, and a four-hundred-yard dash to the hotel.

My legs dragged tiredly through the deep drifts as the lights ahead grew steadily brighter. Fifty yards, no more! At least the wind was on my back, making the going easier. Something like a groan escaped my lips when I realized that if it was making it easier for me, it would be making it easier for them! And whoever they were, they had the advantage. They probably lived in this place. They would know these few acres of navigable terrain like the backs of their hands.

I slowed up momentarily and glanced back. The sight of the yellow light humpling through the snow towards me put new life into my aching limbs, and I surged on with renewed vigour. I had the torch in my left hand as I skidded through the outer door and found the light switches. I reached out and knocked them off, plunging the main entrance and the corridor beyond the inner door into darkness.

Then I was in the dry, throat-picking warmth of the building, torchlight raking left and right. There was a stairway on the left leading to the upper floor. The hallway where I stood led directly to a matching double door on the opposite side of the building. Midway down the short hallway a central corridor ran left and right down the entire length of the building. I turned into the corridor going right, went six paces, and shook the loose snow from my clothing. Not much of a false trail, but the best my scrambled brain would come up with at such short notice. Having done that I moved quickly back to the rear entrance and slipped outside into the cold night. The door led to nowhere: probably one of those design features aimed at the aesthetically pleasing as opposed to the coldly practical.

I moved out into the rocky outcrop as the main building lit up like a Christmas tree. At least it gave the appearance of doing that. What in fact had happened was the outside lights at the rear of the building had been switched on, reflecting off the snow with the augmented candlepower of a high-intensity searchlight. Keeping low, I scurried on into the darkness, swearing softly as my ankles cracked against the unseen rocks.

Only when the raven wing of night folded over me again did I stop. I was breathing hard, the sweat freezing instantly on my forehead. Now what, Spence? Now what? You heard car doors slamming, remember! Doors – plural! So one of them is covering the back of the building, which means you could be walking into a trap at this very moment. I squatted lower, listening … straining to catch the faintest sound. A stumbling footstep; an untimely cough! But there was nothing; nothing but the whine of the arctic wind as it blasted its way over Tunugdliarfik fjord. I was about to move out when I saw the shadow. Twenty yards away. A shadow caught against the distant lights of the hotel.

Good! But how good? I slipped silently to the ground. To the prone position. One more dark shape amidst the icebound rocks. A shape which would soon be covered with a fine dusting of snow. Now it was down to waiting. How long? Ten minutes … twenty … an hour? No more than an hour, Spence or you'll be here for ever. Silently, behind closed eyes, I began counting.

The voice came six hundred and eight seconds later.

My heart jerked painfully. The voice sounded close. I screwed up my eyes and tried to press my body further into the icy hollow between the rocks. Then it was back. Louder this time.

'Kolb … over here.'

I waited, hearing the pulse thundering in my ears. I tried to concentrate on feeling the cold. Tried to find the pain which had been

81

there a short while ago. Anything to slow up the adrenaline. Anything to stop the noise in my head. The noise I felt sure they would hear. And then unmistakably footsteps dragging through the snow.

'What is it?' the new voice said.

'A movement ... down towards the road.'

'Couldn't be.' I vaguely recognized the American accent. The one belonging to the big ugly cop I had met on my first visit. 'Unless there were two of them!'

'How about the inspector?' the first voice said. 'He should be down there by now.'

'That's probably who it was, then.'

'So how about this one?'

There was a grunt. 'Looks like the slick bastard has given us the slip.'

'But how ... it's impossible.'

'To an outsider perhaps; but this one I think belongs to the North.'

The first voice said uncertainly, 'One of our people, you mean?'

'No Fleischer ... I think the slick bastard's even better than our people.'

There was a wordless silence. The only sounds were my own heartbeat and the wind worrying the snow with its endless whining.

After a time Fleischer, the first voice, said, 'So what now?'

'We go back.'

'What about the inspector?'

'Fuck the inspector,' Kolb snapped, 'they don't pay me enough to get my balls frozen off.'

'And him?' Fleischer said.

'Him!' The word was fainter, as if the head was turned away surveying the flickering lights of the hotel. It had been said almost uninterestedly, as if the eyes had been idly imagining the warmth beyond the distant glimmer of windows. Picturing and envying those cocooned within. For some the long northern winters had their advantages, the order of which was usually whisky, women and bed. 'Don't worry, Fleischer. Whichever way, we've got him ... no one gets away from this place.'

Fleischer said something in return. Something I didn't catch. The second voice, Kolb, laughed distantly. It was then I realized they had gone. I didn't move. I lay, snow covered, slowly freezing to death.

And all the time I heard the second voice saying, 'I think the slick bastard's even better than our people.' Somewhere inside I smiled. You're still not good enough Kolb, or whatever your name is. You see, for the last five years I've made a profession out of being a survivor in this hell of yours. You probably imagine it's your birthright. And you know what, Kolb, without realizing it you've become an alien in your own country. You've grown fat and soft, reliant on whisky and tobacco; the white man's ways. You rely on the supply ships now. Once you hunted. But not any more. I resumed the count.

Eight minutes and thirty-two seconds later they were back. Soundlessly they had returned; or perhaps they had never been that far away. Fleischer spoke first. He sounded nervous. 'He's ... he's not here, Kolb; couldn't be. He would have made a move by now.'

Kolb grunted like an animal. 'He's here, Fleischer. Men don't disappear into thin air.'

Fleischer laughed. A thin hysterical laugh. 'When I was a boy,' he said, 'there was a shaman ... up at Godthaab ...'

'There's no shaman here,' Kolb growled. 'No spirit songs, no magic ... just a man.'

'What if he's got a gun? Have you thought of that?'

'He hasn't,' Kolb said with some assurance.

'How do you know that?'

'He doesn't need one.'

'Why?'

'For the same fucking reason bears don't use them,' Kolb reasoned impatiently. 'Animal instinct.' There was an exasperated sigh, or perhaps it was nothing more than a trick of the wind, then Kolb said, 'Let's go, Fleischer. My balls really are frozen off now.'

I turned my head slowly, straining to catch their scuffling footsteps, but there was nothing. Wait, Spence ... animals and back trails, remember? Long, painfully cold seconds later, the distant metallic

83

clunk of car doors carried on the wind. The revving engine followed, and was soon swallowed by the black angry night.

I moved out slowly, silently curving my way back towards the lights of the hotel. A body twisted in gradually developing pain. A pain I grudgingly welcomed. Once that stopped the real problems began.

It was fortunate that at least one of us had been given a room on the ground floor, and doubly fortunate that I had bothered to check which window it was before setting out for the weather station. I rapped twice on the frosted glass and waited. Ten seconds later I tried again, harder this time.

The top section of the window grated open a fraction of an inch. 'Who is it?' Hannah Dawson asked nervously.

'Spence ... let me in. Quick.'

'What the hell's going on?' she said as I pulled myself through the opened lower window. No nervous shaky voice now, just a cold, measured anger. I closed the window and drew the curtains. When I turned to face her she bit her lip. The nervousness returned. And with it I found myself looking at the other woman. The one scrubbed clean of lipstick, mascara and eye shadow. The one stripped of the fashionable clothes and flattering colours. She was standing defensively, arms folded across her breasts, wearing nothing but a flimsy black wrap. And she wasn't beautiful any more. 'What... what happened ... your face, it's covered with ice.'

I pulled my mittens off and with numbed fingers started on my parka. 'Where's Rollo?'

'What do you mean, where's Rollo? I thought you were both going to the weather station.'

'He went, then?'

'Yes. Some time before eight.' Some of the composure had returned when she added, 'Now perhaps you'll tell me what's going on?'

I slipped out of the parka and dropped into the bedside chair. 'Get me a towel first.'

She went to the bathroom as I attempted to rub some kind of feeling into my arms and shoulders. There are times in the North when you

84

feel you will never be warm again. Hannah came back with the towel, handed it to me and sat down on the edge of the bed. I held the towel to my face for a minute or more wincing as the real pain of thawing out began in earnest. After a while I said, 'Palmarsson's dead!'

Hannah's head jerked up quickly. 'Palmarsson the weather man?'

'One and the same,' I said.

'How? What happened?'

I ran quickly over the events of the previous hour, omitting the gorier details of exactly how the Dane had been killed. Even so, by the time I had finished her face had paled considerably, white skin shining taut over high cheekbones.

She said, 'You're sure it was the police following you?'

'I'm sure.'

'What if they follow you here?'

'Not much chance of that. It's virtually impossible to track anyone over rocky outcrop. Then there's the wind, that will have covered any footprints I did make.'

She shivered slightly, folding her arms. That was when the pieces began to fit together in her mind. Her eyes suddenly widened. 'But Rollo ... what if he's still out there?'

'I didn't see him. Perhaps he's back in his room.'

'No. He would have come and told me first,' she said quickly.

I thought for a moment. 'Which leaves the bar. He may have gone back there.'

There was a note of impatience in her voice when she said, 'Shouldn't you go and check?'

'Later.'

'What the hell do you mean, later? He's out there, and there's a killer on the loose, and you're saying you'll go and find him later.'

I looked into the angry eyes. 'Rollo's game,' I said. 'I didn't invent the rules.'

'So what do you propose?' she said at length.

'We wait.'

'For what?'

'The police ... they should be along shortly.'

'You said they couldn't follow you here, that your tracks would be covered.'

'Not that way. No, they'll be doing the rounds of questioning anybody and everybody. And if my guess is right I'll be one of the chief suspects.'

Hannah gave me a quizzical stare. 'How do you make that out?'

'There's a cop name of Kolb, or something like that. Met him on my last visit here. He gave me the impression then that he didn't like the colour of my eyes ... I somehow doubt his feelings will have mellowed.'

'What if they don't come?'

'They'll come.'

'To hell with that,' she said, getting up from the bed. 'If you won't go and look for him, I will.' She moved across the room and started sorting through a pile of clothes.

'And where do you propose looking?'

'His room, the bar ... I don't know. Anything's better than sitting here waiting.'

I said, 'Okay, I get the message. I'll go.'

'You don't have to,' she replied defiantly.

'No,' I said, getting up from the chair. 'I don't have to, but I have the feeling you'd never forgive me if I didn't.'

She lifted an eyebrow at me. 'And that's important?'

I picked up my parka from the floor and looked at her leaning against the wall, her breasts thrusting sharply against the thin material of the black wrap. And I knew it was for all the wrong reasons. She wouldn't like me for that. I didn't even like me for that. 'Important? No, I guess not. But then you wouldn't have believed me if I'd said otherwise, would you?'

'No,' she said in a small voice. 'I don't suppose I would.'

I tried Rollo's room first. He was, as expected, not in. So I went back down the open wooden staircase, past the reception desk, towards the main entrance. If the bar was still open in the annexe building I might find him. If not ... The thinking stopped quite abruptly. At about the same time the two ugly cops came through the door, and I walked straight into their arms.

The taller one of the two was the mean-faced character I had bumped into before. The one whose name was probably Kolb. His companion I hadn't seen before. He was almost as tall, almost as ugly and about half Kolb's age. He had to be Fleischer.

'Captain Spence!' The taller cop's face twisted into a cruel smile. The accent told me it was Kolb. 'You are going somewhere?'

'The bar.'

'But you have only just come in.'

'What the hell are you talking about?'

'I think you know, Captain.'

'Know what?'

His face hardened. 'Your clothing, it is still wet... I think you had better come with us. We have some questions.' He half turned to the other cop and nodded towards the door. 'Fleischer.'

Fleischer opened the door and I was bundled outside. Outside into the blizzard. Outside to where any sound would be lost in the tortured scream of wind.

Kolb's face was close to mine when he shouted. 'You remember what I told you last time, Captain Spence?' The words were torn one by one from his lips. The bad breath had a more lasting quality.

'What?'

'I told you ... last time I told you, you were not welcome in this place ... ever. You remember?'

I was still trying to come up with a suitable answer when he hit me. Low and hard. I doubled up and started going down, that was when his knee connected somewhere around my jaw, and my head snapped viciously back. After that there were hands dragging me roughly through the snow, pushing me on to the floor of a car, and a boot on my neck to make sure I didn't move. Then a short jerky drive over rough unmade roads until we arrived at wherever we were going.

As far as police outposts went, this one had to be the worst: from the smells of bad alcohol and rotting seal meat to the permanent stench of body sweat. It was a place hardly fit for animals. A storm lantern hung

87

from a hook on the ceiling, and swayed drunkenly as the wind whistled through the cracks in the ill-fitting door. The uneven floor, the solitary broken-down old desk, and the two uncomfortable-looking hard chairs were covered in a fine white dust. Except it wasn't dust, it was finely grained snow. Apart from the lantern, which at least offered a promise of warmth, there was no heating.

Kolb pushed me unceremoniously into one of the chairs and moved around the back of the desk. He picked up a black telephone, dialled three numbers and waited. Then he spoke quickly in Danish. The angry-sounding conversation was short lived, ending with Kolb slamming down the phone.

'He's at the airfield,' he said to Fleischer. 'At the operations shack.'

Fleischer said uncertainly, 'What's he doing there?'

'Gunnar said he's on the radio.'

'The radio?'

'Yeah, the fucking radio. Can you believe it … at a time like this?' Kolb pulled his parka hood over his greasy black hair and shuffled towards the door.

'Where are you going?' Fleischer asked nervously.

'To get him. You keep an eye on this one.' The door opened to the full blast of the norther. A few papers scurried along the floor and the lantern cast its swinging light even higher up the dirty grey walls. Fleischer pushed it closed with some difficulty, then hurried to the far side of the desk and the other chair. He dropped into it, placing both hands on the desk top in front of him. In his hands a small snub-nosed revolver gleamed dully in the yellow light.

'So, perhaps you'd like to tell me what all this is about?' I said as casually as my aching jaw would allow.

Fleischer's hands twitched. 'You wait. The inspector will be here soon.'

'Inspector who?'

'Inspector Thiessen.'

'He's the boss, I take it?'

'He's the inspector.'

I tried again. 'So why am I here?'

The gun wavered, then lifted a fraction. 'Shut up,' he snapped.

When faced by a gunman speak to him nicely; be courteous, polite. When faced by a nervous gunman, don't say anything, he's likely to squeeze the trigger without even realizing it. Fleischer, I decided, was a nervous gunman.

Thiessen arrived twenty minutes later. His first action was to apologize for keeping me waiting. Then taking over the chair Fleischer had vacated, he removed his mittens and rubbed his hands together. 'One day,' he grimaced. 'One day we may even have heating in this miserable place.' It was addressed to no one in particular, although I sensed it was by way of another apology.

He reached for a desk drawer and produced paper and a pencil. 'You have been told,' he said, brushing snow from the desk top with his sleeve, 'why you are here?'

'No.'

'No?' He looked genuinely surprised. Then turning to Kolb said, 'You have not explained, Sergeant Kolbrunarskald?' So that was his name, no wonder he was known as Kolb.

'No point,' Kolb rasped. 'It was him.'

Thiessen sighed, frowned, and turned back to me. 'It was me what?' I said sharply.

'Nothing, Captain Spence ... a mistake.' He turned back to the ugly Kolb. 'Take Fleischer to the airfield. You will pick up Kavavouk.'

'Kavavouk ... the old hunter?'

'Unless you know of another by this name,' Thiessen said curtly. 'Of course Kavavouk the hunter.'

'What for?' Kolb replied sullenly.

'Questioning.'

Kolb pulled his parka hood over his head with great reluctance. 'You're wrong, Thiessen ... he's the one.'

Thiessen's face hardened. 'Question my authority once more, Sergeant, and I take the stripes ... now get out.'

Thiessen waited for the door to close before leaning back in his chair. His face visibly relaxed. Softened into a smile. He was somewhere approaching fifty, somewhere in the settled season of middle age. Pale European features, pale eyes, light brown hair greying at the sides. He looked lean and fit, the type who had looked after himself. 'Once more, Captain, it seems I must apologize, this time for Sergeant Kolbrunarskald. The problems of independence ... Greenland for the Greenlanders ... you understand?'

I nodded. 'Happens,' I said.

'Yes, regretfully it happens.' Thiessen smiled, a small sad smile. I sensed this one was a policeman. A professional. No fairy tales for him, no fancy stories. He was too smart for that.

'I take it this is about Palmarsson?' I said suddenly.

There was no surprise in his voice when he said, 'You know then?'

'I was there after it happened.'

'What then?'

I ran through the story for the second time that evening, omitting to mention I had heard the two voices. The voices of Kolb and Fleischer. He wrote quickly as I spoke. When I had finished he looked up. 'And the two men who were chasing you ... you thought...'

'I thought they had something to do with the killing.'

Thiessen nodded. 'But afterwards ... you were leaving the hotel when the sergeant picked you up.'

'Coming here, by way of the bar,' I said. 'After what I'd been through I needed a stiff drink.'

'Yes, perhaps.' A pause, then: 'Why didn't you get the hotel receptionist to phone here first?'

I shrugged. 'You tell me, Inspector. Delayed shock ... I don't know. I do know, however, I wasn't thinking that clearly.'

Thiessen sucked the end of the pencil for a moment. 'But you said nothing to Kolbrunarskald.'

'He didn't seem in the mood for talking.' I rubbed my jaw painfully. 'In fact, if I didn't have this beard you'd see a reasonable-size swelling.'

Thiessen dropped the pencil on the desk. 'He struck you?'

90

'Don't worry Inspector, I won't be making any complaints ... as long as he doesn't try it again.'

'I think it is time for him to go,' Thiessen said quietly. He picked up the paper before him, his eyes scanning back and forth. 'You said you went to the weather station to check for tomorrow. This is correct?'

'Yes?'

'And your purpose for going to eastern Greenland?'

'Eastern Greenland?' I echoed dumbly.

'Yes Captain, your flight plan was for Kulusuk. You diverted here for fuel I believe. And this flight, it has a purpose?'

'Do you have a saying in Denmark, looking for a needle in a haystack?'

He smiled. 'I have heard of it, yes.'

'Well that's what we're doing. Except instead of needles we're looking for aircraft.'

'The missing Mustangs,' he said casually. Then noting the surprised look in my eyes, added, 'I have spoken with Mr Scarth, earlier in the hotel bar.'

'Of course,' I said. Definitely no fancy stories. Just the truth plain and simple. Or at least as near the truth as makes no difference. 'So what happens now?'

'Now? Now I will take you back to the hotel, when Kolbrunarskald returns with the car, of course.'

'And Palmarsson's killer?'

Thiessen spread his hands flat on the desk. 'Whisky has other ways of killing besides destroying the liver,' he said. 'Black market supplies. People have been killed for less ... you understand?'

'Yes, I suppose I do.'

'There is something ...' Thiessen started.

'Yes?'

'Kolbrunarskald ... he is a dangerous man. He would rather believe that you have something to do with Palmarsson's death.'

'Even if he'd caught the real culprit red-handed, you mean?'

Thiessen nodded. 'If the real culprit had been a Greenlander, yes. He would rather an outsider ...'

'Twisted sense of loyalty,' I muttered.

Thiessen half-smiled. 'I like that ... yes, a twisted sense of loyalty.' The half-smile evaporated suddenly, his face becoming serious. 'You will do well to watch out for him while you are here.'

'I can take care of myself, Inspector.'

'Yes Captain, I think you can.'

Thiessen dropped me back at the hotel ten minutes or so later, Kolb and Fleischer having returned without Kavavouk. The bird had apparently flown, leaving Thiessen with another problem.

'You leave tomorrow, I think,' he said as I reached for the door handle.

I looked beyond the windscreen, at the car headlights cutting a blinding white path into the blowing snow. 'Perhaps not, the weather.'

'Ah yes, it is not yet good. The summer is still a long way away. Denmark was always better ... you have been there Captain?'

'No.'

'No, and I have not been to America. But then we do have one thing in common.'

'We do,' I said, opening the door.

'We do,' he replied sadly, waving a hand at the white wilderness beyond the headlights. 'We have both been to hell.'

I turned towards the hotel door and caught a glimpse of lights in the annexe building. Lowering my head I changed direction and struggled through the drifting snow.

The bar was still open and Rollo Scarth was leaning heavily against one end of it. He was the only customer.

'Where ... hell ... you been?' His voice had that slurred meanness of a drunk looking for a fight.

I ignored the remark, beckoned the barman, and asked for a coffee.

'The restaurant is closed,' he said through thin lips.

I dug around in my pocket and produced a crumpled five-dollar bill. 'Coffee,' I repeated quietly, sliding the note over the bar. He pocketed it quickly and went off in search of a pot of coffee.

Scarth was watching me menacingly. 'Well?' he snarled.

I pulled up a stool and sat down. 'Could ask you the same question,' I replied.

He shuffled round until he was breathing whisky fumes directly into my face. 'Don't get smart ... just don't get smart. What ... what I want ... know is what happened to that half-ass ... at weather bureau.'

'You went, then?'

'Course I went ... waited ... how long did I wait?' He thought about it for a moment and gave up on the idea. 'Waited ... hell of long time ... too damn cold.'

'Then you came back here?'

'Course I came back here ... then this dumb police inspector walks in ... asking questions ...'

'About our trip to Big Gunn,' I added matter-of-factly.

Scarth banged his empty glass on the bar top. 'Where ... hell's that bartender guy got to?'

'Getting me a coffee.'

He banged the glass some more before turning back to me. 'How did you know what the cop had asked?' he said suddenly.

'He told me.'

'The cop ... told you?'

'Inspector Thiessen, yes.'

Scarth frowned. 'What about Palmar ... Palmarsson ... did you find him?'

'Yes. At the back of the weather station ... dead. Murdered!'

The glass slipped from Scarth's fingers, rolled across the bar top and fell to the floor. There was a brief shattering of glass. 'Murdered ... murdered ... what the hell d'you mean ... murdered?'

I went over the details for the third time that evening. By the time I had finished Scarth was sobering up fast. 'Why ... why in hell's name would anyone want to do that?'

The barman returned then with the coffee. I poured a cup and steered Scarth towards a table at the end of the room. 'Get me a drink ... large one.'

'Don't you think you've had enough?'

His bloodshot eyes rolled. 'A large one,' he shouted.

I sat him down and went back to the bar and ordered a triple bourbon.

'Well!' Scarth said tightly as I handed him his drink and dropped tiredly into the chair opposite him. 'What ... do we do now?'

'We could try his wife,' I ventured.

'Yeah ... why not. His wife ... she'd know.' His right hand went to his forehead then swept nervously down his left cheek. The cobwebs were back. 'When ... when ... d'we do that?'

I took a swallow of the lukewarm coffee. 'In the morning.'

Scarth emptied his glass and rattled it down on the table. 'Going to bed ... get some sleep.' He rose unsteadily to his feet. 'What time you around in the morning?'

I looked at my watch. It was nearly midnight. 'About seven,' I said.

'Seven,' he mumbled absently, and staggered towards the door.

I remained for another ten minutes or so, drifting back over a lot of yesterdays. Trying to analyse the exact moment in time when the landslide had started. But there was no exact moment. No perfect fix in time. Just a lot of hazy roads; faded position lines scratched across a Mercator's chart without a navigator to transfer them into some semblance of a known position; hazy roads which had drawn me inexorably from mistake to greater mistake. According to the law of averages it all had to change. And when it did ... and when it did!

I finished the coffee, which tasted as bitter as a lot of my memories, said goodnight to the barman, and went outside. Out to the world I knew and understood. The fighter pilot's world of one-to-one combat. The cold, lonely world of the arctic.

I was back in the hotel, at the foot of the open staircase, when I remembered Hannah Dawson. I turned and trudged wearily down the deserted ground-floor corridor to her room. The second knock got a reply. The door opened a few inches.

'Just thought I'd let you know I found him.'

'Where?'

'The bar ... he was there all along.'

'And it took you all this time to come back and let me know?' Her voice was far from being friendly. 'Do you realize I've been sitting here worrying myself sick for practically the last two hours?'

'Well you can stop worrying now. He's back in his room. One more thing, don't bother turning out early in the morning, we won't be going ... the weather.'

'Just like that,' she snapped. 'You sit in the bar for two hours, and when you've had enough beer or whatever, you drop by and tell me you've found Rollo and not to bother getting up early in the morning.' She took a quick, angry breath. 'Did it ever occur to you to apologize for putting me through two hours of unnecessary torment?'

'If that's what you want,' I said tiredly, 'I apologize.'

'Like hell you do ... like hell you do. I told Rollo all along you were the wrong man for the job. You only had to look at your past record for that.'

A knife turned inside me. 'What do you mean, my record?'

Her face edged out of the shadows, the features sharp and cruel. 'What do you think I mean? He had me check up on you before he came to Frobisher ... I know you were court martialled in Vietnam. I also read some of the old newspaper clippings. I even found out after your jail sentence was over how you tried to find employment with at least five airlines, but they, unlike Rollo, saw you for what you were. After that you ran away and were never heard of again ... until Rollo dug you up, that is. And even then he had to get you out of prison.' The steam ran out at that point. She stood quietly shaking in the half shadow of the doorway.

'Habit of mine, Miss Dawson, the result of mixing with the wrong people.' I turned on my heel and started down the corridor. In my ears the sound of the slamming door rang long and hard.

I was in the annexe building dining room at seven the next morning drinking my second cup of black coffee and staring out of the window at the blizzard. The snow had come during the early hours, riding the wind. A white fluid wall which darkened the world, enveloping everything with icy, dense flakes which cut into the skin as sharply as hailstones.

Scarth appeared through the wall minutes later, a large black figure engraved on an eternity of white. From the comfort of the dining room I could see him clearly. His fat, pink face wrinkled in pain as icy gusts of arctic air blasted at his skin. His grey eyes darted back and forth as he avoided the treacherous drifts which were building fast. I moved my attention to the door and waited. A couple of dull thuds and I knew he was inside the first pair of doors. A few more seconds as he stood in the outer entrance slipping off his hood; brushing the loose snow from his clothing; kicking the icy slush from his boots. Then the second pair of doors burst open.

'Jesus Holy Christ,' he exclaimed, shuffling over to the table. 'What in hell happened to the weather?'

I pushed out a chair with my left foot. 'Welcome to Greenland,' I said.

He tugged off his caribou mittens, hung his parka over the back of the chair and sat down. 'Guess you were right,' he said, rubbing his hands together. 'No flying today, uh?'

'Could be longer if this keeps up.'

He swore, picked up the coffee pot and started pouring. 'Okay, down to business. What do we do about this Palmarsson dame?'

'I'll go down to the hangar after breakfast and check out the plane; when that's done I'll find out where she lives and pay her a visit.'

Scarth ran a podgy hand through his white, cropped hair. 'Want me along?'

'Not on this one. I speak the language, and she may not be in the mood for seeing too many people ... especially us.'

'Why especially us?'

'You've got a short memory, Rollo. Erik was getting the information from her to bring to us. As he somehow got killed in the process ...'

'But you said he was killed over black market whisky dealing.'

'I know that, and you know that ... she might think differently.'

Scarth rubbed his eyes. 'But we need that information, Spence. It's vital.'

'Not as easy as you thought, eh?'

'It's not impossible either. I intend to find those planes if it's the last thing I ever do.'

'That might be the most prophetic thing you ever said, Rollo ... how do you like your eggs?'

He half turned and saw the yellow-faced Eskimo waitress. 'Over easy ... and another pot of coffee.

I ordered the breakfast and turned back to Scarth. 'Hannah was telling me last night that you'd been checking me out.'

'Checking you out?'

'Checking my background before you came up to Frobisher.'

He leaned back in his chair and said casually, 'Had to be sure you were the right man for the job.'

'And a two-year stint in prison meant I was, is that it?'

'Horse crap, Spence. I read all the old newspaper reports. I know you were used as a scapegoat for the generals. I was in the Air Force too ... or the Army Air Force as it was in those days, so I know what those bastards are like. Okay, so they sent you in on a strike against a Vietcong arms dump which turned out to be a refugee camp for kids; and if the war correspondents hadn't picked it up they'd have given you a medal. As it turned out they had to appease public opinion. Anyway it was a long time ago.'

'Sometimes it is,' I said absently. 'So when did you do your stint for Uncle Sam?'

'Backend of World War Two. I was eighteen years old at the time. They gave me a couple of stripes and sent me off to England. I was in Supply.' He smiled reminiscently. 'That's how I got into the buying and selling business, lot of black market dealings in England at that time. Did pretty well for a dumb corporal, didn't I?'

'I guess you did. What part of England were you in? I was raised there.'

'Based at a place called Debden, north of London. Ever hear of it?'

'No,' I lied. 'Lived up in the Lake District myself.'

Breakfast came then. Sizzling eggs and crackly bacon, and steaming hot coffee. We ate in silence. In the back of my mind the voice of Silent Sam Mason was telling me that the 4th Fighter Group was based at Debden, operating P-51Ds. Possibly the same type Patterson's Volunteers were flying on their return to the States. And before that Erik Palmarsson had said it was more than just a squadron of planes returning home.

I had the distinct feeling Scarth knew more than he was telling.

I arrived at the Greenland Air hangar at eight forty-five. The truck driver who had given me a lift dropped me at the side door, then accelerated viciously away towards the operations shack. The wind and snow had let up now and a dawn sun glimmered weakly through the white sky.

The Beaver, squat and ugly, was tucked under the main rotors of a giant Sikorsky S-61-N helicopter. I spent half an hour checking oil, fuel, tyres, skis, and squinting through access panels at the big Pratt and Whitney radial to make sure everything was hanging to where it should be hanging. The Greenland Air station manager had been good to his word; all the tanks had been refilled – even the internal ferry one. Satisfied that everything was serviceable, I went over to the operations shack.

Finding out where Palmarsson had lived wasn't too difficult. He was the main topic of conversation that morning. Him and Kavavouk, a tyrannical old man who had long ago given up hunting and turned to more profitable things – the sale of watered-down whisky being one of them. One or two of the Eskimo despatchers reckoned Palmarsson had owed him a small fortune, and when the small fortune wasn't forthcoming Kavavouk turned hunter once more. Which would explain the harpoon, and the old rogue's sudden departure. But me being me, I somehow found it all too pat. Even though I had heard of similar cases up around Frobisher.

The station manager, still sniffing from what could have been a perpetual head cold, finally appeared from his office waving a fuel bill. I told him he would have to go down to the hotel and see Rollo, and while he was doing that he could give me a lift.

He dropped me at the side of the airport road halfway to the hotel. I walked the last 150 yards up the access trail to the prefabricated concrete building. Next to that, and a little further down, stood the Greenland Air quarters which I had passed through the previous evening. This one was exactly the same: a pile of grey concrete slabs screwed and bolted together. Ground and first floor. Rows of neat, square, metal-framed windows and the centrally placed double doors. Through those into the porch way, dust off any surplus snow, and through the inner doors into the hall.

Palmarsson had lived with his wife on the first floor. The last apartment at the airport end of the building, the station manager had said. I went down the long corridor visualizing Akalise Palmarsson – or would she still be known as simply Akalise? Eskimos only had one name, in Canada at least. Then the Canadian government had changed that by issuing them with numbers. Even that changed after a decade or so when the Eskimos were de-numbered and issued with a second name. With Greenland, now independent of Denmark, it would be a different story.

The door opened on the surprise of the century: Akalise Palmarsson. She was tall where Eskimos are normally short; her hands were long and elegant – European hands, whereas Eskimo hands are small. The broad, round, even flattened face with the Mongolian features didn't exist in her case; hers was shaped with a delicacy which was almost oriental. The yellowish complexion only added to her beauty. Obviously she was more Danish than Eskimo. The result was quite breathtaking.

'Mrs Palmarsson!' I said haltingly.

'Yes, I am Mrs,Palmarsson.'

I held out my hand with uncertainty. 'My name is Luke Spence. I was a friend of Erik's.'

She took my hand in greeting. 'Please come in, Mr Spence.' I was ushered into a light, airy room. The furniture was modern, the colours restful pastel shades. 'Would you care for a cup of tea ... or perhaps coffee?'

'Coffee would be fine ... thank you.'

I followed her through to the small kitchen, taking in the slim figure beneath the pale blue sweater and the tightly fitting French-blue skirt. Erik Palmarsson had been a lucky man.

I said, 'I thought I should come and offer condolences ... I'm very sorry.'

She plugged in the electric kettle. 'Will instant coffee be all right? Supplies, you understand.'

I nodded. 'Thank you.'

'It is kind of you to come, Mr Spence.' She had the same kind of eyes Erik had had. Soft, brown, friendly. 'Erik did mention you. You were here a few months ago I believe?'

'That's right. I also saw Erik yesterday afternoon. He ... he agreed to meet me at the weather station last night; when I got there it was too late.' I felt the words drying up. 'I somehow feel responsible.'

Her head tilted to one side. 'Do not feel responsible, Mr Spence; Erik had his enemies.'

'Enemies?'

She gave a feminine little shrug. 'It is not important ... now!'

'Not important!' I exclaimed. 'But you *have* told the police!'

She gave me a pitying smile; one that said I did not understand. 'The police were among his enemies.'

'The drinking, you mean?'

There was no surprise in her voice when she said, 'You knew about that?'

'More or less. My last visit. I was buying him drinks at the Arctic Hotel when the police warned me off.'

'Sergeant Kolbrunarskald?' she queried.

'Yes. The unpleasant Kolb.'

'Unpleasant!' she exclaimed. 'I think more than unpleasant. He is a very dangerous man; you should take care to avoid him.'

'Inspector Thiessen said the same thing,' I remarked

'You have met him also, then?'

'Yes, last night.'

She nodded thoughtfully before busying herself with the cups.

'Have you heard anything else; the inspector mentioned a man called Kavavouk?'

'Kavavouk,' she said dispiritedly. 'Yes, an evil old man ... no, I have heard nothing more.' She stopped shuffling the cups and turned to face me. 'Do you think a man would kill for the price of a few bottles of whisky?'

'Depends on the man ... and how many bottles a few bottles is. Perhaps ... I don't know. What else is there?'

'Maybe nothing ... but now it is too late.'

'Too late, I don't understand.'

'Yesterday you asked Erik for information on some missing aircraft. This is correct?'

'Yes. We agreed to meet at the weather station at eight last night.'

The brown eyes were encapsulated by great sadness. 'I think someone else knew of your meeting and also knew Erik would have the information you wanted.'

'And killed him?' I said incredulously.

'Yes ... perhaps.'

She turned, switched off the kettle and poured the water into the cups. I followed her through to the lounge. We sat on opposite sides of a small coffee table; she self-consciously pulling her skirt over her knees; me wishing I was high in some distant sky. That place I could handle ... this one, I never would.

I said, 'But who's going to kill someone over a bunch of aircraft that crashed in the last war?'

A look of surprise registered in her eyes. 'Aircraft? ... but you know of the gold, surely?'

I sat motionless and felt my mouth sag open. Then slowly and uncertainly I heard my voice saying, 'Gold? What gold?'

'Erik did not tell you?'

'I ... I think he tried to once.' I paused, trying to recreate our last meeting, understanding at last his reference to Jason and the Argonauts and the golden fleece. 'So what you're saying is that the missing aircraft were carrying a cargo of gold?'

'That is the story my father told me. It is something of a legend in eastern Greenland.'

'But you've never seen it ... the gold, that is?'

'No ... I don't think anyone has. Not since it happened anyway.'

'But if whoever killed Erik knew of the gold isn't it possible he will try to extract the information from you?'

She ran her long graceful fingers around the corner of the table. Pensive, thoughtful. 'It had crossed my mind,' she said slowly.

'Isn't there somewhere you can go?'

'I could go to Denmark. My mother had relations there. But I do not much care for the country. I went to school there when I was a girl.'

'Where is your mother now?'

'Dead. She has been dead for many years.'

'I'm sorry.'

'There is no need, it was a long time ago.'

'Is your father still alive?'

'Yes, he went back to the east coast after my mother died; he has brothers there.' She fell silent then, deep in thought. Trying to rekindle the dying embers from a past I had unknowingly raked up.

I finished my coffee and got to my feet. Somehow the time didn't seem right for more questions; it was too soon after Erik's death. 'Thank you for the coffee Mrs Palmarsson ... and the talk.'

She moved as if to rise from her chair.

'Don't bother,' I said, 'I'll find my own way out.'

She smiled sadly. 'Goodbye then Mr Spence.'

I paused. 'If there's anything ... anything at all, I'm staying at the hotel.' I went out, closing the door softly behind me.

When I reached the airport road I turned right and walked the half mile back to the hangar. It was too cold for walking that far, but I needed time to think. I climbed up into the Beaver's cockpit and sat with the silence

102

and the oil and metal smells of aeroplanes. The faint noises started after a while. The distant harmony of the brass section, the marching cadence of the drums; then the whine of jets rose above the military band; then, above that, the clipped r/t chatter as MIG fighters drifted lazily through gun sights. I saw Linc Kullman's F-4 pull up alongside like a Cadillac at a drive-in movie. The bone-domed head nodded a silent hello; the fist stabbed forward, and the warriors went to war ...

The pictures stayed a little longer, willing me back on an impossible journey through time. Then, tired of the game, tired of the ghosts they were, they slipped silently away. Scarth had been wrong about it being a long time ago. Memories know nothing of days and months and years. They are always here and always now. A few minutes later I stirred my stiffening body and made my way to the Greenland Air operations hut. If I spoke to them nicely they might give me a lift back to the hotel.

I found Scarth in the dining room of the annexe building. He was alone. 'The prodigal son returns,' he said, waving me into a chair. 'How did you make out?'

I sat down. 'So so.'

He grunted and went back to butchering his steak. 'You saw the Palmarsson dame then?'

'I saw her.'

'Did you get the info?'

'Not exactly.'

The steak knife stopped cutting and he looked up. 'How much not exactly?'

'She's still in a state of shock,' I said. 'I hardly think this is the time ...'

Scarth cut me short. 'You hardly think this is the time! You hardly think! What you seem to forget, Spence, is that I'm running this show. Damn the time, damn her state of shock; just let's get the information and get to hell out of here.'

'I don't think she'll be as easy as Erik,' I protested. 'You can't offer her a year's supply of whisky and expect all the right answers.'

Scarth's eyes glinted in amusement. 'Wrong again, Spence. As I've told you before, everyone has their price. Tell me where she lives. I'll sort it out.'

'No need,' I said reluctantly. 'I'll go back.'

'When?'

'This afternoon.'

Scarth hesitated for only a second. 'Right, but if you screw it up this time I'm taking over.'

'I'll see you later then,' I said getting to my feet.

Scarth said, 'Aren't you stopping for lunch?'

'No, I'll eat tonight.'

He nodded and turned towards the window. 'Stopped snowing, I see.'

'Runway's closed though.'

'Haven't they got snow ploughs?'

'Yes, but they're expecting the man in the moon to start whittling on his walrus tusk again tonight.'

Scarth said, 'And what the hell's that supposed to mean in plain old-fashioned English?'

'Snow! That's how the Eskimos believe it snows – chips of walrus tusk floating down from the sky.'

Scarth chuckled to himself. 'You're not trying to tell me they believe that crap?'

'Some do.'

'Maybe tomorrow, then!' Scarth said with finality.

'Yes,' I said, gathering up my parka. 'Maybe tomorrow.'

It was in fact two days before I saw Akalise Palmarsson again. She had left on the very afternoon of our first meeting to fly up the coast to Godthaab, on the only helicopter shuttle to leave that day. With her had gone the body of her husband for burial at the Hans Egede church.

Scarth didn't seem unduly worried about the delay and divided his time between eating, sleeping and getting rid of a month's supply of drink coupons. Hannah on the other hand became edgy, even morose. With none of the creature comforts of civilization it was becoming too much for her.

Akalise arrived back on the midday flight. I waited an hour, to give her time to unpack, then arrived at her door.

'Mr Spence! Please come in.' She smiled warmly. 'It is better weather today.'

I looked beyond her, to the large picture window framing a peaceful blue sky, sunlight streaming in. 'Deceptive, I would say.'

The smile was still there. 'I think you know the arctic; yes, it is wickedly deceptive. Sunshine one moment – snowstorm the next.'

'You don't seem surprised that I am still here.'

'No, I am not surprised; I somehow thought you would be. You would like a coffee ... the real coffee this time. I bought it in Godthaab.'

'Thank you ... how did everything go?'

'The funeral, you mean?' She had the Eskimo way of coming straight to the point. The Eskimo way of shedding grief quickly.

'Yes, the funeral.'

'Erik is buried next to my mother. He never met her in life, you see; now perhaps ...' She left the sentence unfinished and busied herself with the coffee percolator.

We were sitting drinking coffee around the glass-topped table. 'You know why I am here?' I said.

She lowered her eyes. 'Yes. The information Erik was to give you.'

'It's more than that, I'm afraid.'

'More!'

'I want you to come with us.'

Her eyes came up and met mine. 'With you ... I do not understand!'

'To Kulusuk.'

'But why?'

'I could say I was concerned for your safety, and after what happened to Erik I am. But there is something more. I think the man I am working for already knows about the gold ... his secretary as well, in all probability. I have the feeling I will need help.'

'Help! But what can I do?'

I outlined my initial meeting with Scarth and what had happened since. By the time I had finished the sun was low in the afternoon sky. She didn't speak at first, which made me think that my suspicions were unfounded, bizarre even. Then she said, 'I think you are right, Mr Spence, you do need help.'

'You'll come then?'

She answered me with another question. 'You think that perhaps it was not Kavavouk then?'

'Perhaps.'

'Who, then?'

I shrugged. 'A difficult question. Perhaps it was someone who had just found out about the gold; about Patterson's Volunteers ... I don't know.' I looked towards the window for inspiration. Nothing came.

'Perhaps your Mr Scarth?' A thinly voiced question.

'He's got the motive, sure; but somehow I can't see him in the role of killer. Especially with a harpoon.' I saw the sudden anguish catch in her eyes. 'I'm sorry, I didn't mean ...'

'It's all right,' she said quietly, 'it has to be talked about.'

'Yes, I suppose so. As I was saying, I somehow can't see Scarth doing such a thing. Which leaves me back with Kavavouk the hunter.'

'What about the police?'

'The police? Surely you can't think they had anything to do with it?'

'Why not?' she said calmly. 'You know the North, you have lived at Frobisher. It is not much different here. Except our police are perhaps not as honourable as the Canadian police.'

I tried to think it out. Sure, Kolb had a mean streak. He would probably kill just for the hell of it. And the gold would have given him a motive. Except he wasn't that bright. He could never put the jigsaw together. Fleischer, I decided, was even less intelligent; he wouldn't be able to get the pieces out of the box. 'It doesn't pan out,' I said at length. 'I can't see Kolb or Fleischer getting involved in this.'

'And Inspector Thiessen?'

I laughed. 'Thiessen? Hell no. I'd put him down as a good cop, first, last and always.'

She sighed. 'Even so I still have the feeling it was not Kavavouk.'

106

'I'm sure you're right. Perhaps once we get to the east coast we will find out.'

'We, Mr Spence?'

I managed what might have passed for a weak smile. 'Assuming you will come ... will you?'

She gave a demure nod of the head. 'I will come, but there is one condition.'

'Which is?'

'You will find the man who killed Erik!' The brown eyes had suddenly lost their warmth.

I knew that the Eskimo religious ideas contained numerous taboos, some of which had to be observed when somebody died. Erik had died violently, his life being taken by a weapon usually reserved for the killing of animals. This obviously had some direct effect on the movement of his eternal soul. I'd heard it all before; different areas had different versions of the same story but at the end of the day it all came back to the same thing. The underworld! The Eskimo heaven where conditions are pleasant and warm, and where the catch is abundant. As one of the taboos had been violated, retribution was the only way Erik's soul could reach there. She wanted me to murder his killer!

I could have argued that Erik wasn't an Eskimo; or handed over the entire proposition to Scarth; or even searched for some other compromise. I could have, if I hadn't found myself looking into her unforgettable face. That was when I heard my voice say quietly, 'Yes, I will find the man.'

I left her shortly after that, and took the long cold walk back to the hotel. Somehow I was half expecting to run into Kolb again. I found myself looking over my shoulder every thirty steps, watching for a dark figure creeping up behind me. Unfortunately it was nothing more than my imagination. Unfortunate because I didn't like being used as a punch bag. But then again there was always tomorrow, and I had a gut feeling Kolb might figure somewhere in that.

The morning was predictably cold. It was seven thirty and still dark, except for the yellow pool of light which spilled out of the open hangar doors. Then even that light faded as the two ground handlers wound the big steel doors closed. It would be better in an hour. Then we would be up at our cruising altitude, droning east towards the sunrise, warmed by the aircraft's heating system. Yes, it would be better.

I stamped my feet and turned slowly around until I felt the wind on my face. Damn! It was out of the east. No more than ten to fifteen knots, but enough to make me wonder about the extra passenger. Narsarsuaq is one of those airfields which keeps you wondering all the time. You approach it from the west coast by taking the middle one of three fjords. Get that simple bit of arithmetic wrong and you end up in a box canyon with insufficient room to turn around and go back. The way you know it is the correct fjord is by the rusting old shipwreck at about the halfway stage. Once that has passed under your left wing tip, on the north side of the fjord, you can breathe a little easier.

The illusion which follows usually gets the heart rate up again: the illusion of flying into a gigantic barrier of ice. Then as if by magic the fjord breaks sharp left. You jink left with it, and then right, and then you're on short finals for runway 06. It starts at the water's edge and runs uphill until it merges with the icefall of the glacier at its eastern end. Whichever way the wind is blowing that is the way you land. Take-off is equally entertaining. You go the opposite way; down the hill. The wind, once again, is academic.

The truck's engine shattered the silence as it burst into life. The gears clunked and grated, then it pulled away in the direction of the operations shack and my waiting passengers. I went over to the Beaver and snicked on my torch. I'd already done the preflight inspection in the relative warmth of the hangar. This final walk round was by way of an encore. In the flying game you only get one chance of missing something. By the time you're up there it's too late.

By the time I had finished, the truck was on its return journey. Scarth hadn't been too happy at first about the extra body. But when I told him that Akalise wasn't too sure of the exact location of Patterson's Volunteers, which meant she would have to see her father, he started to listen.

The truck slithered to a stop and Scarth dropped down from the cab. Through the mouth covering of his parka hood his voice was muffled. 'All set then?'

'Guess so. You'd better sit in the back with Akalise. Hannah can sit up front with me.'

'Got it,' he said, and ducked under the port wing strut.

I climbed up to the cockpit last, having briefed the two Eskimo ground crew on removing the ground power unit. Then it was the usual round of seat adjusted, harness on, trimmers and controls checked, instrument glasses unbroken and reading normal ... and on ... and on. Finally throttle set, prop full fine and hit the starter. She coughed only once before I advanced the mixture to full rich. Then the Pratt and Whitney Wasp settled down to a satisfied steady rumble.

I switched on the radios and rubbed my hands together. Cold-soaked aircraft always had that feeling of the grave. Damp and bone chilling. I glanced at Hannah, parka hood lying neatly on her shoulders. 'Hear me okay?' I said, flicking the intercom switch.

She adjusted the boom mike of her headset nearer to her mouth. 'Loud and clear, how me?'

'Fine.' I turned back to Scarth and Akalise. 'Tied in okay?' They nodded and that was it. Except for the take-off! I hadn't even done a load-sheet calculation this time. We were too far overweight to even consider it. I smiled when I thought of Fullerton. He would have loved me for this one. But this really was the place they had thrown the rule book away. Lots of hidden corners, but no Fullertons. I pressed the r/t transmit button and requested taxi clearance.

I did the power checks at the end of the runway. The engine temperatures were quietly nudging the bottom of the green arc. A quick run through the pre-take-off checks and we were ready to go. Well, Mr de Havilland, there's just you and me now ... just you and me and a hell of a lot of weight.

The tower said languidly, 'November seven three niner one cleared for take-off.'

I eased the throttle open and felt the wheels break from the ice. 'Three niner one rolling.'

There was a double carrier-wave buzz in my headset as the controller acknowledged by blipping his transmit button twice; then the runway lights began drifting lazily past the aircraft. The slope steepened ahead of me, the twinkling lights leading on to the black void at the end of the runway. Tunugdliarfik fjord. I eased the controls forward and lifted the tail off the ground. Slow ... painfully slow ... but she made it.

The airspeed indicator creaked through 55. I tweaked the control column back, or tried to. Too heavy. Too, too heavy ... 60 ... try again ... nothing. I wound on a handful of nose-up trim. Speed 65 ... come on, you ugly bitch, for Christ's sake fly ... 70 ... 72 ... 75 ... how much runway have we used? How close to the fjord? The runway lights were merging into a racing line ... 80 ... I pulled again and suddenly, magically, the nose pivoted up towards the black vault of sky. Hold it down, Spence. Hold it down ... let the speed build. At 100 and no more runway lights I eased the stick back and gave her her head. And like the thoroughbred she may once have dreamt of being she soared up into the darkness with the grace of an eagle.

I headed down the fjord towards the west coast, coaxing her up as fast as she would go. We needed at least 5,000 feet to avoid hitting anything down that fjord. I turned the instrument panel lights off and sweated silently until my night vision isolated the eerie white glow of the mountains as they ran down to the sea. Through 5,000 I let out a shaky breath. Now we needed to get to 10,000 to overfly Narsarsuaq going northeast, and towards the end of the flight we would have to climb further, to 12,000 to skip over the top of the Crown Prince Frederick range. By then however we would have burnt off sufficient fuel to make it. How about now, Spence ... how about now? I continued on the westerly course, step-climbing lethargically to 10,000.

Forty minutes later we crossed Narsarsuaq on course for Kulusuk.

The book cruising speed, for these altitude and temperature conditions, said 137 mph. The best I could wring out of her was 110. And even then I had the feeling she was lying. The controls were too sloppy. Too many pilots tugging at her heartstrings for too long.

I waved the controls over to Hannah. 'All yours.'

She smiled. The bright innocent smile of a penniless child being handed a bag of candy. I watched her for a moment. The light persuasive touch told me all I needed to know. She had a feel for aeroplanes. She would be all right. I relaxed and turned back to Akalise.

'Everything okay?'

She nodded sweetly. 'Thank you, yes.'

'Rollo?'

'Should have bought a bigger airplane,' he growled. 'No damn leg room in this one.' He began to unzip his parka. 'How long?'

'Still-air time from now would have been around three and a half hours, but with the extra weight and about twenty knots on the nose it'll be at least four and a half.'

He ran a fleshy hand through his hair and frowned. In less than a week he had aged considerably, the dry cold winds of the North consuming the natural body oils of exposed flesh. The parchment process had begun, his flabby face changing slowly into a mask of darkly etched lines. 'Four and a half hours,' he said to no one in particular, 'in that case might as well get some shut-eye.'

I said, 'Good idea.'

'Would be if you could turn that damned racket off up front.' His face contorted for a moment as he struggled to find a comfortable position in the too-small seat. Then he laid his head back and closed his eyes. I smiled briefly at Akalise and turned back to the instrument panel.

Daylight started filtering out of the east forty minutes later. A penumbra of light – grey, unwanted – creeping into the cockpit to steal the last hidden corners of darkness. This was the worst part of any pilot's day; watching the cosy red glow of the instruments gradually harden into a room full of grey windows. And then through those same squares of crazed Perspex the harsh light of dawn uncovering the scratched and scuffed surroundings. A junk shop of non-matching instruments; sweat-corroded switches; and matt black paint which had been intended to merge with the original, except no one had yet come up with a matt black paint with a twenty-year-old fade built in. I shuddered at the cold I saw rather than felt, and went back to monitoring the instruments.

Everything was completely normal; even the outside air was silky smooth; too smooth – too normal. I smiled idly at the thought. Age was making me suspicious, or cautious – or both! I glanced at the fuel gauge again. Between half and three quarters. As with any ferry-type operation using internal cabin tanks, you needed to burn off half the contents of the main wing tanks before you started transferring the ferry fuel. This was because the two dry-sump electric fuel pumps, which were lashed down to the cabin floor at the rear of the cabin, pumped at a higher rate than the engine consumed fuel. The reason for having two pumps was safety. They were connected in parallel, so that if one pump should fail the system would still function. Fail-safe! Same reason you have two or more engines on the bigger commercial aircraft.

I turned to Hannah, whose eyes had now drifted up from the instruments and were mesmerically locked on the distant horizon. The easiest way to fly straight and level. Forget the instruments; just keep the nose cowling tucked a few inches below the natural horizon. She gave me a sideways glance, then flicked the intercom switch.

'There it is!' she said.

I followed her eyes back to the east and saw what she meant. Dawn breaking. Not the landsman's dawn, though; this one belonged to pilots – to travellers in that third dimension of space.

The soft blue rim forming an ever-widening circle between the still dark land and the starry heavens above. A brilliant morning star rising rapidly over the eastern lip of the horizon as the blue rim changed imperceptibly to pink to red. And then the sun striding majestically into the beginnings of a new day. This was what the Killer Man had meant by 'just another aviation junkie'. No one pulled out of this game by choice. This was where they had coined the phrase 'getting high'. And once a mainliner ...

'Nice morning,' I said at length.

'Unbelievable I would have said.' She paused for a moment. 'Do you ever get the feeling you'd like everything to stop?'

'Sometimes,' I said. 'With the exception of aircraft engines at ten thousand feet, of course.'

She smiled warmly and returned to the job in hand. It was then I realized it was probably Akalise who was responsible for the transformation. Apart from the change in attitude, I suddenly became aware of Hannah's face. She must have been up very early to apply her make-up with such care and precision. From the pink lip gloss, to the highlighted cheekbones, to the deep blue eyeliner and mascara accentuating the pale blue eyes. And now she was flying the plane and had removed her mittens, the well-manicured fingernails painted the same colour as her lips. If that wasn't enough there was the perfume, lingering faintly amidst the harsher smells of aeroplane cockpits. And all because I had mentioned another woman was coming along.

I looked down at the fuel gauge. Half tanks. I checked my watch and made a note of the time, then I flicked the intercom switch. 'Start easing it up to twelve thousand now.'

Her left hand reached for the throttle. 'Leave the power settings,' I said. 'Ease it up as gently as you can.'

Satisfied she had the right idea, I reached down between the seats and pressed the two circuit breakers firmly in. In a quieter aeroplane I would have heard the electric pumps buzz into action as they started pushing the fuel uphill from the tank behind Akalise and Scarth. But if the Beaver was anything it was not a quiet aeroplane, which left me watching the gauge and my watch. The ferry tank would take twenty minutes to empty. Should the main fuel gauge approach the full mark before that twenty minutes was up I would have to pull the circuit breakers and allow the main wing tanks to drain sufficiently before repeating the operation. Some days were better than others I thought, and sat back and closed my eyes.

It could have only been five minutes, not much longer, when I checked the gauge again. Something was wrong! The needle had slipped fractionally beneath the half. I sat watching for another five minutes, waiting for it to rise. But it didn't – It was still going down. I reached forward and tapped the glass. Nothing changed.

Hannah looked across at me. 'Something wrong?'

'Nothing. Maintain your heading, I'll let you know.'

But something was wrong. Desperately wrong. The needle should have been going up. We were supposed to be refilling the main wing tanks! The system had worked perfectly well under test conditions at Gander and during the flight to Goose and Narsarsuaq. Perhaps the fuel gauge was on the way out! I swore silently and started unclipping my seat harness. Hannah turned, eyes questioning.

'Might have a slight problem with the ferry system,' I said, putting the emphasis on the 'slight'.

'How slight?'

'Fuel doesn't appear to be transferring to the wing tanks.'

'Can you fix it?'

'I'm going back to have a look, which means Akalise will have to come forward to this seat. Keep an eye on her as she climbs over, make sure she doesn't accidentally put her boot through the panel.' I reached down between the seats. 'One other thing. I'm pulling the two circuit breakers now. When I tell you, I want you to remake them. Right?'

'Press them in, you mean?'

'You've got it.'

As the Beaver, along with all small single-engined aircraft, had doubtless been designed by a midget with other midgets in mind, changing seats with Akalise Palmarsson was not easy. I resolved the problem by sitting Akalise on Scarth's ample lap, then clambered back over my seat at a forty-five degree angle. I ended up the only casualty when I cracked my head on the butt of the twelve-bore shotgun which I had thoughtfully stowed in the green quilted head lining of the cabin roof. Scarth made some cryptic remark about arctic survival gear as I wiped away the smear of blood above my left eyebrow. There was nothing of the half-hearted humour in his voice when he added, 'You can fix it, though?'

'Let's hope so ... tell Hannah to remake the circuit breakers, will you.' I leaned over the back of the seat and pulled a long screwdriver out of the canvas tool bag. Then I slid further down behind the seat, head first, put the metal tip of the driver hard against the pump, and pressed the plastic handle against my ear. Nothing! I edged the screwdriver tip further along the pump and tried again. But I was searching for a heartbeat where none existed. The second pump was the same. Double pump failure! Impossible! They were both new, or had been in Gander. The slow uneasy feeling started at that moment. The sick feeling of being in an aeroplane that is running out of fuel, of being out of range of any airfield. The sick feeling which would continue for another hour or so, until the engine surged and coughed and died. Then the slipstream: eerie, hissing, final.

Okay Spence, let's analyse the problem. Both pumps have failed. What is common to both pumps? The question rattled around in my brain. Come on for Christ's sake, you fitted the damned system. I thought some more, then it hit me. Earth! The earthing wire! I had used a common earthing wire. I scrabbled around in the canvas bag and found a torch. That's what it had to be. Someone must have accidentally disconnected it. The refuellers at Narsarsuaq! They had been in the back – probably stood on the wire.

I snapped on the torch and craned my head around the small wooden platform which held the two pumps. The white earthing wire looked back at me. I reached out and tugged it. Tight – perfectly tight. I disconnected it anyway; cleaned the terminals and the earth point on the cabin floor, then put it back together. I checked the pumps again, using the screwdriver as a stethoscope. The silent prayer I offered as I pressed the screwdriver handle to my ear remained unanswered. I hauled myself up over the chair back, screwed my body round and dropped heavily into the seat.

Scarth looked at me expectantly. I ignored him and tried to picture the entire ferry system in my mind. At the end of it I was left with a handful of possibilities. Power supply from the aircraft electrical system, circuit breakers unserviceable, open circuit in the wiring between the circuit breakers and the pumps. I quickly checked each one. But everything was normal. Which left the pumps themselves. The fail-safe system which hadn't failed safe!

By now there was anxiety written all over Scarth's face. He had watched me checking and double checking, and seen my lip-twitching become a voluminous torrent of abuse.

'Haven't we got enough gas in the main tanks to make Kulusuk?' he questioned.

'Sure we've got enough,' I replied cynically. 'That's why I've been crawling around on my hands and knees for the past twenty minutes. Take a look at the airspeed indicator up front. She's still flying like a skua full of bird shot.' I waved my hand around the cabin, 'Too much dead weight ... that and the headwind.'

'Can't we get back?'

'Back! Back to where? Narsarsuaq? I'll tell you something, Rollo; without that fuel behind you we haven't got and never did have a point of no return – not on this particular trip anyway. We've simply flown into the middle of nowhere without a hope in hell of getting out.'

Scarth's hand reached up and brushed down his left cheek. Nervous reaction setting in. I turned back to the ferry tanks. What hadn't I checked? 'Carbon brushes' leapt out of my subconscious like a startled racehorse. I had just witnessed Scarth brushing away one of his imaginary cobwebs and my subconscious had come up with brushes – carbon brushes. Word association, or some dusty white-robed God handing out another clue; it didn't matter. The odds were remote, especially as the brushes, like the pumps, were new. Perhaps they hadn't seated properly; better still the metal springs which held them in place had contracted in the cold. Insufficient tension to hold them on to the face of the commutator!

I climbed back over the seat and started unscrewing the plastic end

116

caps which held in the brushes. There were two to each commutator. I slid them out of the key-ways, inspecting the slightly curved faces with the torch. They were all perfect; in fact hardly worn at all. I took a last look at the miniature faces of coal-black shininess and refitted them. Then I got Hannah to remake the circuit breakers. Nothing moved! Nothing buzzed happily into life. Somehow I hadn't expected it to; but then I knew about aircraft. Their feminine charm was only surpassed by their occasional bouts of bitchiness.

The seat changeover with Akalise worked out more easily the second time around. Or perhaps it was because my mind had more serious problems to consider. My last picture of Scarth as we made the transfer was one of abject misery. His fat face was running free with sweat.

I slipped on the headset and turned to Hannah. 'How's it going?'

'We're not picking up the Kulusuk beacon yet.' Then with an air of careful optimism she added, 'Have you managed to sort it out?'

'In a word "No".'

'What happens now?'

I was thinking, that's what happens now. Not too clearly, but I was thinking. I looked down at the fuel gauge. Barely a quarter remaining.

I said, 'I'll try to raise Sob Story and get a fix. We'll take it from there.'

I worked out a rapid dead-reckoning position on the chart and tuned the radio to the Sob Story frequency. 'Sob Story this is November Seven Three Niner One. How do you read?'

The laconic drawl of the American radio operator came back immediately; it was as though he had been expecting me all day. 'Three Niner One this is Sob Story, reading you strength five go ahead.'

I passed the usual spiel required in a position report and requested a radar fix. There was a momentary pause while he assimilated the information. Then: 'Three Niner One what did you say your position was?'

I thumbed the mike button. 'DR position sixty-four degrees north, forty-one degrees west.'

'Okay pal, believe I have you now, turn right thirty degrees for positive ID.'

I motioned to Hannah who swung the plane right on to the new

117

heading. Then the man from Sob Story was back. 'Three Niner One positive identification ... quite a ways off that position though. Would you believe nearly a hundred miles!'

'I'd believe you if you told me you were Santa Claus ... which way? West?'

'You've got it, buddy. Your new position sixty-four degrees thirty minutes north; forty-two degrees thirty minutes west. Looks like you're bucking some pretty bad winds, uh?'

I pencilled in the new position on the chart and went back to the man from Sob Story. I could even picture him. Private First Class Elmer Jones, United States Air Force; plugged in to a mug of coffee and a radar screen, waiting patiently for Ivan Ivanovich to appear over the top of the world with a few megatons of instant death. The base would be mostly underground, except for the spidery array of aerials and the moon-like white dome merging into the snowscape. 'Three Niner One copied position.' The next part came a little harder. No pilot enjoys putting out an emergency. 'And we have a slight problem.'

'Go ahead on the problem Three Niner One.'

'Roger, we appear to have a ferry tank malfunction. Cannot transfer fuel to main tanks. We need to know terrain conditions in our present position for precautionary landing.'

'Stand by on that.' Rapid fire now. He was concerned. 'Three Niner One confirm altitude one two thousand?'

'Affirmative.'

'And your flight conditions.'

'Roger, we're visual at this level but have blowing snow beneath. No ground contact.'

A new voice came back; deeper; more authoritative. 'Three Niner One state full call sign, number on board, endurance, and whether ski equipped.'

'November Seven Three Niner One, four souls on board, one hour, and affirmative on the skis.'

'Copied Three Niner One ... could you also confirm you have signed a copy of the Hold Harmless Agreement?'

That sounded like my old Air Force. Living in a cloud-cuckoo-land of paperwork mountains. They'd probably ask Ivan the same question when he came over the top at Mach 2. 'Affirmative,' I replied tiredly.

'Roger Three Niner One ... stand by.'

Hannah said, 'What's a Hold Harmless Agreement?'

'Oh, nothing much ... just a piece of paper which confirms that we release for ever the United States, its agencies, and United States personnel, from every liability arising out of the use of any Air Force services. In other words the buck stops here ... in this cockpit.'

'I see,' she said. She didn't, of course. Or perhaps she had noticed the bitterness in my voice and was just being kind.

'Three Niner One this is Sob Story!' The officer of the watch was back.

'Go ahead Sob Story.'

'Roger Three Niner One; your present position puts you over the eastern edge of the snowfield ... suggest we take you west about twenty miles, then turn you back on a slow descent. Estimated height of the field in that area seven thousand feet above sea level. Set altimeter now at 28.85.'

It wasn't as bad as I had thought. The blowing snow covering the tundra could only be a few hundred feet deep at most. What the hell was I talking about! Descending blind into 300 feet of whiteout without knowing what was underneath ... until you hit it! Bad? It was bloody suicidal. Then again there was a way; fifty-fifty perhaps, but as no one was offering better odds ...

'Roger Sob Story altimeter set 28.85. What heading do you want us on?'

'Three Niner One turn left on to two seventy true.'

I checked the chart. Magnetic variation 38 degrees west. I flicked the intercom switch. 'Get all that Hannah?'

She nodded unhappily. 'I think so.' The colour had drained from her face now; all that was left was the pink lipstick shining sadly in the sunlight.

'Good, compass heading three zero eight.'

'He ... he said two seventy.'

'That's two seventy true,' I corrected. 'Variation is thirty-eight degrees west. West is best, east is least – remember? So we add the westerly variation to obtain our compass heading ... yes?'

'Sorry ... I forgot.' She started the Beaver off in a gentle rate-one turn; leaving me to work out my own rules in what could be my last game of chance.

Eleven minutes later we had completed our turn back towards the east. Into wind. I half turned in my seat and shouted to Scarth. 'All set, we're starting our descent now.'

'Ready when you are,' he rasped. The sweating had stopped when I told him the plan. It seemed even his fear had a price. Either that or this was the first time he had faced death and now found he had the guts to meet it. Whatever it was I didn't give a damn, just as long as he didn't crack up at the critical moment. I took the controls from Hannah and eased back the throttle.

'Sob Story Three Niner One leaving one two thousand now.'

'Three Niner One copied ... good luck, sir.'

'We make our own, Captain, but thanks anyway.'

'How did you know the rank?'

'Educated guess ... used to work for the same outfit.'

Nothing else came back, but I knew he was there. Waiting, praying. His voice had softened over the last two transmissions; emotion finally breaking through the veneer of military discipline. I had seen grown men cry doing his job. Talking their own kind down to certain death.

I ran through the pre-landing checks and lowered the hydraulic skis. The moment of truth! Scarth had wound out the HF trailing aerial; all fifty feet of it. The aerial extended down through a hole in the cabin floor, the end of it being weighted and fitted with a small plastic drogue. Not that the aerial would hang straight down – it would curve gently back in the slipstream. Say a depth of thirty feet. I had instructed Scarth to hold the reel handle lightly. When he felt it jerk, the drogue would have made ground contact. That was his signal to scream out.

I retightened my seat harness until the shoulder straps dug painfully into my shoulders; then told Hannah to make sure she and the passengers did the same. She hesitated. Her face was deathly white now; haunted, gripped with fear.

'Tell them!' I yelled. She turned reluctantly and passed on the instruction. The next moment we joined the spectral world of the whiteout. Okay Spence ... big moment. Airspeed seventy-five. I twitched the nose gently up and decreased the rate of descent.

Heading steady 090 ... speed coming back ... seventy ... sixty-five. Touch of throttle ... hold sixty-five. The hairs on the back of my neck were standing up. Cold, clammy. My feet lifted nervously off the rudder pedals, searching for a higher place. Then my entire body was straining against the harness in a desperate bid to climb out of itself.

The altimeter hesitated at 200 feet and stopped. Come on, you bastard ... go down. Down! But it wasn't the plane, it was my hands. Pulling instead of pushing. I felt the cold sweat on my body as I forced the controls forward. The altimeter jerked past 100. It was useless now. Totally useless. Now it was down to Scarth ... and the aerial.

There was a moment of full power and sunshine rushing through my mind, but the moment died with the realization that I would have to come back. And that was the inescapable truth ... I would have to come back. They've got you this time, Luke Spence. They tried in Nam – the MIGs, the missiles, even God wanted you back. And you escaped them all. You outsmarted every last one of them; and they, reaching out, watched you go. But not now. Not now.

'Contact ... contact!' Scarth's piercing scream could have been heard a mile away. I instinctively slammed down full flap and closed the throttle. The Pratt and Whitney died instantly. All that remained was the lumpy burbling sound of all big radials as the plugs started fouling up. I eased the control column further back and watched the airspeed fade rapidly down the dial. Come on ground ... come on. Jesus God! Too high! ... too bloody high. I felt the buffeting on the controls ... she was stalling. It was too late ... too late for power ... too late to check the controls forward and break the stall. Too late for a lot of things. Suddenly we were falling. Falling through a white, swirling, endless eternity. Arms across your face ... arms across your face ... arms across ...

121

The spine-jarring impact ended with Hannah's scream. Then we were bumping wildly over the uneven surface. I reached out and pulled the mixture control to idle cut off. The propeller kicked once on the compression cycle and shuddered to a stop. It was only then that I realized that the bumping had ceased. We had stopped moving. We were down. And all that was left was the wind and the snow; those two sorrowful companions of the North; beating their endless tattoo against the airframe.

Hannah's quiet sobbing brought me back. That and the gyros, and the ice crystals, and Scarth's excited voice, and Akalise's serenity. I slowly removed my headset. Then Scarth was leaning forward, pounding me on the shoulders. 'Pretty neat trick with the aerial; yessir, pretty neat trick.'

I unclipped my seat harness and half turned in my seat. 'You liked it, then,' I said.

'Now we're down,' Scarth said, 'I loved every damned minute of it. Guess you must have used it before!'

I said, 'First time. As a matter of fact it was something I read in a book a long time ago ... ever hear of a guy by the name of Ernest Gann?'

'Nope, can't say I have.'

'Well when you get back to New York send him a thank you note ... it was his idea.'

'His or not, it was still a neat trick,' Scarth conceded.

I looked across at Akalise. 'You okay?'

'Yes, Spence,' she said softly. 'I'm fine.' Not Mr Spence any more, just Spence. From her lips it sounded special; like the light in her eyes.

I turned back to Hannah and patted her on the thigh. 'Next landing is yours,' I smiled. 'Seem to have lost the knack.' A smile shone through the tears.

An hour later the storm died, giving way to a curving white emptiness which seemed to last for ever. Above, the dazzling sunshine arcing coldly through the blueness of space. I could have waited after all, I thought, feeling the painful warmth throbbing back into my feet and hands. But it was done; to the most part at least.

I had carried out a superficial check of the aircraft, and apart from a small dent in the leading edge of the left ski, found everything serviceable. Following that I had followed the trailing aerial back, fitted a new plastic drogue, and then held it clear of the ground while Hannah contacted Sob Story with the news of our safe landing.

Now I was sitting in the back of the plane with Scarth, thawing out over a cup of coffee.

'See what you meant about this place,' Scarth remarked, refilling his cup from the thermos.

'This place?'

He rubbed a patch of near-freezing condensation from the window. 'That!' His gaze was directed at the bleak wilderness beyond the Perspex. 'Lonely kinda takes on a new meaning, wouldn't you say?'

Akalise, who was sitting up front with Hannah, leaned over the back of her seat. 'It is the elder world, Mr Scarth.'

'Maybe. It's not my world, that's for sure.'

'No,' she replied. 'It is the land of the great white bear, the arctic fox, and my people ... few white men ever survive.'

Scarth turned uncomfortably in his seat. 'Any ideas on the fuel?' he said to me.

'Not unless you've got a five-gallon drum secreted about your person. That way at least we could transfer the ferry fuel to the wings.'

'So what the hell happens now?'

'I'm going to check out that system again.'

'But you checked everything before!'

'So ... I'll check again. Unless you've got a better suggestion?'

He gave a resigned shrug and went back to his coffee.

'Anything I can do?' Hannah said.

'As a matter of fact there is. You can crank up the engine before the oil starts thickening up. Not too much throttle though, we're on skis remember ... no brakes.'

I climbed over the rear seat and went to work removing one of the electric pumps from its mounting. The fault, whatever it was, had to be there.

Ten minutes later Hannah cut the engine. The heater had taken the chill off the cabin, for the time being at least. Slowly and methodically I began to reassemble the pump. I'd still drawn a blank. There was no apparent reason why it shouldn't work. Perhaps the other one would show some distinct signs of failure! I took a handkerchief from my pocket and wiped the faces of the carbon brushes. Not that I could see any grease on them, but it was possible. Anything was possible. And grease would act as an insulator.

I was putting the handkerchief in my pocket when I noticed it. Or didn't notice it, which was more to the point. Rub a white handkerchief over soft black carbon and what do you get? Simple – a dirty handkerchief! But the handkerchief wasn't dirty. In fact there wasn't a mark on it. I picked up one of the tiny brushes and rubbed again, harder this time. Not a trace of carbon deposit showed on the white linen. The brushes! There was something wrong with the brushes. I leaned over towards the window and held them up against the light.

If you hadn't been looking for it, you would never have noticed. And that is exactly what had happened. Sabotage! Neat. Ingenious. And in the final reckoning almost the perfect crime. Except the saboteur hadn't taken into account the change in the upper winds. But how could he have known; even the weather station had got that wrong.

Sweet Jesus, that was the only reason we were still alive. Because we had ended up 100 miles off course; 100 miles the right way. On track we would have been on the coastal side of the crown Prince Frederick mountain range which runs up to Kulusuk. We would never have made it back to the snowfield to attempt a forced landing. Thank you winds of the North; for being such wonderful fickle-minded bastards.

I smiled to myself and took a piece of fine emery cloth from the tool bag. Whoever you are, you clever sod, you were not quite clever enough. Not this time at least. And the next time, if there is a next time, I'll be waiting.

I carefully doctored the brushes belonging to the first pump and refitted them; then repeated the operation on the second pump. Now the moment of truth. I hauled myself back over the seat.

'Okay Hannah, let's have some power.' She flipped on the battery master switch as I leaned forward between the two pilots' seats and pressed in the circuit breakers. The two electric pumps whined happily into life. I pulled the breakers and sat back in the seat; smug satisfaction all over my face.

Scarth turned excitedly. 'You did it,' he yelled. 'What was wrong?'

Hannah and Akalise joined in the congratulations before I had time to answer. Then I said to Scarth, 'What do you know about electric fuel pumps?'

'Next to nothing.'

That was good enough. 'The failure was due to the carbon-brush springs contracting ... arctic conditions. Brushes weren't seating on the commutator.'

'I thought you checked them before?'

'I did, but have you ever tried working upside down by torchlight in a noisy aircraft in flight, with only minutes to sort everything out? Besides, I had to strip the pump right down before the problem became apparent.' A qualified engineer would probably have fallen about in fits of laughter over that kind of statement. But as Scarth wasn't a qualified engineer, it didn't seem too important. What *was* important was the fact that someone else was aware of the missing gold. Someone not on this aeroplane. What other reason could they have had for wanting us dead?

Minutes later I was outside with Akalise, pacing out a reasonably long take-off run into wind. The air was clear and cold; the wind practically nil. When we were a suitable distance from the aircraft I told Akalise what had really happened.

She stopped suddenly, her face pinched and drawn, and very concerned. 'You are sure?'

'I'm sure,' I said. 'Whoever was responsible had coated the ends of the carbon brushes with varnish.'

'But how would this make the pumps not work?'

'Surprisingly simple, really. The varnish has to be a type used by aircraft electricians. And varnish is an insulator. Without those brushes the pumps would never work; which is precisely what happened. But whoever was responsible had thought of just about everything. He could have removed the brushes and left it at that; but then he couldn't be sure that I might not have a spare set somewhere on the aircraft. So what he did was to varnish them over, which made them appear to be quite normal. In fact it was only by chance that I realized what was wrong.'

Akalise looked totally baffled. 'It sounds very complicated. Then there is the question of who would have done such a thing?'

'Couldn't have been Scarth,' I ventured. 'Which leaves a number of people back in Narsarsuaq.'

'The police,' she said simply. 'Kolb.'

'No. He wouldn't have had the know-how to fix those pumps.'

'Unless he was helped by one of the Greenland Air mechanics!' A flat statement with more the ring of truth about it than I cared to admit. Perhaps the ugly sergeant wasn't as dumb as I figured.

'We'll talk about it some more when we get to Kulusuk. In the meantime don't breathe a word of this to Rollo or Hannah.'

'You still suspect...'

'I still suspect.'

We started walking again, checking the surface for hidden wind ridges of solid ice. After a while Akalise linked her arm through mine. 'I have not thanked you yet for saving my life,' she said.

I looked down at the beautiful brown eyes, shrouded by the soft fur of her parka hood. The sun spokes gave them a laughing quality. It was as if from great sorrow she had found a greater happiness. 'There's a long way to go yet,' I said weakly, wishing I had the courage to say what I really felt. Perhaps those words would come later; when it was all over. We turned and started back towards the aircraft.

Kulusuk was exactly as I had imagined it: a rough unmade airstrip and a scattering of wooden huts. Beyond the huts to the east that scream of sea known as the Denmark Strait, frozen solid as far as the eye could see. With the coming of the summer and the thaw, there would be the eternal groan and grind of the ice breaking up into a flotilla of bergs – an armada of white ghost ships running south to the shipping lanes. Summer would also be the time when Kulusuk once more would become an island.

To the west of the airstrip the bluish-white ice mountains soared jagged towards the sky. A few miles southwest of the strip, at the lowest point in the range, a million-year-old time capsule, Teardrop Glacier. Exactly as I had imagined it? No, it was more than that. It was beautiful. Savage, frightening – but wickedly beautiful.

I parked the Beaver in the lee of one of the wooden huts and set the other three on unloading the aircraft, while I tied the kapok-filled covers over the engine. Not much of an insulator in these temperatures, but it would keep off the chill. Even so we would need to carry out engine runs every four hours to prevent the oil from solidifying. Hannah could help with that. For the first time I was glad that she was along.

Akalise appeared from under the starboard wing as I secured the final tie line. With her was an old and wizened Eskimo. He was very skinny, and from his smell he sweated a lot. 'This is Che-mang-nek,' Akalise said, introducing him. 'He looks after the airstrip.'

I slipped off my mitten and took the proffered hand. It was gnarled and bony, and had a grip of iron. 'It is a pleasure to meet you, Che-mang-nek,' I said in Inuktitut.

'You are welcome,' he said in a hoarse whisper. It was said as a courtesy, no more. I read the true message in the narrow yellowish eyes; the message that contradicted the words.

He turned to Akalise, his own kind, and said something I didn't quite catch. But then I wasn't really listening. I had noticed something about him that wasn't quite right. His mouth perhaps. The way he spoke. The way his mouth hardly opened when he did. It was something I had not seen in an Eskimo before. One of those niggling little things that you cannot quite put your finger on.

Akalise said, 'I will go with Che-mang-nek now, to the village at Big Gunn. He has a dog team here.'

I looked up at the sun sinking behind the mountains. 'How far is it?'

'About two hours' journey.'

'But it will be dark soon.'

She smiled. 'Do not worry. He makes the journey every day. It will be all right.'

'Your father ... does Che-mang-nek know him?'

'Yes, he knows him.' She turned to go and then stopped. 'Mr Scarth and Miss Dawson have moved the baggage into the next cabin.' She pointed. 'There are no beds, but there are stoves and also a plentiful supply of driftwood.'

I watched them go then, down the line of wooden shacks to the *komatik* – the sled. I saw Akalise pull a heavy fur over her, as the long whip cracked, bringing the whining dogs to their feet. On the second stroke of the whip the dogs leapt in their traces and broke the runners free. The outfit picked up speed over the dry snow; the little Eskimo, one foot on each sled runner, giving a final crack of the whip. Akalise didn't look back and soon the black moving shapes topped a gentle shadow-painted ridge and were gone.

Damn! I hadn't asked her when she would get back. I took a last look around the Beaver and stomped off to find Rollo and Hannah.

The mouth-watering smell of meat stew hit me as I went through the outer door. I kicked the surplus snow from my boots and went in. Hannah looked up from the primus stove and flashed me a brilliant smile. 'Tinned stew and cold salted beef, how does that sound?'

'Sounds good to me. Where's Rollo?'

'Out back ... looking for the john.' She laughed at the thought. Then added, 'Water, there's no water ... have we any in the emergency rations?'

'We have,' I said. 'And that's where it stays. I'll melt some snow.'

She pulled a face. 'Coffee made with melted snow, sounds revolting.'

'Tastes better than it sounds ... in fact if you took the idea to California you'd probably make a lot of money out of it. Yeah I can see it now: Eskimo Nell's Coffee House; only instead of snow you use imported Greenland ice, tastes the same. Then you hang the sign outside – "Every cup of coffee guaranteed a million years old".'

Hannah smiled. 'That's not as dumb as it sounds ... what do we do for light, by the way?'

I went over to one of the packs and found the candles I'd bought in Gander. I lit one from the primus stove, poured a little hot wax on the centre of the deal table, and stuck it down.

Hannah looked up at the weak halo of yellow flame. 'Couldn't we have two or three? Then I could see what I'm doing.'

'This is the North, Miss Dawson,' I said chidingly. 'Not downtown Manhattan. The key word here is frugality. Frugality in all things, and hoard like a miser ... rainy days are ten a penny.'

'I get the idea you enjoy all this.'

I turned towards the door. 'I'll get the snow,' I said, and went outside into the gathering darkness.

It was two o'clock in the morning and I had just shut down the Beaver's engine. I clambered down from the cockpit and started replacing the engine covers, muffling the sighs and pings of contracting metal. A chill wind whispered in off the ice and ran like a playful child down the deserted airstrip.

I turned quickly at the first sign of noise, snatching up the shotgun which was resting against the port main wheel. Polar bears don't usually attack people, except perhaps in winter when food is scarce and the sea frozen over. I swung both barrels round and fixed them on the dark shape.

'Don't shoot!'

'What the hell are you doing out here?' I snapped, lowering the gun.

Hannah Dawson moved slowly forward until a thin sliver of moonlight touched her face. 'Heard the engine stop. I ... I couldn't sleep ... I've put the coffee pot on the stove.' She wrapped her arms tightly round herself. 'God, this must be the coldest I've ever been in my life.'

I lowered the gun to the trail and put my left arm around her shoulder. 'Another lesson,' I said softly. 'Never go outside in winter unless there's a damn good reason.'

The main room of the cabin was pleasantly warm as we shed our outer clothes, the hissing flame of the primus spreading a soft blue light over the room. Scarth had taken one of a pair of black antiquated paraffin stoves into the small back room, and made up his bed there. If Hannah and I were going to be up and down throughout the night running aircraft engines, he didn't want to be disturbed. He had gone to bed with half a bottle of whisky and within minutes was sleeping soundly.

'Coffee smells good,' I said, throwing some driftwood on the dying embers in the fireplace.

'You were right about the snow,' she replied, filling two tin mugs.

I took the coffee and squatted down on my sleeping bag next to the hissing primus. In the blue glow Hannah began to undress. 'Old sea ice is better, though,' I said, watching her. 'As I mentioned back in Gander; if it's two or three years old it's generally fresher than spring or river water.'

She slipped out of the last of her clothes and turned towards me. Through the soft blue flame my eyes searched up the long shapely legs, across the flat belly, to the large, full breasts. Beyond that the curve of shoulder and face were lost in the shadow. She paused for a moment longer then dropped gracefully to the floor and slipped into her sleeping bag. 'Sounds fascinating,' she said sexily, 'quite fascinating.' We drank our coffee in silence.

Hannah pushed her empty mug across the wooden floor towards the primus. 'Pity we didn't bring any pillows.'

I smiled to myself at the thought – only a woman could think of pillows in a place like this – then climbing to my feet I turned my parka inside out and moved over to her. 'Lift your head,' I said, kneeling down beside her. 'Arctic fox. May not be goose down, but it's the best I can do.' I rolled the white fur beneath her head. She dropped back unexpectedly, trapping my left hand beneath her shoulder. I moved it out slowly, enjoying the silky warmth of her skin. Then I saw the eyes. Beckoning. Challenging! Willing me on with the same wicked beauty of the ice mountains beyond the airstrip. And no seasoned Northerner takes chances with that kind of beauty. I pulled my hand reluctantly away and got to my feet.

130

Hannah said in a half whisper, 'So the loose woman doesn't get raped tonight, uh?'

'Not tonight, Miss Dawson ... not tonight.'

'Not any night, Captain Spence!' I couldn't tell if that was a question or a simple statement of fact. She sometimes had that way with words. I kicked off my boots, turned off the primus, and struggled into my sleeping bag. Sleep, deep and blessed, came shortly afterwards.

Akalise arrived back from Big Gunn at noon the following day. With her, apart from Che-mang-nek, was a boy. I had just replaced the engine cowling after carrying out a more thorough inspection than the one up on the snowfield. After that heavy landing I had at least expected to find some slightly wrinkled skin or the odd popped rivet or two. But there was nothing, not a trace of damage. Mr de Havilland, it seemed, had built his aircraft to take more of a beating than I was prepared to hand out.

The dog team came to a halt near the cabin. I watched as Che-mang-nek undid a bundle and threw a frozen fish to each of the animals. They devoured them instantly and continued circling him, whining for more. The old Eskimo was unmoved and went back to help the boy unload the sled. He knew that a dog on the trail runs better on an empty belly. The dogs gave up after a while and started digging holes in the snow, using their muzzles and paws. Then having made their own igloos, they slid in to sleep; the entrances crumbled behind them with the heat given off from their bodies. An icy gust blew in from the ice, rattling fine granules of snow against the Beaver's fuselage, then on, over the animals and down the airstrip, rolling the snow like some giant carpet. When I looked again the dogs had gone. I turned back to the Beaver and with cold, mittened hands began to fit the engine covers. I didn't hear Akalise come up behind me. One moment I was totally alone, the next I felt her presence. Felt her eyes watching me.

'Welcome back,' I said, without looking round.

She laughed; a warm friendly laugh. 'Do all pilots have such good hearing?'

'No,' I said, turning to face her, 'more of a sixth sense. They always know when a ...' I let the sentence die. She was more than a few cheap words.

'What do they always know?' she asked coyly.

'It's not important. What is important though is, it's nice to see you; my feet are frozen; and how about a cup of coffee?'

The laugh was back as she linked her arm through mine and tugged me impatiently towards the cabin.

'Not so fast,' I said, checking her. 'What happened with your father?'

The happiness faded to a look of concern. 'It is not good!'

'What! I thought he knew the exact location of the crash site.'

'Oh it is not that. No, what I mean ...' she paused. 'Tell me Spence, do you believe in the shaman's power being able to foretell great evil?'

'A big question for a white man,' I said. 'Let's say I don't disbelieve. Why do you ask?'

'It is said there are bad spirits beyond the mountains ... the spirits of the dead pilots.'

'Do you believe that?'

'Yes,' she said simply.

'And your father told you this?'

She nodded. 'Yes.'

'Have you ever considered he told you that because he knows we are going to look for the aircraft ... and the gold?'

'No Spence, it is more than that. After the war an American came to look for these same aeroplanes. Apparently he came every summer for fifteen years. My father's people said nothing and offered no help, but the American kept on searching. Then on the last summer he went up to the snowfield through Teardrop Glacier ... he never came back!'

'So he ran out of luck ... got lost or something. It does happen, you know.'

'No, it wasn't like that. He didn't get lost. You see when he didn't come back to catch the supply ship to Iceland, my father sent three of his best men up to the snowfield to look for him. They found him at the place the aeroplanes had crashed. He was sitting, huddled by one of the machines, completely frozen ... all of his equipment – his tent, his food – had disappeared. He was frozen to the metal of the aeroplane.'

A cold shudder ran through my body. 'What happened to him ... is he still there?'

'No, my father's people carried him as far as the mountain range and built a stone grave around him ... as he died so he was buried. Since that day no Eskimo will go to the snowfield ... it is a bad and evil place.'

'Does that mean you won't go?'

She gave me a searching look. 'If you ask me, I will go.'

'What about the evil spirits?'

'We made a pact, remember? I will not go back on my word.' There was a strangely distant quality in her voice when she added, 'Neither will you, Luke Spence.'

'Let me get this straight!' Scarth's face had the dark intensity of a thundery sky. 'You're telling me that the planes are up on the snowfield, behind the mountains, and that an American died up there looking for them. Right so far?' No one had the opportunity to answer before his right fist crashed into the table, rattling the empty tin mugs. He continued by answering himself. 'Right! We all agree on that ... now comes the best part. Being American he didn't die of any of the normal physiological ailments; unless of course you're implying a sudden attack of old age ... which I somehow doubt. No sir, being an American he had to be different. He had to bump into a bunch of his fellow countrymen who then robbed him of his survival kit and left him to perish.' Scarth's eyes swept quickly around the room. His voice was full of irony when he added, 'Being a dumb American myself I might just have bought that. I mean, I might just have accepted that a Greenland snowfield isn't that far removed from Fifth Avenue on Christmas Eve ... except! Except you had to add that the Americans he met were dead. More than fifteen years dead! Come on Spence, what's with this crap you're giving me?'

'No crap,' I said quietly. 'That's what they believe.'

'Okay, so that's what they believe. As for me I don't buy a single damned word of it ... anyway, what's stopping us going up alone?'

'Too many things,' I replied. 'First we need to send a dog team and Eskimos up to the snowfield to mark out a safe landing area near the crash site. Two, if the landing area is any appreciable distance from the crashed planes we need the sled and the dogs as transport. Three, and most important, we need someone who can handle dogs and knows the terrain. Not forgetting the digging, and once we find those planes there'll be plenty of that.'

Scarth was only half listening. He turned suddenly on Akalise. 'But you've agreed to go ... why?'

'I promised Spence. I am keeping my word, that is all.'

Hannah gave Akalise a dark brooding look before Scarth said, 'You're quite a lady, Mrs Palmarsson. Yessir, pity the rest of your people don't have your guts.' We were silent for a few moments then Scarth, a slow smile spreading across his face, said to Akalise, 'Where's that little Eskimo guy ... Che ...'

'Che-mang-nek,' she prompted. 'I think he is with the boy in the next cabin.'

'Does he speak English?'

'No ... I think not.'

'But you can translate for me?'

'Yes, this is possible.'

'Good. If you bring him here I think I can persuade him to come along.'

Akalise regarded Scarth for a moment. It was as if she was reading his mind; probing the very depths of his soul. 'You are thinking to belittle him in front of everyone, Mr Scarth; perhaps saying he has not even the courage of a woman?'

'Something along those lines. Why not?'

'It will not work. My people are not like your people.'

'So what are your people like, Mrs Palmarsson?'

'I can quote you an example from a man called Lars Dalager – he was a Dane who opened the supply routes from Denmark in the eighteenth century. He said, "The most efficacious measure by which the Greenlanders may be won, is a rational association with them, because

134

they are more likely to follow examples than to obey the most profound admonitory sermon.'

'And what the hell does that mean in East-Side lingo?'

'It means,' I said, 'that we make Che-mang-nek a suitable offer for the use of his dog team, then prepare to go alone to the snowfield. We let it be known that Akalise is going to lead us.'

Scarth said cynically, 'And at the eleventh hour this guy jumps up and says he's changed his mind, uh?'

'He will, Mr Scarth,' Akalise said firmly. 'You see, the boy with Che-mang-nek is his son.'

Scarth digested the words thoughtfully; then clapped his fat hands together. 'Of course! Jeez, that's it. In the eyes of the son the father ...' He didn't need to finish the sentence.

Hannah, who had moved over to the solitary iced-up window, had been watching developments with the air of a bemused onlooker. She suddenly jolted everyone back to reality with that one basic unanswered question. 'I'm assuming,' she said, 'that the American who came back after the war must have known something about arctic survival – especially as he returned every summer for fifteen years. What worries me is how a man with that sort of knowledge can lose all his survival equipment.' Her attention focused on me. 'What do you think, Spence?'

'I think that if the shaman – the Eskimo witch doctor – says there are spirits up there, there are spirits up there. Easy as that. Don't ask me to give you a logical explanation though, because I couldn't even begin to. Suffice to say I've been around these parts long enough, and seen enough unaccountable happenings, to make me realize that our kind of logic doesn't count for much.'

Scarth let out a deep raucous laugh. 'You reckon you've been around these parts long enough! I'll tell you what pal, you've been around these parts too long, period; and if I was you after this little trip is over I'd make tracks for civilization pretty damn quick.'

'And the eternal money tree, you mean?'

The slate-grey eyes glinted greedily. 'And what's wrong with that?'

'Too many people playing the same game ... come to think of it, the only game.'

'And here? What have you got in this frozen-over hell, apart from a bunch of superstitious Eskimos and a few polar bears?'

'Something you wouldn't know about. Freedom.'

Akalise left the following day at noon. With her was Che-mang-nek. Her simple philosophy, or the one she had borrowed from Dalager, had worked like a charm. Even Scarth's international language had turned up trumps yet again. He had offered Che-mang-nek a handful of dollars for the use of his dog team and the wily old Eskimo had snatched his hand off. After that it was only a matter of time before Che-mang-nek arrived at the face-saving suggestion of accompanying Akalise. His son, eyes gleaming with pride, would stay and guard the airstrip.

The plan was basic in the extreme. Akalise and Che-mang-nek would take the dog team up to the snowfield and mark out a safe landing area as close to the crash site as possible. If the weather held they should be on station within two days, with me carrying out daily recce flights to check on their progress. At first Scarth had insisted on going with the sled. When I pointed out his physical condition was against him – running frequent four-hundred-yard stretches with the team to keep warm – he reluctantly gave up the idea.

'You've got all the information on marking out the airstrip?' I said to Akalise as we walked towards the sled.

'That's the third time you've asked me!' The mock severity softened when she added, 'Do not worry ... I will do as you have told me.' She said it as if she always would.

'Take care of yourself.'

'And you, Luke Spence ... and you.' She lifted her face towards mine. As if drawn by a magnet I reached down and kissed her fully on the mouth. The stars in heaven were never as bright. Then for what seemed the millionth time in my life I watched somebody go; not necessarily a woman, but somebody. Something about pilots and airports, and airports and goodbyes.

'Touching little scene,' Hannah Dawson said, appearing at my side.

'Glad you liked it ... but I'm sure you didn't come out here just to tell me that.'

'Perceptive as always. No, I was wondering if you would let me fly from the left seat when we go up on the reconnaissance flights ... it's just that I might not get the opportunity to fly a ski-equipped plane again.'

I looked into her blue eyes, searching for the other reason. The reason, or one of the reasons I had put to Akalise back in Narsarsuaq. But all I found was an open innocence. A low-time pilot wanting to get her hands on the controls.

'Why not?' I said, walking back to the cabin. Two words which could end up as the signature on my death warrant.

It was following our midday meal that Scarth had a rush of blood to the head and wanted to know how to build an igloo. Trying to explain that a little knowledge is a dangerous thing was waving a red rag to a bull where Scarth was concerned. He typified the self-made man. In his mind money had the propensity of God-like powers. It was all seeing, all doing, all powerful. I took my long snow knife from my kit and worked with him until darkness came. By then I had to reluctantly admit to myself that he was an able student. Perhaps he was right after all; perhaps they were all right. Perhaps money lifted that final psychological barrier, releasing some superhuman force from an unknown cosmic consciousness: that same power which manifested itself in a knowing aura around all successful and wealthy people. The truth of course could have been far simpler. He was picking my brains for survival techniques, for the day I wouldn't be around any more.

Following an early supper I pulled on my cold-weather gear and went out into the night. The misery of removing iced-up engine covers slowly died as the Beaver's engine began to push a little warmth back into the cabin. It wasn't much, not enough to remove your parka, but it was something. I turned the instrument-panel lights down until the red glow resembled the dying embers of an old, burnt-out log fire, and sat with the strangely satisfying rumble of the Pratt and Whitney. Once there had been other airports, other planes, other pilots. Pinpricks of navigation lights weaving gently down dimly lit taxi-ways. Faceless voices. Distant friendships. Even Nam hadn't destroyed that; except perhaps at the end. The kids! My big investment! Not that seven years of pay cheques to a Vietnamese orphanage would ever bring them back. But it was all I could do. One day it would be all over. One day I would lay the ghost for ever. I gunned the engine, as if trying to blow away the memories in the slipstream. Blue flames flickered from the exhausts, then, as I throttled back they were gone, taking my children with them.

When I returned to the cabin I found Scarth sitting on an empty packing crate by the table. He was writing in a pocket-sized notebook, his eyes straining in the feeble candlelight. Hannah was perched on the other end of the table dealing out hands of cards to imaginary players. She looked up as I entered the room.

'There's still some stew left,' she offered.

'Thanks,' I said, rubbing feeling back into my face.

Scarth stopped writing and looked up. 'How's the machine?'

'Battery's a bit low, but we should get another two or three starts out of it before I have to change it.'

'How many spares did you bring?'

'Two.'

He thought for a moment. 'Is that going to be enough?'

'Depends. Needs a good long flight, really, to put a bit of life back into it.'

'Guess you're right,' he murmured, and returned to his notebook.

'Working out how much profit you'll make if we pull those planes out?'

He continued writing. 'When, not if. No, I've already done that. What I'm doing now is costing out helicopters and ships.'

'You're going to lift them out and put them on a freighter, right?'

'You got it.'

'When?'

'August; that's when the ice breaks up sufficiently ... isn't it?'

'Usually. But what if it doesn't? Happens some years, you know.'

Hannah put a tin plate of warmed-over stew in front of me. I smiled and turned back to dearth. 'Smells nice,' he said, turning to Hannah, 'any left?'

She grimaced, nodded, and went back to the primus and the pot of stew.

'You didn't answer my question,' I said. 'What happens if it doesn't break?'

'It will,' he replied, adding up a column of figures.

'Then there's the Greenland government,' I continued. 'What happens if they don't give you permission to take them out?'

Scarth stopped writing and placed the pencil carefully on the pad. 'You know something, Spence, if I thought your way I'd be selling bootlaces in the Bronx. So just to put your mind at ease, I have a lawyer back in New York who's taking care of that side of things. Funny thing is, when I first took him on he was much the same as you ... a first-rate schmuck. You know, that guy couldn't even walk and chew gum at the same time. Now of course it's different. Now he doesn't look for problems where they don't exist ... you want to try it some time.'

Hannah pushed a plate of stew in front of Scarth. 'You talking about Melville?'

'Yeah, I'm talking about Melville.'

'You're mistaken, Rollo. Just because a man keeps on saying yes, doesn't necessarily follow he's changed for the better. He's probably realized that that word is a ticket to easy street. And I should know, I work with him most of the time.'

'So you work with him, and you maybe think the guy has his off days. So who doesn't? But whichever way you look at it, he's still a fine lawyer. Damn fine.' Scarth snatched up his fork and began to shovel the stew into his mouth.

Hannah looked at me, shrugged her shoulders, and gave a tired smile. 'Coffee?'

'Thanks.'

'Rollo?'

'No, but you can get my whisky. It's in the back room.'

'Hell of a way to spend the rest of your life,' I said to Hannah.

She glanced towards the back room. Scarth had finished off his stew, drunk himself legless, and was now sleeping it off. 'It's not for always,' she replied. 'One of these days I'll pack my bags and vanish into one of those spectacular Hollywood sunsets.'

'Nice world, isn't it? Everyone looking for a way out.'

'You're wrong,' she said wistfully. 'I think we all know the way ... it's finding the money to get there.'

'And that's what you're doing?'

'Isn't everybody?'

'Not me.'

'So what's at the top of your wish list?'

I smiled at the reference. 'I thought they took those away when you stopped believing in Santa Claus ... then again, perhaps you're right. Perhaps we want every day to be Christmas.'

'You still haven't told me.'

I shrugged. 'A new beginning in exchange for an old ending, perhaps.'

'Money will buy you that,' she said.

'Not my kind of new beginning it won't.'

'It was the war, I guess.'

'The only one we ever lost. Did you know that?'

'It wasn't that though, was it?' Then more perceptively she added, 'But it was more than the newspaper reports, wasn't it?'

'What gives you that idea?'

Her eyes were turned away when she said, 'Something that Linc said that night back in Gander; something about, under that ravaged exterior you're as soft as a kiddy's teddy bear.'

I laughed. 'As Rollo would say, crap.'

'No crap, Spence.' The voice was serious now. 'What really happened?'

'What do you mean what really happened? You read the clippings.'

Her face moved slightly, closer to the yellow halo of candlelight. She said quietly, 'It wasn't you, was it?'

'Wasn't me what?'

'Wasn't you who bombed that village.'

I rubbed my eyes tiredly. 'Course it was me ... I was there. In the sky... in an F-4 ... what more is there to say?'

'How about the truth?'

I looked at my watch. 'Better get some sleep; it's your, engine run in two hours.'

She watched me move over towards the sleeping bag, her eyes wide in disbelief. 'You went through all that for somebody else ... let them destroy your life.'

'You're tilting at windmills, Hannah. Let's leave it now, shall we?'

'Was it a woman?' she said, as I slipped into the kapok-filled warmth.

I laid my head back and closed my eyes. 'Sure it was a woman,' I said sleepily.

'The truth?'

'Cross my heart ... the truth.'

Two days after Akalise and Che-mang-nek had departed we struck camp at Kulusuk and loaded and refuelled the Beaver. There was no wind, but it was bitterly cold: twenty-six below, cold enough to make even the straightforward task of breathing a painful experience. It would be worse up on the snowfield, a dreary exercise in endurance. No one spoke as I spiralled the Beaver up to 12,000 feet and set course to Akalise's last known position. Thirty minutes later we crossed over the mountain range.

I felt a momentary stab of concern when I realized I couldn't see anyone, just an endless desolation of snow and ice. It was the sort of place you could drop the entire city of New York into and never find it again; and here was I looking for two infinitesimal figures, a dog team and a few tents. I pulled on my snow goggles to reduce the glare and began a methodical box search. Even so Hannah beat me to it.

'Over there!' she yelled excitedly, pointing frantically towards an area below the starboard wing tip. I dropped my gaze and instantly picked up the thin plume of orange smoke climbing lazily into the midday sky. I cut the power and let the Beaver drift down towards the camp. Five minutes later the skis rattled over the ice. We were down.

'Nice landing,' Scarth shouted as I taxied back to where Akalise and Che-mang-nek had pitched the tents. It was the sort of remark that experienced pilots let go, being as profound as telling a pedestrian he's good at walking.

I killed the engine as we neared the site. 'Well,' I said to Hannah. 'What do you think of it?'

She looked at me through darkly shadowed eyes. Except they weren't shadows, they were the dark half-moons of tiredness caused by irregular sleeping patterns. Her mouth twitched, the corners breaking into a series of age lines. 'I get the idea God gave up when he got this far.'

Scarth gave a hollow laugh from the back of the plane. 'What's the problem? Looks a nice enough day to me.'

'Don't be deceived,' I said. 'See that?' I pointed to the outside air-temperature gauge. 'It's forty below out there ... you'll get the idea when you step outside.'

Scarth sneered and moved to open the door. His hands were bare. 'Mittens!' I yelled. 'At the risk of boring you I will repeat a former instruction. After that you're on your own. Do not touch cold metal with bare hands. At anything less than minus thirty they'll freeze together instantly. If by chance you forget and find one of your hands in that unhappy situation, urinate on it. If you're dumb enough to get both hands stuck, make sure you've got a friend along.'

'Is that it?' Scarth growled unhappily.

'For now.'

He pulled on his mittens, kicked the door open and clambered down into the snow. Hannah and I followed.

'Engine covers?' Hannah said, pulling the wolverine fur of her hood closer to her face.

'In the baggage locker. When you've done that get into the tent and warm up.'

Akalise was waiting for me by the side of the main tent. The smile in her eyes faltered as I drew nearer, being replaced with a look which could only mean one thing.

'Problems?' I asked.

'I am afraid,' she said in a small voice, 'that we have lost most of the supplies.'

I looked at her in disbelief. 'Lost! How the hell did that happen?'

'We were coming up through Teardrop Glacier ... it was a difficult passage ...' she paused.

'Go on,' I said.

'I went to the front of the team to pull the lead dog on, while Che-mang-nek pushed the sled from behind. The next moment he called out... I saw two large crates fall into the ravine.'

'So it was Che-mang-nek?'

'He was just pushing. He said perhaps the ropes were badly tied, or ...'

'Or what?'

'Or the *tarneqs* ... the souls of the dead pilots!'

'*Tarneqs* be damned. Are you sure he didn't untie them?' I said angrily.

'Why would he do that? He is only an Eskimo ... he has come to help.'

I flailed my arms across my chest in a miserable attempt to keep up my body heat. 'Maybe, maybe not. Anyway, can you give me a hand to unload the aircraft? We'll go through the inventory then.'

We were sitting in the main tent fifteen minutes later, warming our hands on mugs of coffee. The general air was one of depression. Mine was something more. That something about Che-mang-nek I had noticed on our arrival at Kulusuk, the something that had told me he wasn't all he seemed to be: the incident at Teardrop Glacier seemed to confirm my suspicions. But suspicions were all they were; in the meantime we had a mission to complete. 'So,' I said, breaking into everyone else's private thoughts, 'I figure we can last out for a maximum of five days with the present supplies. No more.'

Scarth shuffled uncomfortably. 'We stay here until we find the planes,' he snarled.

'In that case, Rollo, you'll be by yourself.'

'Like hell I will. I employed you to do a job. You stay until it's finished.'

'You're crazy, do you know that? Bloody crazy. Over half the food supplies have gone, most of the paraffin, and the other tent. That one, in case you've forgotten, had insulated walls ... take a look at this one. Go on, take a look.' But as usual I was wasting my time. I doubted he was even listening. I doubted he saw what I saw, or felt what I felt. The temperature at the bottom of the tent could have been as much as thirty below, while the temperature at the top, due to the heating of water and the breathing of four occupants, was above freezing. The result was a heavy mist which almost prevented you from seeing the person sitting on the opposite side of the tent. But worse than that, because of the single wall in direct contact with the arctic cold, the vapour condensed into water. I could feel it now; running down my neck in a cold drizzle.

'What about igloos?' Scarth suddenly exclaimed.

Akalise looked at him. 'Not igloos on a flat snowfield, Mr Scarth; snow caves under the ground.'

'How safe are they?'

'Safe enough,' she replied.

'Where's Che-mang-nek now?' I said.

Akalise turned to me. 'He should be finishing; I told him to prepare three caves.'

'Why not one big one?'

'Smaller ones are easier to make. A big one needs to be deeper for strength in the roof.'

I half smiled to myself. She was a better snow engineer than me simply by birthright. 'I'm sure you're right; anyway you and Hannah can have one of the small tents each; they're insulated so you'll be warm. Rollo and I will take the snow caves with Che-mang-nek.'

Scarth gave me an uncomfortable look; his mouth opened in protest and then snapped silently shut.

I waved away the fog with my hand. 'You okay Hannah?'

She leaned forward, her face tired and drawn. 'Exhausted,' she sighed.

'My fault, shouldn't have had you running about out there. We are, after all, seven thousand feet above sea level.'

'I'll be all right in the morning. Now if you could point me in the right direction I think I'll turn in.'

I staggered to my feet in the confined space. 'I'll do better than that, I'll show you.' I pulled the flap back and went outside. I could feel my hair freezing before I had the chance to pull on my hood.

'Soon be dark,' Hannah said, following me out.

I looked towards the distant horizon, where the sun was playing its lonely game with the tall shadows. 'Another hour,' I replied. 'You take this tent. And make sure you brush off as much surplus snow as you can before getting in.'

'I will. How about you?'

'What do you mean?'

'Will you be all right in the snow cave?'

'Warmer than you, probably.' I held the flap of the tent open as she eased herself into the restricted space. 'When you've taken your boots off, put them in the sleeping bag with you. That way they'll stay supple.'

'What about the engine runs?'

'Don't worry about that, you can have the night off.' She smiled gratefully and started pulling off her boots.

I went back to the main tent. Akalise had gone to check on Che-mang-nek's progress; Scarth was still sitting in the same place, only now he was adding a generous measure of whisky to his coffee.

'I wouldn't do that if I were you.'

'But you're not, Spence. That's where we're different. You look for problems and find them; I ignore them and they leave me alone.'

'If you say so, Rollo.'

'I say so,' he said. 'Anyway, how far did Akalise figure we were away from the crash site?'

'Two to three miles.'

'Yeah, that's right. Pity we couldn't have landed right alongside.'

I said, 'Sastrugi ... it's pretty bad that way, she reckons.'

'I heard that... anyway, how long to get there?'

145

'With the sled and the dogs, could be a few hours … depends on the sastrugi.'

Scarth snorted. 'Why the hell don't we walk?'

'And who's going to carry the gear?'

'What gear?'

'Shovels, picks, that kind of thing.'

He swallowed some more coffee, then said, 'So, what time do we leave?'

'First light. Now if you'll excuse me I've got an engine run to do.'

It was nearly an hour later when I heaved the aircraft's battery into the tent. It was too much extra work in this type of climate and at this altitude, but it was either that or be left with an ornamental aeroplane. I wrapped the battery in a fur and took it to the snow cave. Then I returned to the main tent.

Akalise was still working, organizing a daily ration rota. She appeared tireless, but that was an illusion. I could see the fatigue in her eyes. She turned and smiled as I entered the tent. 'Sit there,' she said. 'I will make you some coffee.'

I smiled weakly back and squatted down by the hissing primus. 'Mr Scarth and Miss Dawson are asleep, I think,' she added.

'Take them a few days to acclimatize to the altitude.'

'Yes.' She looked up from the coffee pot. 'I am sorry about the supplies; I know things will now be even more difficult.'

'Don't worry … it was an accident. Anyway, once we've located the crashed planes and put down markers it won't be so bad.'

'You have thought some more about what happened?'

'Happened?'

'On the flight from Narsarsuaq.'

'The fuel pumps, you mean? No … not really. You?'

She lifted her hands in a gesture of hopelessness. 'Only again the police … Sergeant Kolbrunarskald.'

I warmed my hands by the primus. 'You said something to me back in Narsarsuaq; something about the missing gold being almost a legend in these parts.'

146

'That is so.'

'Would Kolb have known about the legend?'

'I'm sure he did. Most who live in Greenland do.'

'So why didn't he or others like him come to look for the planes years ago?'

Akalise smiled. 'The treasure of legends is hard to find, Spence ... also for those who really believed it existed, there are the *tarneqs*.'

'So why now? Why now, after all these years, should someone be suddenly interested?'

She shrugged. 'Independence perhaps ... perhaps Kolb has been waiting for this moment. Before, if they had found the gold it would have been claimed by the Danish government ... now it is different.' She passed me a mug of coffee.

'Yes, I think you could have something. I noticed Kolb, and Fleischer come to that, didn't much like taking orders from Inspector Thiessen.'

'He will not last much longer,' she said. 'Soon he will go away.'

'Back to Denmark?'

'I don't know. I never knew him that well. He was, I think, a lonely man.'

I finished the coffee. 'Which leaves Kolb and the plane crash that never was,' I said quietly.

'The plane crash ...' she started. 'Oh, I see.'

I pulled my mittens on. 'I'm going back now ... get some sleep. Have you finished?'

'Yes, I have finished.'

I reached across and she moved silently into my arms. Her dark eyes glittered brightly in the meagre light of the primus stove. Then her lips were on mine, soft and searching and willing.

We left early the following morning: Scarth, myself and Che-mang-nek. The sastrugi – wind-made ridges of ice – lasted for about a mile. One mile too far for Scarth. One mile of razor-sharp ice and the beginnings of frostbite and snow blindness. That mile had consumed nearly two hours; in which time we had humped, dragged, and all but carried the

147

sled. That mile, coupled with the altitude, had also consumed most of Scarth's strength. He was still a big fat man; hopelessly out of condition. And this was his first real test. I told Che-mang-nek to stop and sat Scarth on the sled.

'What the hell,' he gasped. 'What ... hell we stopping for?'

'You need a rest. We'll go on in a minute.'

'Rest be damned. It'll get better soon ... you see if it don't.'

'Who told you that? On second thoughts don't tell me. You bought God off, right! You pushed him a handful of dollars and he agreed to keep you informed on terrain conditions.'

Scarth smiled feebly. 'You're learning, kid. You took your time, but now you're getting the message ... now give me a hand to get to my feet.' I pulled him up, taking his right arm across my shoulder. 'Know any marching tunes?' he said gruffly.

'Marching tunes?'

'Yeah! Music to walk by.'

'Remind me next time ... I'll have a military band specially flown in.'

He smiled at the thought, as I half carried him over the uneven ice.

It ended 400 footsteps further on. There was no warning it would; no way of seeing in that glare; but suddenly the sastrugi became smooth, roiling white tundra. I sat Scarth – who had made a point of saying I told you so – on the sled and covered him with a caribou fur, then climbed on in front of him. The long whip cracked and we were moving; slowly at first, then faster; until the biting wind cut through to the bone. Somewhere ahead lay the planes. The Mustangs. Patterson's Volunteers. I felt my pulse begin to race at the thought. How long ago was it that the immaculately dressed Scarth had walked into the airport coffee shop in Frobisher with the half-baked idea of stepping over to Greenland to find a squadron of aircraft which had been missing since the war? And now it seemed we were almost there.

Of course they would be iced in and covered in snow. Even the pilots could still be sitting at the controls; frozen in some hideous time trap – never growing older. Completely unchanged from the day they had force-landed.

148

The dogs slowed to a walk and then stopped. Che-mang-nek was at my side before I had time to move. 'This,' he mumbled, waving his arm in a wide circle. 'This is the place!'

I eased my frozen body off the sled and exercised my arms, trying to push the blood towards my unfeeling fingers. My feet were the same. I had passed through the transition of pain to one of complete numbness. I moved back to Scarth, rubbing the snow off the dark lenses of my snow goggles. 'This is it, Rollo. End of the rainbow!' It wasn't until I had said it that I realized the double-edged connotation.

He tugged off a mitten and held the palm of his hand to his cheek. 'Can't feel my face,' he said.

I pulled his hand away and saw the telltale white patches. 'Mild frostbite. Keep your hand there for a while. Remember what I told you. Keep pulling faces ... try not to let the facial muscles stay in one position for too long.' I helped him off the sled.

'So this is the place?' He sounded unconvinced as his screwed-up eyes did a slow sweep of the area. 'Doesn't look very promising to me.'

'If you put your snow goggles back on you'll see the shadows.' I pointed ahead of the dogs who were whining to be fed.

He pulled the goggles into place. 'Still can't see them.'

'You'll have to wait for your eyes to readjust. Anyway, where there are shadows there is higher ground. Not much higher but high enough.'

'The whaleback dunes, you mean?'

'It's possible.'

A slow grin spread across his face. 'So what in hell are we waiting for? Let's get started.'

We had been working steadily for more than two hours, using the long metal spikes. Working in methodical ten-yard-square boxes; and when each box was complete marking it off with orange marker flags. I stopped and looked around me. Looked at the futility of it all. I almost laughed when I realized we could probably do this for a thousand years and still come out empty-handed; except without realizing it we would have cornered the world market in orange marker flags.

149

'Anything your way?' I yelled to Rollo.

The dark-lensed eyes swivelled towards me. 'Nothing ... not ... damn thing.'

I moved towards him. 'No more today,' I said. 'We'll head back.'

For once in his life he didn't argue, just leant down, picked up his tools and followed me towards the sled. Che-mang-nek, who had refused to help because of the evil spirits, watched us approach.

'Do you think this is the right place?' Scarth rasped.

'If we had a hundred guys digging I'd tell you ... this way we could be literally feet away ... or ...'

'Or what?'

'Or someone isn't being altogether truthful.'

'The Eskimo, you mean?'

I said, 'We did lose half the supplies, didn't we? And I tied most of the stuff on to that sled myself.'

Scarth grabbed my arm and pulled me to a stop. 'You tied it ... you didn't tell me that before ... do you mean that that little bastard is out to sabotage this entire operation?'

'Supposition, nothing more.'

'Supposition horse shit ... so what else haven't you told me?'

'Nothing else.'

Scarth pummelled his right fist into his left mitten. 'Leave him to me. I'll sort the little runt out.'

'And what good do you think that will do?'

'You have a better way?'

'I'll speak to Akalise when we get back.'

Scarth snorted and started off again through the snow.

The journey back took longer, for no other reason than tiredness. By the time we had transited the sastrugi for the second time Scarth was at the point of total collapse. Too much effort expended on his first day. I loaded him carefully on to the sled. 'Not much further now,' I said. He didn't answer. Cold soak affects the body that way, switching off the systems one by one. It's not an altogether unpleasant way of dying, the pain and uncontrollable chattering of teeth giving way to an undreamt of warmth, and a sudden desire to sleep. When the eyelids close it is usually for the last time. Scarth wasn't a thousand miles away from that state now. The white growth of beard accentuated by the caked ice clinging to it, the lips swollen and badly split showing a mess of congealed frozen blood, the puffy eyes closing out the world, and the bridge of his nose cracked open in an ugly purple slit. Elsewhere, white patches of frostbite were taking a positive hold, turning him into an old, old man.

I climbed on the sled in front of him and heard the welcome sound of the long whip breaking the dogs into a whining run. Somewhere above, the sun glowed a dull red through what appeared to be endless layers of white gauze. Down here the wind, constantly changing direction, twitched and skipped against the loose snow. It was a sign I knew well. A sign that would put the fear of God into the hardiest of arctic men.

Hannah Dawson shrank back in horror as I dragged Scarth into the main tent. 'What happened?' she cried. 'What happened ... his face!'

I looked slowly from her to Scarth and back again. 'Greenland's what happened, Hannah. Remember what I said back in Gander ... in that plush, centrally heated airport terminal. I said this trip wasn't a church social outing ... now perhaps you might believe me.' I turned to Akalise who was squatting by the stove melting a pot of snow. 'Could you leave that for the time being and give Hannah a hand to get him out of his wet clothes? And see to his hands and face ... you know what to do.'

Akalise said, 'And what about you?'

'Me? Don't worry about me, I'm like Che-mang-nek ... live for ever.' I lifted the tent flap and stopped. 'When you've made him as comfortable as you can, I suggest you go around all the tents and check the guy ropes. There's a storm coming up that might just blow us off the face of Greenland.'

By the time I had secured the Beaver the wind had come up. It didn't seem very strong at first; more of a squally breeze puffing like an old man out of breath; but that was only the beginning. I hauled myself up into the cockpit and checked the altimeter, the instrument which acts on the same principle as the aneroid barometer. The glass had fallen by as much as thirty millibars which meant that the mother and father of all depressions was moving in. And fast. Not that I had needed to check it – the smell of the storm filled my nostrils.

I hurried back to the tent. Hannah was alone, tending the pot of melting snow. 'Where's Akalise and Rollo?'

'We've put him in her tent,' she said in a subdued voice. Then: 'God, his feet! His feet were turning black.' Her eyes fixed on mine, pleading, begging ... imploring. Praying I would tell her it couldn't happen this way. This fast.

'He'll be all right,' I said. 'Akalise will probably get in the sleeping bag with him. Only way to get rid of frostbite ... animal warmth.' My mind went back to that time five years earlier, the time of the long walk back from the plane crash; and the agony which followed. Especially the agony. 'I'll take care of that,' I said, moving over to the stove. 'Go and tell Akalise I've got some morphine in the plane's first-aid kit. If he gets in too much pain I'll give him a shot.' She went out as the wind picked up and the tent began flapping wildly.

The snow had melted by the time Hannah returned, boiling at a much lower temperature because of the altitude. But warm coffee was better than no coffee. 'How is he?' I asked.

'Akalise thinks it's not that bad. She said morphine shouldn't be necessary.'

'Thank God for that,' I murmured. 'I wouldn't wish that kind of pain on my worst enemy. Now if you'd like to take over from me I'll check to see if I still have two feet left inside these boots.'

'What about food?'

'What have you got?'

'Same as yesterday. Tuna fish, chocolate, plenty of bars of margarine. Oh and quite a few tins of sardines. Outside of that there's coffee, sugar and sealed packs of glucose candy.'

I began to tug my boots off. 'Coffee and tuna sounds real good, and in the meantime you can throw me one of those bars of margarine.'

She handed me one of the frozen packs. 'What are you going to do with that ... or is that a dumb question?'

'Eat it,' I said, pulling off the top of the wrapper. 'Why do you think Eskimos consume vast amounts of whale blubber? It's not for the fun of it, you know. They do it because their bodies demand fat. In your case of course you can also rub it over your face ... skin protection.' I took a bite from the margarine and went back to removing my boots, before adding, 'That way you'll leave looking just as beautiful as when you arrived.'

Hannah looked at me, head angled to one side. 'You know something Spence, you're not quite the bastard you'd have everyone believe, are you?'

I smiled. 'Still tilting at windmills, Hannah. You'll feel differently when it's all over and you're back in New York.'

She didn't answer. Not with words at least. But I read the old familiar challenge in her eyes. We looked steadily at each other for a long time, the only sound the hiss of blowing snow as it drifted against the tent wall.

'Coffee then?' she said finally, and busied herself with the mugs.

I pulled off my socks and set to work on my feet, kneading as much of the frost out of them as I could. Hannah shuffled towards me on her knees, holding the mug of coffee in front of her. She stopped dead when she saw my left foot, her eyes drawn in horrific fascination. 'What happened ... you've only got three toes!'

I looked down at the scars the rough and ready surgery had left. The ugly scars which had once been the two smaller toes on my left foot. Then I reached over and unclipped the Fairbairn knife from my right boot. 'Once had to walk a long way in a place like this,' I said, turning the knife over in my hands. 'And I made one basic mistake. I didn't check my feet often enough. The result is what you see.'

'You ... you cut them off yourself?' she whispered in disbelief.

I stared unemotionally at the glinting blade. 'Yes, and you know what was almost funny about it ... I probably didn't have to. But I was more concerned about gangrene setting in. Couple of days later I was in hospital in Frobisher. That was when I really started thinking about survival techniques.'

Hannah said, 'In case it ever happened again, you mean?'

'In a way; but it was more than that. It was when I read that the first Eskimos appeared in these parts over five thousand years ago. Apparently they came over the top of the world from Siberia. That made me realize why this really is the elder world.'

'You really think they're special, don't you?'

'Oh yes, they're special all right. I've even heard of polar bears shambling away when they've come face to face with an Eskimo. You see the Eskimo would once have been an alien in an inimical world, but not any more. Now they belong as much as the bear and the fox and the seal.'

'And you, Spence ... are you an alien?'

I returned the Fairbairn to the clip and took the mug of lukewarm coffee. 'Perhaps, perhaps not ... I don't really know.'

It must have been around midnight when I heard the noise. It was distinctive; the shuffle of an animal or a human. I picked up the shotgun and slipped off the safety catch; then I aimed both barrels at the entrance to the tunnel. I had never heard of a polar bear coming this far inland in winter to search for food; but just because I hadn't heard it, didn't mean a thing.

Thank God I had left the primus on. Thank God for that aura of faint blue light. Okay, so it's a bear! What are you going to do? Both barrels at once? What happens if it still keeps coming? I was in a trap. A cleverly constructed ice trap, and there was only one way out. Tiny beads of perspiration broke out on my forehead as my eyes unblinkingly held the tunnel entrance. All around me, the damp soft heat became heavy with expectancy.

Hannah Dawson's face popped out of the two-foot-high tunnel Fifteen seconds later, her mouth falling wordlessly open at the sight of the two barrels focused between her eyes. I lowered the gun slowly and let out a long sigh of relief. 'One of these days, Hannah Dawson, you're going to get that pretty little head of yours blown clean off. Next time you might try shouting.'

She crawled into the living area on all fours and pulled herself up on to the sleeping bench. 'I'll try to remember that,' she said, a note of relief in her voice. She looked around the cramped quarters. 'Small, isn't it?'

'Big enough for sleeping.'

'What about the roof, won't it cave in?'

'Shouldn't, it's arched to take more weight. Also allows moisture to run down the walls. Prevents dripping.'

'Clever.'

'As I said before, the Eskimos have been at it a long time. So what's the problem?'

'Problem? Oh I see ... why am I here, you mean. No particular reason, except for the wind up there. The walls of my tent keep cracking and popping. It's not so much the noise that's driving me mad, but the thought of everything blowing away ... and me with it.'

I said, 'It sounds worse than it really is.'

She fixed her blue eyes on me. 'How long will it last?'

'Could be gone by tomorrow. Two days at the most.' I reached down and put the coffee pot on the primus. 'If you're thinking of staying a short while you'd better take off your outer clothing and your boots. You'll feel the benefit when you go back outside.'.

'It's kind of cosy,' she said as she wriggled out of her waterproof over-trousers.

I poured a mug of coffee and passed it to her. She was sitting on the sleeping bench furs, knees drawn up to her chin. And even in white oil-wool stockings, brown cord trousers and a bright red sweater, she still managed to look appealing. Or perhaps I had been in all the wrong places for too long. Who the hell was I comparing her with anyway? Who could I remember with the sexual awareness of Hannah Dawson?

She said, 'What happens about the engine runs tonight?'

'Easy, we won't be doing them. I drained the oil out of the sump when I tied the plane down earlier; and the batteries are wrapped up in those furs in the corner.'

'Will it start when you put some fresh oil in?'

'Should do. I've got a blowtorch up in the main tent. I'll hold that up the exhaust stack for an hour, while you heat the oil over the stove. Then you pour in the oil while I reconnect the battery.'

'And that will do it?'

'Might have to thin the oil down with a bit of petrol; then if we all pray together as I hit the starter ...'

She laughed and passed me the empty mug. Her voice was uncertain when she said, 'Do you mind if I stay here tonight? I ... I don't think I could face being in that tent alone.'

'I don't mind, but in between those caribou furs there's one sleeping bag only ... unless you want to go back and get yours.'

She looked at me, her face bathed in perspiration. What had been a damp, soft heat, was steadily rising to that of a sauna, the result of a second person's body heat and breathing in a snow cave built for one. 'I'll be all right,' she said meekly.

Then, with our eyes still holding each other she began to undress. 'You remember back at Kulusuk, when I said so the loose woman doesn't get raped tonight?'

'I remember.'

'Do you also remember that I said not any night?'

'Vaguely.'

She unclipped her bra and lowered it from the fullness of her breasts. 'So what would you say if I told you I'd changed my mind?'

I didn't answer. Instead my eyes took in the milky whiteness of her skin, the gently flowing curves, the seductive thrust of her body. 'Well?' she said softly, a wicked smile spreading across her face. 'Are you still fighting it?'

There was a long pause as I felt my resolve slowly weaken. Weaken, until the tantalizing sight of her body became too much, then I reached out and took her savagely in my arms, crushing her against my chest. Her fingernails raked savagely down my back; while her legs kicked violently beneath me. Animal aggression in every movement. 'Bitch,' I yelled, pinning her arms.

156

'That's more like it, Captain Spence.' She kicked again. 'Real fighting this time ... every inch of the way.'

'You don't have to spell it out,' I said, forcing my body down on to hers. 'I'm playing with fire.'

She laughed. A deep, throaty, sexy laugh. 'Fire! Oh no, Luke Spence ... it's more than that ... you're playing with the furnaces of hell.'

The heavy-breathing, sweat-wrung passion drowned out the rising and falling moan of wind across the mouth of the tunnel, as it did the soft hissing warmth of the primus which added to the intensity of the moment. In fact everything was lost in the bittersweet minutes that followed. Everything, including the soft shuffle of feet and knees along the tunnel's icy floor. Everything, including my name as it was uttered in a shocked whisper ... and again ... and again ... and again. Then I heard it loud and clear. Heard the pain. Felt the shock. Saw the shadowed vision of sadness as it disappeared back into the tunnel. The sadness of not understanding. The sadness of betrayal. The sadness of Akalise Palmarsson.

I found her in the main tent, shivering over the stove. 'What was it?' I said, securing the wind-lashed flap.

She half turned and looked up at me. 'Nothing ... I went to check Miss Dawson was all right ... the storm seemed worse. When I found she was not there I thought she had gone outside ... got lost perhaps. That is what I came to tell you ... I am sorry I disturbed you.'

'It's not what you think ...' The words choked in my throat. Who the hell was I trying to kid? Of course it was what she thought. Sex, plain and simple. I changed tack. 'How's Rollo?'

'Much better now ... he sleeps.'

There was a long uncomfortable silence. She wasn't looking at me, but I knew what she was thinking. I ended it by asking about Che-mang-nek. About the crash site. If he would knowingly lead us to the wrong place.

There was another long pause before she said, 'What reason would he have for doing such a thing?'

'You tell me. Afraid of the *tarneqs*. Afraid that if the gold is taken away the spirits will be angry.'

She bowed her head slightly. 'The fact that he is here at all shows courage. I somehow doubt he would try to cheat you.'

'But you can't be sure?'

'Sometimes people are not all they seem to be,' she said bitterly.

I watched her for a moment, searching hopelessly for the words, the right words. But they didn't come. I'd somehow known all along they wouldn't. I left her then and went back to the screaming night. Back to the snow cave.

Hannah was still there, wrapped up in the soft furs. 'What was all that about?' she enquired as I struggled with my boots.

'Nothing ... nothing important, that is.'

She chuckled softly. 'I don't believe that for one minute. Anyway, she's not your type.'

I stopped tugging at the boots and turned towards her. 'And what is my type?'

She shrugged and the fur slipped gently from her bare shoulders. 'We go well together, Spence ... why don't you come back to New York with us?'

'And work for Rollo, you mean?'

'You could do worse. Besides, he pays well.'

I nodded. 'Sure he pays well, but I somehow doubt I could keep you in the style to which you've been accustomed. I'm just a pilot, remember, and unless the big world has changed dramatically in the last seven years I seem to recall we all had two things in common.'

'Which were?'

'Number one, easily seduced by pretty aeroplanes, and number two, always short of enough money to pay the rent.'

She smiled. 'I don't think you'd have to worry about paying the rent; I've got my own apartment.'

A short silence. Then I said quietly. 'That reminds me of a third thing. Pilots don't much go in for charity.'

158

She looked up sharply. 'Who the hell said anything about charity?'

'It wouldn't work, Hannah. Well, perhaps for a time, then some young handsome millionaire would come along and offer you that Hollywood sunset you've always dreamed about, and that would be that.'

I reached out and ran my hand through her long tangle of silken hair. She stiffened. 'You could at least give it a try,' she said huskily. 'Surely it's worth that?'

'I think you'd better get dressed and move back to the tent; I'll come and check the guy ropes are secure.'

'Yes, perhaps.' Then more perkily, 'I suppose if I'd been a sweet little executive jet with a sparkling paint job the answer would have been different.'

I smiled! 'We all have Hollywood sunsets, Hannah ... ours are on different days, that's all.'

The storm blew itself out the following night. By then Scarth was up and around and enthusiastic to get started again. We left early the next day and found nothing. A bitter, fruitless journey full of cold and misery. The haystack, it seemed, was growing all the time, and one needle or sixteen, it just wasn't enough. Two more days' supplies and we would have to return to Kulusuk. I said as much to Scarth that night.

'I've been thinking about that,' he rasped. 'You could fly down to the strip and perhaps get some supplies from Big Gunn. From the Eskimos.'

'It's winter, Rollo. The Eskimos are probably worse off than we are. If they had a bad summer, their supplies will be at about rock bottom by now.'

'And if they had a good summer?'

'No summer is ever that good. Food is always scarce.'

'But it's worth a try, wouldn't you say?'

'We'll talk about it tomorrow night,' I said.

He grabbed my sleeve and jerked me around. 'We'll damn well talk about it now. I want you to go down to the strip the day after tomorrow ... understand?'

'And if there are no supplies to be had?'

'Then you come back and pick us up.'

'What then?'

'We go to Iceland and re-provision, simple as that.'

The next day started as our previous two trips. The perilous journey over the sastrugi, followed by the bone-chilling wind as Che-mang-nek whipped the dogs into a howling run. We arrived at the site late morning. The orange marker flags from our previous probings were half buried in the drifting snow. I took my spike, pickaxe and spade, and started where I'd left off the previous day. Less than one hour later the spike clanged dully with that metal-to-metal sound, sending miniature shock waves up my arms.

'Rollo,' I yelled. 'Over here.' I threw the spike aside, picked up the spade and started digging the hard snow with a new-found energy.

Scarth stumbled and fell against me, then began to paw at the snow like a man possessed. Slowly but surely the ice desert gave up her secret – or at least one of them – aluminium twinkling brightly in the sunlight. I worked progressively until I had uncovered the exhausts. Six ice-crusted swept-back stubs. I chipped away the ice until they became six blackened, beautiful, swept-back stubs. I fell away and sat in the snow. 'It's a Mustang … Rollo, it's a bloody Mustang.' I turned towards him as I spoke, but he was too engrossed with clearing the snow and ice down the long length of engine cowling. I watched mesmerized as he gradually uncovered the front part of the cockpit. The perspex was opaque; milky white. The canopy closed. Sealed as tight as a tomb. Scarth's hands dropped lower and began frantically rubbing the metal directly beneath the cockpit.

'Come on you son of a gun … come on … where the hell are you …'

Without warning he let out a wild, bloodcurdling scream which echoed thinly across the white emptiness of the ice desert. Then he fell back against the fuselage, his body racked with convulsive laughter.

I had started at the sudden sound. Even Che-mang-nek, who was sitting patiently on the sled, had jumped to his feet. I edged forward. 'What is it?'

160

Scarth choked back laughter. 'What... what d'you reckon the odds were on finding these planes? Go on, give me a figure.'

'I couldn't even begin to count that far. Why?'

'Okay, there were sixteen planes, or so we were told. And the squadron was known as Patterson's Volunteers; so what odds are you going to give me now?' He moved slowly away from the side of the cockpit, his body uncovering the neatly stencilled black writing. The longest odds in the world. I pulled my snow goggles down around my neck and read the words again. Over and over and over again. The words that said LT. COL. GEORGE PATTERSON. Beneath that in smaller blocks the legend 4th FIGHTER GROUP.

'I don't believe it,' I gasped. 'I just don't believe it ...'

Scarth obviously did. He started jumping up and down, banging me wildly on the shoulders. 'I told you we'd find them didn't ... I told you.'

I laughed as his infectious enthusiasm swelled over on to me. 'And here was I thinking you were crazy to even undertake ... you know, I still can't believe it. I mean I'm standing here looking at it and I still can't believe what I see.'

Scarth said excitedly, 'It's there all right. And somewhere not far away are the rest of them.'

'How about the cockpit ... can we get it open?'

Scarth backed against it protectively. The laughter faded. He said edgily, 'No ... it's frozen. We'll need special tools to do that.'

'We could always break it open; the Perspex's shot to ribbons anyway.'

Scarth lifted his mittened hand to his forehead and brushed away the eternal cobweb. 'It stays,' he snapped. 'It stays.' His voice had dropped back to its usual gravelly cadence when he added, 'Don't worry about it; I'll get the proper gear flown in ... anyway, this calls for a celebration. Any coffee left in that thermos?'

'Why not?' I said, and followed him towards the sled.

Che-mang-nek gave us an uncertain look as we approached, before drifting silently away. 'Shifty little character,' Scarth remarked, watching the Eskimo move down towards the dogs.

'Quite possibly,' I replied, at the same time thinking, he's not the only one. The 4th Fighter Group had been the clincher. Silent Sam Mason – Debden, England – Lt. Col. George Patterson – and now Rollo Scarth. They'd all been there, all been at Debden. Had all known something about the consignment.

I poured the coffee and handed the plastic cup to Scarth. 'What now?' I said. 'I mean, that's only one aircraft. If the rest came down with old George there I'll bet you a plugged nickel to a lousy dime they're going to be scattered over a good few square miles.'

'Aw come off it, Spence. For Christ's sake stop worrying. Your part of the job's over. From here on in it's all downhill.' He scanned the barren white landscape. 'If I can locate another two or three minimum I'm still on a winner.'

'What about the re-provisioning flight?' He was a million miles away. I repeated the question.

'Er ... what was that?'

'Provisions ... Iceland or wherever?'

'Yeah, yeah, no problems. Think we'd better do what you suggested.'

That should have told me something. The Rollo Scarths of this world never do anything that is suggested – unless by themselves. Instead I said, 'What was that?'

'Iceland. You can fly over there in the morning and get a plane load of supplies. You've got enough fuel for that, haven't you?'

'Plenty.'

'Good. I'll give you the money tonight.'

I looked up at the sky; at the thin band of cirrus closing on the cold white sun. 'Think we'd better be heading back ... long way to go.'

Scarth drained the remains of his coffee, wiped his mouth with the back of his mitten and hauled himself to his feet. 'Where's that bloody Eskimo ...' he stopped. We both saw him at the same time. Standing by the Mustang's cockpit. A small, lonely figure. Totally motionless. 'Get away from there,' Scarth yelled.

I reached out and grabbed his arm as he started towards Che-mang-nek. 'I'll get him,' I said quietly. 'You load yourself up on the sled.'

'We go now,' I said, moving up to the old man's shoulder. He didn't move. His eyes were fixed on that cockpit as if the very spirits had dared and won, turning his body into a biblical pillar. Only this time it was a pillar of ice. 'We go now,' I repeated. 'We go.'

He turned slowly, in his eyes that distant quality of day-dreamers — staring but unseeing. On his cheeks the frozen tears shone with the brilliance of diamonds. 'No spirits,' I said quietly. 'Just an old aeroplane ... understand?'

His eyes focused on mine, as if seeing me for the first time. The unaccountable sadness hardened then and he brushed past me without uttering a word.

The celebration that night was a short-lived affair. Four heavily clad figures huddled around the warming hiss of the primus. Scarth had topped up his coffee with a shot of whisky and sat deep in thought. From the smile in the tired eyes, the thoughts were about money. Nothing else would raise even the faintest spark of humour in Rollo Scarth's life.

Hannah, on the other hand, had received the news of locating one of the aircraft with a sigh of relief. To her it meant only one thing. Going home. Back to civilization. Back to hot baths, silk caressing perfumed skin, food served on fine china plates, soft comfortable beds with pillows.

Akalise had continued as if nothing had happened. She had kept her distance from me, as she had ever since that night she had found me with Hannah Dawson. Her placid serenity had become an unwelcome shield. Invisible, impenetrable, as if she had locked her heart away ... for ever.

Scarth ended the short silence when he turned to me and said, 'Will you get the plane started okay?'

'I'll make a start on it when I've finished my coffee.'

'But it shouldn't be any problem?'

I shrugged. 'If it is you'll be the first to know.'

Hannah leaned forward. 'We're leaving, then?'

'Spence's leaving,' Scarth said.

The relief in Hannah's face clouded over instantly. 'What do you mean, Spence's leaving?'

'He's going to Iceland,' Scarth replied, 'to pick up some provisions.'

'But you've found the planes, surely there's nothing else you can do now. Not until you get the helicopters in to airlift them to the coast.'

Scarth put down his mug and rubbed his face tiredly. 'We've found one of the planes, Hannah, that's all. I need to locate another two or three minimum before we pull out and set up the next stage of the operation.'

Hannah persevered. 'But how long's that going to take?'

'Depends. Day or two. Week at the most.'

'A week!' she cried. 'Another week of this!'

Scarth ignored the remark and looked back at me. 'Anything I can do to help with the plane?'

'Know how to use a blowtorch?'

'Course I damn well know ...'

'In that case you can help.'

Hannah said, 'Can I go with you ... to Iceland?'

'Ask the boss.'

Scarth intervened. 'No ... you'd better stay here.'

'Why?' Hannah snapped.

Scarth avoided her eyes. 'Because ... because I damn well say so. Anyway, he's only going there and back.' There was a smile in his eyes when he added, 'Besides I want you to come with me in the morning to the crash site.'

I looked up with interest. 'I don't think that's wise, Rollo. What happens if the weather turns?'

'We've got the Eskimo,' Scarth remarked sourly.

'That's not the point.'

'What d'you mean it's not the point? Look Spence, you do your job and I'll do mine ... now where's the bloody blowtorch?'

164

We got the plane started two hours later. Two hours of holding the blowtorch up the exhaust stack. Two hours of heating congealed oil. Two hours of warming batteries next to the primus. Two hours of desolate resolve; of freezing, of swearing, of praying. I ran the engine for thirty minutes after that, letting the heater take the cold soak out of the cabin. When that was done I clambered stiffly back to the snow and went to the main tent. Scarth was there with Akalise. Hannah, angry with the world, and everybody in it, had turned in an hour earlier.

'Sounds healthy,' Scarth remarked as I slipped off my mittens and took the mug of warm coffee from Akalise.

'No problems. I'll get a couple of hours sleep now and give it another run.'

'What time you leaving?'

'About six.'

'In the dark?'

'Akalise can lay some flares out for me.' I turned to her. 'Is that okay with you?'

She nodded. 'Yes, that is all right.'

Scarth was thoughtful for a moment. 'When will you be back?'

'Following morning ... it's about four and a half hours to Reykjavik. By the time I've loaded up with supplies I'd never make it back in daylight.'

'No, guess not.' Scarth reached into his pocket and produced the thick bankroll I had seen in Narsarsuaq. 'How much you need?'

'Well, I have to refuel as well... say five hundred dollars.'

Scarth counted off a number of hundred-dollar bills. 'There's a thousand,' he said, handing me the money. 'And I want receipts for everything.'

'You'll get your receipts,' I said flatly.

He struggled to his feet. 'Good, in that case I'm turning in. Big day tomorrow. Might even find the other three I need.'

And pigs might fly, I thought. The irony was that for Rollo Scarth they probably would. 'Keep your eye on the sky,' I said as he unfastened the tent flap. 'If it starts clouding over get back here as quick as you can.'

'Don't worry about me, Spence; as I told you once before I don't have problems.' With that he was gone into the dark night, leaving the tent flap fluttering gently in the icy breeze.

I turned to Akalise. 'Will you be all right by yourself?'

'Why should I not be?'

'You recall what I said to you in Narsarsuaq, and your reason for being here?'

There was a moment's hesitation, then: 'But you have found one of the planes ...'

'Yes, but there's something you don't know.' I went on to explain Scarth's reluctance at trying to open the cockpit of the Mustang, a reluctance bordering on anger. And how he had suddenly been willing for me to go to Iceland for supplies.

'You think,' she said, 'the gold is hidden in the cockpit?'

'Seems that way.'

'And you think he wants you out of the way ... then he will hide the gold?'

'Perhaps.' I reached across the tent for my flight bag, in the bottom of which was a two-inch-high secret compartment. One lined with tinfoil. I emptied the bag and prised away the false floor. There, wrapped in an oily rag, was the Browning Hi-Power. It had been illegal in Canada, as were all small arms. But no one in their right mind ventured out over the arctic wastes with no means of defence. I had bought it from a Canadian soldier one night at the 'animal pit' – the local bar. It still had the government issue number engraved on the side and was anodized against corrosion. It also had thirteen 9-mm shells in the clip. The fourteenth was in my pocket, jingling about with the nickels and dimes. It was an old habit left over from Nam. Always keep one in reserve for yourself. One day you may need it. The tinfoil-lined compartment was the easy answer to airport security checks. The Achilles heel of X-ray machines, and probably how so many terrorists smuggled arms aboard airliners to perpetrate successful hijackings. I unwrapped the gun. 'Can you use one of these?' I asked.

Akalise looked startled. 'No ... I have never ...'

'I think it would be better if you kept it with you. I'll show you what to do … just in case.'

She shrank away, horror etched across her face. 'No, Spence … I could never use such a thing. I could never take life, even if my own were in danger.'

'But what if it was a bear?'

'It isn't though, is it? It is a man.'

I smiled weakly. 'Perhaps you're right.' I glanced down at the heavy automatic in my hands. 'Veterans of wars turn to the tools of war to solve all of life's problems, without realizing there are other ways.'

She looked at me with renewed interest. 'You were in a war?'

'Vietnam … a long time ago and a long way away.'

'Yes,' she said in a small voice. 'I heard of it.' She paused before adding disbelievingly, 'You killed people?'

I tried to avoid the innocence in her eyes and wrapped the Browning back in the oily rag, then put it back into my flight bag.

She repeated the question and I lifted my head. 'Yes … I killed people.'

There was a look of not understanding. It affects some people that way. Especially people who have never known or seen war. And suddenly without realizing it I had taken another step down the stranger's lonely road. Another step away from Akalise Palmarsson.

It was a flicker at the blurred edge of my vision. By the time my eyes had turned to the engine gauges it was gone. Everything, it seemed, was normal. No, not normal. Once the pilot of a single-engined aeroplane sees the needles of critical gauges flickering, nothing is ever normal again. Not until he is on the ground, at least. Not until he, or an engineer, has located and rectified the problem, or confirmed the problem could never have existed. And I had another hour to go before landfall. Another hour of engine noise, slipstream, and the occasional word to a bored-sounding Icelandic controller. Another hour over the icy cold waters of the Denmark Strait. I watched the gauges for another five minutes. Nothing happened. Not a damned thing. My imagination

... fatigue ... or just an old lady getting crotchety. Perhaps old aeroplanes also suffered at time's tyrannous hands, being slowly but surely strangled into the final stages of senility.

I turned my face back towards the east and let the warmth of early morning sun through glass lull me back to the state of semi-sleep I had been in five minutes earlier. Thirty minutes later the needle flickered again. And this time I had it. Oil pressure. Only now it wasn't just flickering, now it was dropping. Slowly but surely it was dropping.

The sleep that had been in my eyes disappeared instantly. It was as though someone had thrown a bucket of ice-cold water into my face. Suddenly I was wide awake. More awake, it seemed, than at any other time in my life. I reached across and tapped the glass of the offending instrument. Nothing changed. The needle continued to twitch down the dial. I glanced at the oil temperature. Still stable. Still in the green. But for how much longer? Never think those thoughts in aeroplanes. Never. The needle nudged sluggishly. And again. And again. Then the temperature was slowly climbing. Climbing towards the red line. And when it gets there it is only a matter of time before everything that was turning and burning seizes up solid. After that ...

I checked the altimeter. Flight level nine zero. Nine thousand feet. Range from the Keflavik VOR approximately fifty miles. About forty-five miles too far. I tugged my harness straps tight. Damn, damn, damn. How? What had happened? We couldn't be losing oil. I had poured it into the engine myself. And I had re-secured the filler cap.

The oil pressure was nearly off the gauge now, and the oil temperature had teamed up with the cylinder head temperature, both closing unmercifully on the red line. That was when I went for broke; opened the throttle and hauled the Beaver into a steady climb. When that engine stopped I wanted as much altitude as I possibly could. Every extra minute of gliding time would be worth an extra mile and a half.

Then I put out a mayday call, and suddenly the man from Iceland radio didn't seem quite so bored any more. Now he was alerting emergency services, and depending on the type of character he was, possibly cursing my thoughtlessness at getting him involved in a pile of extra paperwork. As it turned out I was completely wrong. I knew that when he passed me a radar range from Keflavik. Fifteen miles! Not fifty as I had roughly estimated. Thank you God – this time for tailwinds; and thank you Iceland radio for a radar set which gave out good news.

'November Three Niner One, do you read?' The Icelander was back.

'Three Niner One, fives, go.'

'Roger ... do you intend landing at Keflavik?'

I looked down at the solid layer of cloud beneath. 'Three Niner One, what cloud base you got?'

'Three Niner One switch to Keflavik approach 119.3 over.'

'Nineteen point three ... Roger.'

I clicked the dials around and called up Keflavik. Their cloud base was solid at 800 feet. Reykjavik was marginally better, they said: 1,200 feet.

I glanced at the altimeter: 12,000. 'Approach Three Niner One, what's my range now?'

'Three Niner One we have you at seven miles ... be advised Keflavik weather now eight oktas at three hundred feet, visibility three thousand metres.'

'And Reykjavik?'

'Standby. I'll call them.'

I stood by, and felt the old familiar sweating as my metabolism accelerated me through a few unwanted years. The engine throbbed very healthily ... but for how much longer? I reached forward and tuned the ADF to 370 khz. The morse coding boomed out loud and strong – dah dit, dit dit dit – NS. And the November Sierra beacon was on the threshold of runway 14 at Reykjavik. The radio compass indicated it was thirty degrees left of the nose.

'Three Niner One Keflavik.'

'Go.'

'Roger Three Niner One, Reykjavik still reporting eight oktas at one two zero zero feet.'

I swung the Beaver thirty degrees to the left. 'Roger copied. Radar range now?'

'No return on radar Three Niner One ... you are overhead.'

'Three Niner One, we're diverting to Reykjavik.'

'Three Niner One understood ... advise ready for descent.'

I looked at the engine gauges. I was nearly red-lining everything that could be red-lined, with the exception of airspeed. That was when I throttled back. 'Three Niner One we're starting descent now.'

'Roger Three Niner One change to Reykjavik approach on 119.1.'

I changed frequency and gave Reykjavik a call. Ten miles out. Passing 11,000 feet. I feathered the propeller and switched off the fuel. All that was left was the rushing slipstream. But I had the height, and there was no point wrecking a perfectly good engine by running it until it seized. I slipped into the dark oily clouds minutes later and swore at my total stupidity. The windscreen began icing up immediately. And I had stopped the bloody engine, and the bloody screen blower heaters depended on that engine. I hurriedly reset the prop lever, throttle and mixture control and tried to restart. The prop continued to windmill uselessly.

I dropped out of the cloud moments later and from the side window saw the grey unfriendly waters. Grey, dirty, unloving – reaching out. The grey merged into the shore, a darker grey of old volcanic ash streaked with snow, and just beyond that shore the dull red rooftops of buildings. I kicked the right rudder and yawed the Beaver round until I saw the glistening black runway beginning where the sea ended. I called finals and lined up the aircraft on the runway heading of 140 degrees, holding slightly right of the centre line. The ice was still solid on the windscreen as I dropped on to the runway, bounced once, and finally settled in a drunken, weaving ground run. It was only at the end of that ground run, when the plane had stopped, and the adrenaline flow was on the long journey back to normality, that I realized why I had been unable to restart the engine. I had forgotten to switch the fuel back on. I shuddered quietly to myself. The result of what could possibly be termed too much experience was catching up with me. The result which was perhaps responsible for the majority of aircraft accidents. A killing word which pilots call complacency.

The mechanic was a scrawny, underfed-looking individual. Thin face, hawkish nose, dirty fingernails. His overalls were coated in what could have been a few years' oil and grease. He smelt of the engines he lovingly tended.

'You are lucky I think, Captain,' he said with something of a smile.

I looked at the de-cowled Beaver's engine. A couple of hours ago I hadn't thought that, but now perhaps he had a point. After landing, the aircraft had been towed away to the Loftleider hangar on the northwest side of the field, and I had been taken to the operations building next door to the Loftleider Hotel on the east side of the airport. After checking in with customs, phoning air traffic and passing them the usual details for their occurrence report, Sveinn Bjornsson, the flight services manager, had produced a cup of hot black coffee. As he handled ferry pilots who were forever transiting Reykjavik, he was well used to the odd moment or two of drama. After the coffee he had run me over to the hangar in his maroon station wagon.

I looked at the mechanic. 'Don't need a new engine then?'

He patted the Pratt and Whitney affectionately. 'Not this time,' he said. 'But I think you have perhaps halved its normal life.'

'The same way it did to me, you mean?' He smiled, before I added, 'So what was wrong?'

He turned to the engine. 'That union,' he said, pointing into the oil-spattered bowels of the engine. 'The one on the bottom of the oil tank, it was not wire locked ... it somehow worked loose in flight.'

I looked closer, at one of the hundred and one items I had carefully checked at Gander before our initial departure. It had been wire locked then.

The mechanic said, 'How far have you come?'

'From Greenland ... Kulusuk, east coast.'

The mechanic's eyes widened. 'Then you were doubly lucky. If that was anywhere near loose before you left I am surprised you got so far.'

'Must have worked loose towards the end of the flight,' I said as casually as I could.

'Yes, perhaps.'

But it hadn't. It had been loosened before I left the ice desert. And Scarth had been responsible. I could see it all now. Scarth finds the planes, but doesn't want anyone to know about the gold. So after I had done the second engine run and returned to my snow cave, he had gone out and removed the locking wire from the union at the base of the oil tank. He would know that much at least, being a dealer in warbirds – and warbirds like the Beaver have radial engines, with in some cases similar oil systems. Having removed the locking wire he would have unscrewed the union a couple of turns, knowing that when the engine got hot so would the oil. And as the oil heated up it would naturally thin out. What he hadn't realized was that he had slackened the wrong union. He had slackened the one on the suction line. The one that led from the oil tank to the engine-driven oil pump. Once the oil leaves that pump it is forced into the engine galleries under pressure and returns under pressure from the engine to the tank to be recirculated. If he had slackened the union on the return line – the pressure line – the engine wouldn't have lasted more than half an hour. The oil would have forced out of the tiniest gap in double-quick time. I settled up with the mechanic, who said he would wash off the engine, refit the cowlings and give it a ground run before returning it to the light aircraft park in front of the Loftleider Hotel, and went off to find Sveinn Bjornsson. The Iceland air tasted a lot sweeter than I thought it should.

It was later in the hotel, as I stood beneath the steaming shower, that I started having doubts about Scarth and his possible motive. As supplies were critical he would be putting his own life on the line. Unless he had arranged for a second plane to move in. No, impossible. He couldn't have known beforehand that half of the supplies would be lost at Teardrop Glacier, couldn't have worked out a time scale. Which left Akalise, Hannah and Che-mang-nek. I ruled out Akalise immediately. She wouldn't know a damned thing about aero engines. Hannah, on the other hand, might have done, but what would have been her reasoning? Which left Che-mang-nek. The Eskimo who had lost half of the supplies at the glacier. The Eskimo who maintained the airstrip at Kulusuk. The Eskimo who might have learnt something about aircraft over the years. The Eskimo who would blame the *tarneqs*. And they were all that was left ... the spirits of the dead pilots.

I was in the hotel coffee shop an hour later, enjoying a late lunch of steak and eggs, when Sveinn Bjornsson arrived. He bought a coffee and came over to join me.

'A good lunch, I think.'

'Something that's hard to find in Greenland,' I said.

Bjornsson smiled before reaching into his inside pocket. 'Your list.' He handed me the piece of paper. 'I have managed to get most things, they will be delivered this afternoon.'

'Good of you.'

He dismissed the remark with a wave of his hand. 'No problem, all part of the service.'

'How much do I owe you?'

'Later,' he said. 'When I have refuelled your plane. You can pay for everything then.'

'When do you want me to file a plan? I'll be leaving at six in the morning.'

'Six. I will file for you. What level do you want?'

'One zero zero.'

'And the destination?'

'Kulusuk.'

He took a notebook from his pocket and scribbled down the details. 'Oh yes, one more thing. There was a pilot asking for you.'

'For me?'

'He was in my office half an hour ago. You have not seen him?'

'No. What was his name?'

Bjornsson scratched the back of his head thoughtfully. 'I forget now. He was an American, though.'

I pushed the plate aside. 'Is he night stopping?'

'He's been here for two days. Engine trouble.'

173

'The time of the year,' I said absently. 'Anyway, if you see him tell him I'm in room forty-six.'

'I already did,' Bjornsson replied.

I got to my feet. 'I'll call round and see you later then ... pay you some money.'

Bjornsson smiled again. 'You'll be paying in American dollars?'

'Yes.'

'Good.'

I left him with his coffee and drifted through to the lobby. I had planned on getting a couple of hours' rest in a real bed, then I saw the hotel barber's shop and changed direction. Half an hour later I emerged with a halfway decent hair cut and a neatly trimmed beard. Then I called in at the small shop next door and purchased a bottle of imported French perfume – Chloe. A present for Akalise. Under the circumstances I felt sure Scarth would have no objections at the misuse of company funds.

I bumped into Al Stepanovitch five seconds later. He looked greyer and older than when I had last seen him.

'Spence.' I stopped. 'Al Stepanovitch ... we met at the hospital in Gander.'

'Yeah, I remember.' I held out my hand. 'How's it going?'

'So so. Hear you had a bit of drama with that Beaver of yours.'

'Drama?'

'Engine quit, I heard.'

'Just saving fuel,' I said noncommittally. 'Was it you looking for me earlier?'

'Yeah. Some bad news, I'm afraid.'

'Bad news?'

'Jacqueline,' he faltered. 'Jacqueline Kullman. She's dead.'

I stared at Stepanovitch in disbelief. 'Dead! Dead. How? When?'

Stepanovitch shuffled his feet uncomfortably. 'Last week. Suicide.'

'Suicide ... Jesus Christ ...'

'I know,' Stepanovitch said reassuringly. 'Bob Young and me both felt the same way. Hell, she seemed okay when she left Gander. We said we'd call in and see her when we got back from Europe. You know, check everything was okay.' He paused and looked around the lobby. 'You're not flying again today, are you?'

'No.'

'What say we grab a beer then?'

We were sitting in the corner of the bar. Apart from the occasional voices of two American tourists and what might have been three Icelandic businessmen the room was peacefully quiet.

'So,' Stepanovitch continued in a low voice which matched the surroundings. 'We got back a day too late. She took a bottle of sleeping pills or something.'

I turned the beer glass around on the table. 'I guess Linc meant more to her than anyone realized,' I said quietly.

'Yeah ... guess so.'

'I suppose that's the end of the seaplane company. Pity in a way, it seemed a good idea.'

Stepanovitch took a pack of cigarettes from his pocket, lit one, and drew deeply. 'It still is,' he said, exhaling as he spoke. 'That's why I'm glad I've found you. You see they had no kids and both of their folks are dead.' He stopped and looked at his cigarette for a moment. What came next was as much a shock to me as it probably had been to him. 'Jacqueline left it all to us.'

'Us?' I echoed in astonishment.

'You, me and Bob Young. She left a will. Said as we'd all been good friends of Linc ... you know the sort of thing.'

'That's crazy,' I said. 'Surely there has to be some closer kin?'

'Apparently not. Lawyer checked it all out ... still is, as a matter of fact. Course if anyone turns up they could contest the paper, but in the meantime we've got a seaplane company.'

'Where's Bob Young now?' I asked.

'Back at Key West, flying tourists out to Dry Tortugas. That's a little island in the Gulf of Mexico.'

'Yeah, I know it. And you, what are you doing now?'

'Taking a Turbo Commander through to Wiley Post, Oklahoma.

Brought it through from Germany two days ago, left engine's down on power. Should be fixed by tomorrow, though.'

'Then what?'

'Once I get it to Oklahoma I'll head down the Keys and see how things are doing. Course I'll let the lawyer guy know I've run into you ... papers to sign. Guess you'd know about that, uh?'

I finished my beer. 'So as it stands we have one Cessna floatplane and three pilots, is that about it?'

'Not quite. Bob and I have pooled together to buy a second plane ... and if you could come up with a deposit we figured we could take out a mortgage on a third. Plenty of work down there.'

'It's possible,' I said guardedly, remembering the contract I had persuaded Scarth to have drawn up in Gander. 'I'm heading back to Greenland first thing in the morning. Should be through in a few days, one way or the other. What say I call you next week ... I'll be in Gander by then.'

'You've got the number?'

'Jacqueline gave me a business card.'

'Same number,' he said.

'Who took care of the funeral?'

'Bob and me.'

'You gave her a good send off?'

Stepanovitch smiled sadly. 'The best ... we sent some flowers for you.'

'Thanks ... hell of a way for it all to end.'

'Yeah ... hell of a way.'

The bar started filling up then. 'I'll be going then Al, expecting some supplies at the flight services office. If I don't see you before ...'

He held out his hand. 'We'll be hearing from you.'

'Yeah, you'll be hearing.' I walked out of the bar thinking of sabotaged oil systems, and wondering if he would.

The supplies arrived mid-afternoon. Bjornsson helped me to load and refuel; then we headed across the patched-up tarmac ramp to his office. The total amount for fuel, airport charges and supplies, came to 680 dollars. An expensive few hours in Iceland. But then in Scarth's world it was no more than the loose change in someone's trouser pocket. With that done I wandered back to the hotel and sat in the empty coffee shop, staring through the grimy window at odd aeroplanes taxiing in and out. I remained at that window after the cloud-filtered daylight had gone, and the aircraft were distant pinpricks of navigation lights arcing across an empty black void.

I turned in shortly after that. Me and a celebration bottle of beer – a farewell toast to Jacqueline – lying in the semidarkness. Through the gap in the curtains a sliver of light lay angled across the floor, and from a distant somewhere came the faint, almost indistinguishable sound of music. I listened as the song changed and a female with a pretty voice began singing: 'I'll be seeing you ... in all the old familiar places ... that this heart of mine embraces ... all day through ...'

It was a lullaby that sent me to sleep. And in the crook of my arm the empty bottle was telling me the celebration was over. Tomorrow I was going back.

PART THREE

The dawn caught up with me as I approached Greenland's east coast. I was at 12,000 feet. Far ahead towards Canada the lower sky was still settled in darkness. I throttled back and drifted slowly over Teardrop Glacier. Five more minutes west of the range and I would be there. I started the stopwatch. Four minutes later I pushed the props to high-rpm and commenced a slow descent. If I was anywhere within ten miles of the camp they would hear me. When five minutes had elapsed I began circling, easing the prop lever from high to low and back again. Three minutes after that the thin line of orange smoke drifted up gently to the west. Another three minutes later, the skis made contact with the snow.

Someone was running towards the aircraft as I swung it into wind and cut the engine. It was only when she climbed up to the cabin door that I saw the deathly white face of Hannah Dawson. I pulled on my fur-lined hood as she wrenched the door open, letting the bitter swirl of wind into the cockpit.

'Thank God you're back,' she cried.

'What's wrong?'

She lowered herself to the ground and I followed. 'Well?' I said, grabbing her by the shoulders. 'What is it?'

Her lower lip was trembling when she looked up at me, her face the ashen colour of those suffering from some long, incurable illness. 'Rollo,' she said shakily. 'He beat Akalise.'

'He what?' I shouted.

'Beat her ... said she knew about the gold ... the crashed planes ... they were carrying gold. That's what he said.'

'What else?'

'That she and the old Eskimo had hidden it...'

'Where is she now? Akalise.'

'I managed to get her into her sleeping bag ... I think ...'

I didn't wait to hear any more, I was running towards the tent.

She was lying semiconscious, her face badly bruised. From the side of her mouth a thin line of dried blood ran darkly towards her neck. I choked back the anger and turned to Hannah who was crouched by the open flap. 'Get the first-aid kit from the main tent.'

I removed my mittens and stroked the hair back from Akalise's forehead. 'You okay?'

The dark eyes didn't move, but her hand came up and found mine. 'Spence? Spence... is that you?' A small frightened voice.

I squeezed her hand gently. 'It's me,' I said softly. 'Everything's going to be all right now.'

'Spence,' her head turned towards me and the tears ran unchecked in the pale light.

'It's all right,' I said reassuringly. 'Nothing else will happen now. I'll take care of everything.'

Her hand tightened on mine with a grip of steel. 'My eyes,' she said suddenly. 'I can't see ... I'm blind.'

I was still in a state of numbed shock when the tent flap opened and Hannah Dawson pushed the first-aid kit at me. I looked at it dumbly for a long time.

Hannah said, 'You all right?'

I motioned for her to move away from the tent, then turning to Akalise, rearranged the folded parka beneath her head. 'Just rest for a moment... I'll be right back.'

Her grip tightened. 'It will come back ... my sight will come back ... Spence?'

I leant down and kissed her gently on the forehead. 'Sure it will. Now you rest a moment, I won't be long.'

'Blind ... blind!' Hannah reeled as the realization hit her.

I steeled myself against the anger and shock, which was playing havoc with my thinking. 'Tell me exactly what happened, after I had left, that is.'

'But I did.'

'Okay, so let's try again. From the beginning.'

Ten minutes later I had the story, or as much of the story as I needed. 'So he left with Che-mang-nek about an hour before I arrived.'

'Yes.'

'And he'd already told you I wouldn't be coming back?'

Hannah shrugged. 'Yes, but he was saying a lot of crazy things by then.'

182

Not so crazy, I thought, but that could wait. What was more to the point was that I now knew Scarth was responsible for the sabotaged oil system on the Beaver. 'Did he take the shotgun?'

'Yes, he was carrying it.'

'Right. We have some work to do. First we unload the supplies from the plane. Then you carry out engine runs every three hours. In between times keep Akalise warm and make sure she eats and drinks. Got it?'

'What are you going to do?'

'I'm going after him.'

'On foot?'

'On foot ... now let's get moving; we're wasting daylight.'

I set out thirty minutes later. Apart from the snowshoes and the lightweight pack on my back I had the Browning Hi-Power, and Scarth would need to deliver a pretty convincing argument to stop me from using it.

By the time I had crossed the sastrugi the sun was high in the morning sky. There was also a light wind which stirred the loose snow, partially covering the tracks of the dog team.

I stopped and checked my pocket compass. The tracks, or what was left of them, were still heading due south. Towards the crash site. I returned the compass to my pocket and picked up my step.

I heard the dogs long before I saw them, their familiar whine reaching out across the windswept white desert. Five minutes of tracking that sound told me something was wrong. Huskies don't keep up that kind of noise indefinitely – not unless they smell danger.

Then with mirage-like quality, through the thin veil of dusty snow, the black shapes suddenly materialized. Black on white. The only colours of the arctic. The shapes gradually took on forms: a sled. And a figure huddled against it. Everything was very still. I stopped and took the Browning from my pocket. The safety was off. Then I called Scarth's name. There was a long brittle silence, a silence occasionally caught with the whine of dogs.

'Spence?' Scarth's voice rang out from my ten o'clock. It was full of uncertainty. Full of disbelief.

'Surprised?' I shouted.

'Surprised ... what d'you mean?'

'What the hell do you think I mean? The oil tank on the Beaver.'

Silence.

I put the Browning back in my pocket, slipped my hand out of the mitten, and eased my finger on to the trigger. 'One thing that puzzles me though ... how did you intend getting out without a plane?' Covering his position, I moved silently out to my right.

Some of the old confidence was back when he said, 'Take the sled back to the coast. Wait for the supply ship.'

I moved another three steps. That was when I recognized the huddled figure by the sled was Che-mang-nek.

'So what happened to the Eskimo?'

'I shot him,' Scarth rasped.

'Still haven't found the gold, uh ... and you figure shooting unarmed Eskimos is going to help?'

'He jumped me ... the little bastard jumped me.'

'And the gold?'

'Knew about it all along didn't you, Spence ... like that Akalise dame.'

'She told you?'

'No. He told me. Che ... the Eskimo ... he speaks English. But then I guess you knew that as well.'

I didn't, but it didn't matter. I had to work my way to the cover of the sled before Scarth decided conversation time was over. I moved three more steps.

Scarth shouted, 'So where is it, Spence?'

'The gold, you mean?'

'Of course the fucking gold ... where is it?'

'You tell me. You're the guy who's covered all the angles. I'm just a hired hand.'

'Don't get smart with me, Spence. I know you damn well know ... and just to keep it interesting I've got a shotgun pointing in your direction.'

184

I glanced towards the sled. Six more steps, not much more. 'Okay. How about the cockpit?'

'Empty.'

'How about the pilot?'

'He's gone as well.'

'Hannah told me you found two more planes yesterday!' Another three steps.

'Empty as well ... no pilots ... nothing.'

I took the Browning from my pocket and brought it to bear on the voice. Then holding it two-handed I let off three rapid shots. All high, but enough to send him diving for cover. Then I was off, stumbling towards the sled. I hit the snow as the birdshot rattled off the other side of the wooden frame.

'So you've got a gun, eh? How many rounds, Spence? That was three you let off and you missed by a mile.'

I put the Browning back into my pocket, blew on my hand, and slipped the mitten back on. Then I slid forward on my stomach until I was next to Che-mang-nek. His head turned. 'You okay?' I whispered in English.

He considered the question for a long moment, before replying. 'Leg ... not bad.' I looked down at the caribou-skin trouser leg. It was impossible to tell the extent of his injuries. That would come later.

'So how did you know about the gold?' I shouted, suddenly worried at the short silence. Wanting to hear Scarth's voice from the same direction.

It came. And it was. Behind the fuselage of the Mustang, at a guess. 'It's a long story, Spence ... I'm not going into all that now.'

I poked my head up above the sled. The wind was still lifting the snow in a dry fog. The visibility was perfect ... for me at least. 'Okay,' I yelled. 'Let's say you heard about it at Debden, England, at the end of the last war.'

Silence. The bastard was moving round, trying to outflank me. 'Don't try it, Scarth. I've got better eyesight than you.'

'You can't see me, Spence ... you're lying.'

185

'But you can't be sure, can you? And Browning nine millimetres leave pretty big holes.'

'Okay ... okay. So what's the deal?'

'Tell me about the gold first.'

'Debden, England, as you said. I was there at the end of the war. Patterson's Volunteers flew in from Europe somewhere ... to refuel. The cockpit fuel tanks had been removed ... the word was they were carrying gold ...'

'Then what?' I prompted.

'What do you mean, then what? Then we heard the squadron had disappeared up in Greenland ... end of story ... until I met that guy down in New York, at least.'

'Jack Lovatt, you mean?'

'Yeah. Jack Lovatt.'

'So why did you kill him?'

There was a long brain-ticking silence. 'Me ... kill him? You're crazy.'

'Too long, Rollo. You took too long. You see, Jack Lovatt was a snowmobile expert, he would never have run out of road, no matter how much ice.'

'He was too talkative,' Scarth said at length. 'Couldn't have the story being blabbed about. Not after all those years. Y'see I worked it out. Sixteen Mustangs each carrying say fifteen ingots each. That makes a total of two hundred and forty. And at today's prices that comes to around fifteen million dollars.'

'I'm impressed. So how did you get rid of Jack?'

'Got one of my men to fix the brakes ... police missed that. But then those dumb bastards miss most things.'

'And I suppose me not getting that job with Big Pete LeFrance in Goose was more than coincidence?'

Scarth laughed loudly. 'As I said, Spence, everyone has their price. I paid him not to employ you ... I needed you more.'

'And Akalise?' I shouted bitterly.

'She should have told me where the gold was.'

'Did it ever occur to you she didn't know?'

186

'She damn well knows all right ... just being tight-lipped.'

'So you beat her up.'

Scarth thought for moment. 'Look Spence, I'll do a deal with you. Straight down the middle ... and ... and you can forget the cost of setting up the operation, I'll bear that. What do you say?'

'How does "no deal" sound?'

'Okay ... okay. Sixty-forty to you.'

'As I told you before, Scarth, you're dealing in the wrong currency. You're not buying yourself out of this one.'

There was nervousness in his voice when he said, 'What do you mean I'm not buying myself out of this one?'

'Because,' I said flatly, 'I'm going to kill you.'

'You're crazy!' A note of hysteria now. 'Kill me over a bunch of planes. Look ... you take all the gold.'

'It's not about gold, Lovatt was a friend of mine ... then of course there's Akalise.'

'Akalise?'

'She's blind.'

'Blind ... blind? She can't be.'

'She can be. And she is. And you're the lousy bastard who did it.'

'Perhaps it's only temporary ... you know the sort of thing. Look, we'll fly her out to New York. I'll get a specialist to sort it out ...' Suddenly his voice was moving. I kicked off the snowshoes, removed my right mitten and covered the gun in my pocket. Then I started crawling slowly to my left. I made about ten yards in what seemed as many minutes, every movement creaking loudly in the freeze-dried snow. I could even hear my heart beating like a drum ... a shaman's drum.

Then I heard the heavy breathing. The heavy breathing which joined together with the occasional tapping sound. The drumbeats became sharp and rapid. Faster ... faster ... the taut sealskin trembling like a kite's sail in a high wind. The shaman exorcising an unfriendly spirit. I had heard about it; the arctic was renowned for its fables. The dog man who came in the guise of a handsome young Inuit and lay with the women. They gave birth to dog children. Then there was the great

187

female spirit Nuliayuk, who lived in a house beneath the arctic seas. Savage sea wolves guarded the entrance to her house, and all the seals that she hoarded. Only a shaman could journey to her and bargain for a better catch.

I stopped crawling, and lay flat on the snow. I was sweating and trying to look ten different ways at once. I was up against more than Scarth and a double-barrelled shotgun. I was up against a monstrous, glowing shaman who was working for the other side. What other side, you crazy bastard? The *tarneqs*, Spence! No Eskimo will go to the snowfield ... the dead pilots, remember? I felt my legs twitching as they tried to get me up. Up into a running position. Run ... run ... run for your life ...

I rubbed my face in the snow and pulled myself back from the edge of panic. Come on, Spence. Come on, old Vietnam buddy. Hand over hand, over hand. Forget the shaman ... it's all in the mind anyway. What was it Kolb had said to Fleischer all those hundreds of years ago: 'no spirit songs ... no magic'. And there's no magic here. All in the mind. That's it, hand over hand, over hand.

I began circling further left; going the long way around to the back of the Mustang. Scarth, I figured, was moving the other way. Each trying to outflank the other. Continuing around in a giant circle ... until the faster one came up behind the other. Then it would all be over ... one way or the other.

The wind blew the dry snow against my goggles and I paused to wipe them. That was when I realized I had taken my right hand from my pocket and hadn't put the mitten back on. Now the hand was dying. I pushed it, and the gun, back into my pocket. Thirty seconds later I was ready.

I turned until I was facing Scarth's estimated position, then easing up into a low crouched position I let off two rapid shots, before breaking into a low run for the sled. The double explosion rocked the very ground as I dived for cover alongside Che-mang-nek. I rolled once and came up with a rough bead on the flash. It had come from slightly right of the sled at a range of about twenty yards.

Rapid fire – go. I let off five rounds at the position, then rolled right before letting off another two: one left and one right of the estimated target. Twelve rounds gone. One remaining. I rolled left, back to the cover of the sled.

'Come on, Scarth ... you haven't got a chance. You might be a whizz with the money, but Uncle Sam taught me how to kill ... and not only from the sky.'

He didn't answer. Not a sound. Nothing but the whisper of the easterly wind as it carried the loose snow on its never-ending journey. I took a quick look at Che-mang-nek. He was lying quite still, his face pale and trembling. This was it. Another of life's big moments. All you've got to do, Spence, is move out to the right, then forward. In twenty yards or maybe a little less you'll discover one very fat and very dead body. Come on, move! No time for thinking about it. You've still got to get back to base camp.

Even the dogs had stopped whining now, or perhaps they had stopped a long time ago. I couldn't really remember. The snowfield began to creep in on me as I took a deep breath and moved out on my stomach. Ten yards out I found the reason for the dogs' earlier whining. A dead husky, full of bird shot, lay frozen in the snow. Scarth must have killed it when he was gunning for the Eskimo. The other dogs, with the smell of dead meat in their nostrils, would be waiting for the man scent to go before moving in like a pack of jackals. The gunfire would have moved them further out. But they were still there. Waiting.

I don't know how long it took me to reach the position where Scarth should have been, but whichever way you looked at it, it was too long. My right hand, bared and gripping the automatic, was dying again. What was more alarming, Scarth wasn't there. There was blood, though. Not too much because in those temperatures it congeals and freezes almost instantly. But there was still enough to tell me Scarth had been hit. The dark stains led away in a thin irregular trail across the snow. I put my right hand back into my pocket and spent the next two minutes preparing for the final journey. The one which would lead me to the wreck of the Mustang.

I found the shotgun first, halfway along that final journey. He was in a worse state than I had imagined. Any man being hunted doesn't throw away his lifeline to survival. I picked it up, checked to see if it was loaded – it was – then trudged slowly forwards; the shotgun making easy purposeful sweeps ahead of me.

I found him pressed up against the side of the open cockpit, bared hands reaching unfeelingly towards the emptiness within. I dropped to one knee, stood the gun against the fuselage and eased his body around to face me. The pulse was very weak. Too weak for anything but dying. After a while his eyes flickered open. They looked almost surprised. It was somewhere amidst the surprise that he died. In the near distance a husky whined plaintively.

'The one thing that money doesn't buy, Rollo ... I always told you that you were dealing in the wrong currency.' I loaded him into the cockpit then, and after a lot of struggling managed to force the canopy closed. That way at least he wouldn't end up as dog meat ... and in a way he had found a part of what he was looking for.

The journey back was a nightmare of dying, over and over again. Without the sled, I had loaded the little Eskimo up on my back and started the long walk. By the time I had covered half a mile he had become twice as heavy. The wind had stopped now, and the tundra rolled on in an endless blanket of white.

Before departing I had taken the bars of margarine and the frozen tuna from my pack and fed the old Eskimo and myself. The coffee in the thermos had been hardly warm. We had finished it. Now dying of thirst, I battled on. I should have brought more fluid with me. I had been around long enough to know that the arctic desert is no different from the Sahara – both places are totally dry. Both places are without water. The fact that one is hot and the other cold has nothing to do with it.

It was night when we approached the sastrugi. I lowered Che-mang-nek to the ground and massaged his shoulders and legs, watching my tiny puffs of breath freezing in the clear frosty air. I looked at my pocket compass and took a bearing from Vega and the Great Bear. The Eskimos called Vega Narlarsik – the moon's brother; and the Great Bear Nalerqat, which meant that by which you steer. Both of these heavenly companions were used as lodestars long before the white man discovered their importance. Now on a clear and cold night they would help us to find our way back.

We were halfway over the sastrugi when Che-mang-nek whispered, 'The good shadows!'

I stopped and looked towards the heavens, seeing the thin glimmer of light, like moon glow from behind some vast tall cloud. The Northern Lights – the Aurora Borealis; or as the Eskimos called them, the good shadows. They had been placed there to help the Eskimo, not only to light his way but to give him the strength to endure the bitter wind and the hard going. They proved the existence of a kindred spirit. We would be all right, no harm would come to us this night. The lights became brighter as we moved slowly north. Brighter and more majestic. Green waving curtains; hanging, wavering gently as if disturbed by some magical ionospheric wind. I paused more than once during the last mile, taking in the heady display; the unbelievable beauty of it all. Then with a sigh at having to leave it, I lowered Che-mang-nek to the ground, took the Browning from my pocket and fired a single shot skywards. Then I waited. Twenty seconds later the orange flare flickered welcomingly in the distance. My last instruction to Hannah before setting out. One she had waited for all day. I reloaded Che-mang-nek on my back and set off for the base.

I watched her come towards me as I neared the camp, a dark bulky figure, strangely witch-like in the green glow of the aurora. She stopped a few feet away as I lowered Che-mang-nek to the ground; the smile of relief was mixed with questioning glances.

'Thank God you made it,' she exclaimed. 'I was getting worried.'

'You got the feeling second hand,' I assured her. 'I had it a long time ago.'

'Did you find him?' Hannah started, looking beyond me into the semi-darkness.

'I found him.'

'What ... where is he?'

'Dead,' I said tonelessly. 'I killed him.'

She took the news without any show of emotion. As if she had been expecting it all along. After a while she lifted her chin and said quietly, 'What happened?'

'Happened? Gold fever and the arctic at a guess; a touch of madness.' Then more quietly. 'He shot Che-mang-nek and one of the dogs. He was never coming back, Hannah ... I think even he knew that.'

'You buried him?'

'In a way ... yes, I buried him.'

I looked down at the unconscious bundle of rags at my feet. 'Let's get Che-mang-nek to the tent, he doesn't look too good. How's Akalise?' I asked, lifting him on to my back.

'She's sleeping.'

'Did she eat anything?'

'About as much as a sparrow. I think she cried herself into a state of total exhaustion ... she was asking for you.'

'I'll look in later. Better if she gets a good night's sleep.'

'What about her eyes?'

That was one question to which I didn't have an answer.

I was tending the old Eskimo's leg, carefully picking out what bird shot I could. Hannah was melting snow. When that was done I could wash the wounds before applying the iodine. I looked across at Hannah, at the haggard face, the untidy hair which kept falling across her eyes. The hands that had become red and ugly. And I remembered how she had been at our first meeting. 'We'll be leaving first thing in the morning,' I said.

She looked up and smiled tiredly. 'Yes, I suppose so.'

'Thought you'd have been happy to be going back?'

She brushed her hair away from her eyes again. 'It's not that, it's just ...'

'No job, you mean?'

'Something like that.'

'But you'll find something, surely.'

'Another rich man to latch on to, you mean?' It was said without bitterness.

'Not necessarily … there has to be something else.'

'There probably is,' she said softly. 'It's just that I've lived the good life for too long … I think I'll find it hard going back.'

'But you've got your apartment… and you must have some money saved.'

She laughed. 'You don't know the rich, Spence. The first rule is, they don't throw their money around. They don't even pay well. What they do do, however, is allow you to use their Cadillac, buy new dresses on their account, drink their champagne, pay for your holiday in the Bahamas … what they don't do is give you enough money for you to be able to do it yourself.'

'And the apartment?'

'Company owned. As I said, the trappings but never the means.'

'Will six thousand dollars help?'

She stopped stirring the melting snow. 'Six thousand …'

'Rollo's bank roll. No point leaving it with him.'

'What about you … what have you got out of this?'

'How does a de Havilland Beaver sound?'

There was disbelief in her eyes. 'He gave you that?'

'Drew up a contract in Gander. Only way I'd agree to come.'

'Doesn't sound like the Rollo Scarth I knew and hated.'

'Perhaps not… how's that snow?'

'Near enough.'

I washed and dressed Che-mang-nek's wounds and finally put him to bed in Hannah's tent. Then I returned to the main tent and took off my boots. I couldn't remember the last time I had been able to feel my feet.

Hannah was making coffee, and that was when I told her the entire story. From my meeting with Erik Palmarsson right up to finding the first plane. She listened to it all with an almost hypnotized fascination. When I was through she poured me a mug of coffee and handed it to me.

'So the emergency landing that day wasn't just an accident ... a faulty fuel pump or whatever?'

'No.'

'So who was responsible?'

'I don't know. Akalise and I talked about it. Our only answer was Kolb, the police sergeant at Narsarsuaq.'

'And the gold?'

'If it ever existed.'

'And if it did ... where is it now?'

'There were no pilots in the planes. Perhaps they took it when they left.'

'Do you believe that? I mean how far would anyone get in this place? I've been here long enough to realize the impossibilities.'

'They might have been rescued ... or that American who came for fifteen summers after the war might have been taking the gold away little by little. Whichever way, I don't think we'll ever know for sure ... not now.'

'A pity,' Hannah said reflectively. 'How much did Rollo say ... fifteen million?'

'Something like that.'

She sighed. 'What I could have done with that ... God, I'd never have to work again.'

'The price is too high, Hannah. I think even Rollo realized that in the end.'

'Yes ... perhaps,' she said, pulling on her mittens. 'I'll go and run the engine, then.'

'Thanks. When you've done that, you'd better get some sleep. Use my cave ... I'll move in with Akalise ... just in case she wakes up during the night.'

She moved across and unfastened the flap. 'Do you want me to do the next run ... in three hours?'

'I'll take care of it,' I said.

She smiled gratefully. 'Goodnight then.'

'Goodnight Hannah.'

There was a smoky yellow light in the east as I removed the covers from the Beaver's engine. We hadn't struck camp yet. My first priority was to get that engine running. The last run had been nearly six hours earlier. Then, full of good intentions to wake up in three hours' time, I had crawled into the tent beside Akalise and fallen into an exhausted sleep. I awoke five hours and forty-five minutes later with Akalise calling my name. I'd damn well overslept.

Hannah appeared at my side. 'What are the chances?'

'Not good ... I'll pull the prop through about sixteen blades, then we'll give it a whirl.' I moved to the front of the engine. 'Check the magnetos are off before I start, will you?'

Hannah climbed up to the cockpit. 'Switches off,' she shouted.

I started the long sweating process of swinging the propeller, loosening up the guts of the Pratt and Whitney. On a seven-cylinder, 450 horsepower engine, it was no mean feat, even though I was what the Eskimo would term a heavyweight.

I dragged myself up to the cockpit five minutes later, the sweat cooling on my body. Not the best way to start the day – any day, come to that. I flipped on the battery master, and the magneto switches, said a little prayer and pressed the starter down. The propeller groaned and turned slowly, stopping at the compression cycle. I released the starter and tried again. A whirr of starter motor and the prop kicked back.

Hannah was standing under the left wing. She looked as worried as I felt. I tried a couple more times before I knew the battery was shot; then I knocked the switches off and climbed down into the snow. 'What now?' she said.

'I'll take that battery out and try the other one ... you can put the engine covers back.'

Twenty minutes later we were ready for another try. 'Well, this is it,' I said to Hannah. 'If this doesn't work we're walking.'

She grimaced. 'I'll say a little prayer ... do you think that will help?'

'Why not?' I replied, ducking under the port strut. I stopped; frozen in my tracks. It couldn't be. I couldn't have imagined it. I pulled my hood from my head and listened. It was. An aircraft engine. 'Hear that?' I yelled, and ran back towards the tail.

I took a small piece of sky at a time, and searched it as well as the early-morning light would allow. In the same way I had once quartered the sky for enemy aircraft. Then I had him, a small black speck growing gradually larger. The speck becoming a high-wing single-engined aircraft. And it 'was coming towards us.

'Who is it?' Hannah said.

'Probably some ferry jockey on his way from Iceland to Sondrestromfjord. Quick, get one of the flares from the tent.'

She gave me a desperate look. 'There aren't any more ... I used the last one last night.'

'Jesus!' I looked round. There had to be something. There was.

'Get those engine covers,' I yelled.

'What are you going to do?'

'Never mind that, get them.'

I rushed back to the main tent and found an empty tuna can, then returned to the plane and started draining fuel. Hannah came round to the engine, holding the covers. 'Oil,' I yelled. 'Get a couple of cans from the tent.'

I soaked the kapok-filled covers with as much petrol as time would allow, then took them a safe distance from the aircraft. When Hannah returned with the oil I poured that over it. Then I lit a match and threw it at the canvas. The match went out. I moved closer and did the same thing. This time it went. An instant whumph, the heavy thump of concussion in the air, the force of which lifted me off my feet. The oil caught more slowly, sending a black column of smoke drifting lazily up into the sky. The aircraft was about a couple of miles to the north by this time. He looked lower than he should have been for a Greenland crossing.

'He's seen it,' Hannah cried, jumping up and down.

I watched as the aircraft banked gently to port. It was a Cessna. But what was more I could see the skis hanging beneath the wheels. 'Ski-equipped,' I said. 'Probably get a lift out of here if the worst comes to the worst.'

'Our lucky day,' Hannah said as the bright red Cessna grew gradually larger in the morning sky. As it happened she couldn't have been further from the truth.

I watched it do a low, fast pass down the makeshift airstrip. It was a Cessna 185; its Continental flat six engine pushing out close on its maximum 300 horsepower. The McCauley constant-speed propeller went into fine pitch as the plane rocketed past; then it was climbing high and fast, breaking to the left.

Mad bastard, I thought as the pitch note changed and the aircraft levelled off in a tight left turn. The next run-in was slower; not much, but slower. It was also approaching from the same direction. The pilot was holding it steady at about one hundred and fifty feet, when I saw the co-pilot's window open. An arm eased it out until it remained trapped by slipstream under the Cessna's wing.

I didn't see the gun, but I heard the chattering explosions and saw the tiny puffs of snow stitching a neat line towards the Beaver. 'Down!' I screamed, diving at Hannah and sending her sprawling in the snow.

The Cessna's engine went into an urgent scream as the pilot pulled up and away. I was on my feet in less than a second. 'Hannah ... get Akalise and Che-mang-nek,' I yelled, running towards the main tent. 'I'm going to try to start the Beaver. If I do you've all got five seconds to get aboard.' I grabbed the shotgun and what was left of the cartridges and ran back to the aircraft.

Okay, Mr de Havilland, and whoever makes the bloody batteries, let's see what you're made of now. I banged on the switches, primed the engine and hit the starter. The engine turned and coughed. Better ... bloody better. Next time! I reset the throttle and tried again. The starter motor whined from high to low, the prop turned, paused and then kicked through the compression cycle. The engine burst into life, huge clouds of grey smoke billowing back in the slipstream. I jockeyed the throttle and the mixture control at the same time and somehow kept it from dying. Then I turned to the tents and saw Hannah steering Akalise towards the Beaver. Behind them, limping painfully, was Che-mang-nek. Too slow. Too damned slow. My eyes swept back to the windscreen and picked up the red Cessna as it started another low run from the far end of the airstrip. I set the throttle, grabbed the gun, and leapt out of the door, feeling my left knee concertina under the impact before I rolled painfully to my feet.

'Get down,' I yelled at Hannah. 'Back there ... move.' I pointed aft of the tailplane, then started running as fast as I could out on to the open airstrip. A twelve-bore might not shoot down an aeroplane, but it would sure as hell put the fear of God into whoever was flying it.

It was closing on me at something like a hundred and fifty knots. Height this time was less than fifty feet. I broke open the gun, checked it was loaded and snapped it shut. Then I lifted it to my shoulder and took a direct bead on the cockpit. Now it was a matter of waiting. Two seconds can be a long time when you're standing in the open in the middle of a strafing run. Those two seconds were the longest in my life. At the end of it all I knew it was down to timing ... and luck. And I hadn't been having too much of that lately.

The firing started one hundred feet or more ahead of me; the copper-jacketed killers from hell walking up through the snow with an almost dreamlike quality. I waited, almost too long; then I let him have both barrels and took off in a flying leap to the right. Somewhere in my peripheral vision I saw the Cessna buck and twitch, then it was veering away. The spread of bird shot had done it. I'd let the plane drift up as close as possible and gone for the right side of the cockpit. The gunner's side. I might just have hit something. The problem was he had hit me. I didn't know yet how badly; but I'd felt the thump in my left arm. It was still numb; the pain would come later. I scrambled to my feet and started running towards the Beaver.

I took a wide berth of the spinning silver disc of prop. 'Let's go,' I yelled. 'Let's go ... move ... move!' Hannah loaded Akalise and Che-mang-nek up into the cabin, then quickly followed. I climbed in last of all and gunned the engine even before my backside had hit the seat. Hannah was in the right seat, struggling with her harness. 'Never mind that; can you reload that thing?' I nodded at the shotgun I'd thrown across her lap.

'I think so.'

I took the box of cartridges out of my right pocket, threw them into her lap and pushed the throttle all the way forward. The Pratt and Whitney missed a few beats somewhere along the way; it was still too cold for that sort of handling, the temperatures still off the dials. Then we were running. I kicked in a touch of right rudder and held her straight down the strip.

'Can you see him?' I shouted at Hannah.

'No ... no ... yes. There!'

I looked up and right and saw him barrelling in from the same direction as his last two runs. And he had speed and height on his side. I lifted the Beaver off and held it down, letting the speed gradually build. It wouldn't be fast enough, but it would have to do. The Cessna jerked left in a flat turn; trying for a run down my right side. I snapped the Beaver over to the right, and went straight for him. He wasn't expecting that. You could tell when he hesitated for more than two seconds. And that two seconds gave me the upper hand in more ways than one. The most important being, I now knew I was up against a gifted amateur. And gifted amateurs in aerial combat never fare well against old pros.

By the time the Cessna driver had realized what was happening and started to go further left to allow his gunner the right line, it was too late. We were upon him. Now he was pulling more than sixty degrees of bank to avoid a collision. The gunner would have had a bead on nothing more than the empty sky.

I watched as he pulled up and away. He drifted through the place where there would have been a 'sight'.

And suddenly I was switching the fire-control system to auto-acquisition, getting a good radar lock-on. I waited a few seconds to ensure that the release conditions would be met before ripple-firing two radar missiles. I was in a good position on that MIG; about a thousand feet below and six thousand feet behind on the side of his turn. That was when Harry Marlin's voice broke in my headphones. 'Salmon Two ... MIGs in your six o'clock ... break right, Spence ... break right.'

I slammed the F-4 into an 8-g turn and went into afterburn. Harry being Harry went in as though he was in a remake of some old Korean war film. The two MIG pilots who ended up scattered across five miles of sky would have probably wished he was.

Harry said, 'Okay Salmon Two, let's go north.'

I flick-rolled the F-4 on to its back and scanned down the sky. Harry was coming up fast. I snapped level and formated on his left wing. I could later understand how the mistake had been made, after the confusion of the engagement, but right then, right at that moment, there was no time to even think of mistakes.

We dropped down, heading for the coordinates the FAC over Military Region 1 had passed. The coordinates of the SAM site. I started to get the feeling something was wrong when there was no AAA Fire. When no white and grey puffs filled the sky. Target acquisition was simple with no other aircraft to watch ... no AAA.

Harry went in first. I watched him unload two Mk 84, 2,000-pounders. Watched and closed and saw no secondary explosion ... no secondary ... no secondary. I jinked right and down, and as I flashed through the pall of black smoke saw a fleeting glimpse of white-clad figures ... and more ... and more. It was a bloody village. Not a missile site. We'd hit the wrong target ... the wrong bloody target.

I jettisoned my bomb load over the jungle and climbed to join Salmon One. He was in afterburn over Thud Ridge when the ground fire started. That was when he got the 85-mm in the tailpipe.

'Salmon Two to Salmon One ... you've got a flamer, Lead.'

Harry switched off his afterburner and the flames went out. That was when I got my hit. That was when my back-seater Billy Miller stopped talking to me – for ever.

'You okay Two?'

'Okay ... think Miller's hit ... you?'

'Yeah ... stay with me ... lost some of my instrumentation.'

I pulled up alongside. 'Sure we were right on the coordinates?'

Harry's bone-domed head swivelled my way. 'Let's get outa here before we start worrying about that kinda shit.'

We were across the Thailand border when I pressed the r/t button again. 'What were those coordinates, Lead ... I'll check them out.'

The muffled voice passed them. And I checked. And Harry had somehow got it all back to front. Two plus two doesn't ever make six – except perhaps in the heat of battle.

'How's it look, Two?'

'Fine,' I lied. No use worrying him with that now. He still had to get a damaged F-4 on the ground. 'Think we'd better start on down now?'

'Yeah ... you'll have to give me the green light on the landing gear. No cockpit indications.'

The rain – the gentle oriental rain – had started now. Except at 300 knots it sounded far from gentle. Final approach came up four minutes later. I dropped down and scanned Harry's landing gear. Everything seemed about right. Get closer, Spence ... get closer ... make sure. I slipped in tight, until my canopy was wavering a few feet beneath his tailpipe. But instead of landing gear, all I saw was a burning village and what looked like the scattered, broken bodies of children.

'How is it, Two?'

I eased gently out and drifted back up to his wingtip. 'Okay Lead ... everything hanging.'

'No damage?'

'No damage,' I affirmed.

But there had been. Somewhere beyond the sullen flames and choking smoke and the hollow eyes of dying children, there had been. And as I watched Harry Marlin's guts being spilled down the wet Udorn runway I heard my voice echoing the words over and over again. No damage ... no damage ... no damage ... no damage.

Hannah Dawson was yelling at me. 'Spence ... Spence ... what's wrong?'

I shook my head and tried to get rid of the muzzy feeling that was clouding my vision. 'Stopped one ... in the arm,' I said, feeling pain and nausea sweep suddenly over me.

'How bad?'

'Never mind that. Make sure they're strapped in tight,' I jerked my head back to indicate Akalise and Che-mang-nek, before adding, 'and keep a lookout down your side.'

It was a safety precaution only, because I already knew that when the Cessna reappeared he would be coming down my side – the left side. He had to, the gunner was in the right seat. I lifted the left wing and did a rapid box search. Then I cranked my head around and looked back down the left side of the fuselage. That was when I realized I hadn't been wrong.

I checked we still had full power, then eased the nose down a fraction and retrimmed. Not that we had much terrain clearance. Three hundred feet at the most. I pulled my snow goggles into place and concentrated on not flying into the ground, then I snatched a quick glance over my left shoulder. He was coming up fast. Too fast. I managed a wry smile. You've got it all wrong, sonny. You've got the armament and the speed, but you're going about it all the wrong way. He kept coming. I waited until he was about three hundred yards out, then I eased the nose up towards the sun and left it there. The airspeed faded gently back from 120 mph. Now he was really gaining. Now he was being blinded by the sun. Now he was seeing the Beaver expand rapidly before him. Too rapidly! Now he was cursing and pulling off the power, but he was too late. He was overshooting.

He was nearly abeam the Beaver's tail when I chopped the power and rammed down full land-flap. We went up like an elevator in the Empire State Building. Somewhere below, the Cessna rocketed past an empty patch of arctic sky. I slammed the power back and began taking in the flap, little by little. Then I started to climb. Next time he might not fall for the same trick.

I pressed the intercom button. 'Have you loaded the gun?'

'Yes. Do you want it?'

'When I say.'

The Cessna was climbing widely to the left; all the way round. Surely to God he wasn't going to use the same dumb tactics? I sat listening to the urgent blat-blat-blat of the Pratt and Whitney and watching the Cessna curve gracefully around at a 360-degree turn. The gifted amateur had obviously decided he was. Decided he could use the same approach; make the join up, and then sit off my left wing tip doing everything that I did while his gunner took pot shots at me. Sadly he was very wrong. Four MIG pilots in Vietnam would have testified to that – if they had still been alive, that was. I maintained the climb. He was still completing his turn to come up behind me, only he hadn't noticed. Hadn't noticed that I had taken the initiative by gaining height. I opened the storm window on my left side, and took the shotgun from Hannah; then I swung the Beaver viciously back through 180 degrees. Less than half a mile, closing at something like three hundred miles an hour, and I had an extra thousand feet. Six seconds from the kill.

That was when he screwed it up in a bad way. After two seconds of thinking he decided to break left and maybe give the gunner a chance. By the time he had started to act another two seconds had elapsed. Once he had commenced the turn and realized the gunner was unsighted because of his high wing it was too late. We were there, sitting slightly above his right wing. Not for long though; once he stoked up the fires he would pull away. I poked the shotgun out of the storm window and pushed the Beaver down. The skis just about bounced off his right wing tip as we slid down in front of him. Keeping the aircraft steady with my left hand I took a rough aim, somewhere between the propeller and the cockpit and fired both barrels. The gun smashed into my right shoulder, then I was yanking the control column back and to the right. We almost stalled out of that manoeuvre, almost but not quite.

'Get this bloody thing out of the way!' I yelled at Hannah. She pulled the shotgun back to her side of the cockpit, while I slammed the Beaver over on to her left wing tip. It took me a few seconds before I relocated the Cessna. It was drifting down the sky in a gentle left turn. I followed it. He was diving for speed. I realized that as he gradually pulled away from me. Then he swung on course for the east coast and slowly disappeared into the yellow morning.

'He's gone,' Hannah cried excitedly. 'He's gone.'

'For the time being,' I said thickly. 'But unless I hit something with that shot I've got the feeling he'll be back.'

Hannah's eyes strained against the eye-aching glare, trying to relocate the unknown enemy. 'Who was it ... the sergeant you mentioned last night?'

'Could have been him doing the shooting.'

'And the pilot ...'

I leaned back in the seat for the first time since take-off. 'Haven't a clue,' I said, feeling limp and strangely distant. It was as if I shouldn't have been in that place with aeroplanes and strange faces. As though I didn't belong. Hannah said gently, 'How bad is it ... is there a first-aid kit on board?'

'Should be ... in the back ...' I looked down at my left arm. Just below the shoulder was a tear in the parka. No bloodstains that I could make out. But I could feel it, warm and sticky and burning. The shock was wearing off. I probed gently with my right hand and found another tear in the back. It had gone straight through. That was something, at least. Not much, but something.

Hannah leant across and handed me a wad of bandages. 'Anything I can do?'

'Take the controls ... no smelling salts in that kit, I suppose.'

'No. Just bandages and iodine ... the other box did. But we left that behind.'

'Never mind ... take the controls.'

'I've got it.'

I unzipped my parka and my inner jacket, then realizing I couldn't get out of them in that confined space, stuffed the bandages down the top of my sleeve. All around me everything was covered in a fine mist. A fine cosy mist. And the fine cosy mist was quietly closing in. I banged my left arm hard against the side of the cockpit and winced at the sudden pain. The mist cleared temporarily.

'I take it we're going back to Kulusuk?' Hannah said.

I grimaced at the new-found pain. 'Seems as good a place as any.'

'What about the Cessna?'

'We'll cross that bridge when we come to it ... even so you'd better reload that shotgun for me ...' I reached out and rested my right hand lightly on the control yoke, while Hannah busied herself with the gun.

I wanted to turn back to Akalise and talk to her, but there were no words at that moment. Just a sea of pain and an urgent desire to be violently sick. Somewhere below, her savage beauty wasted on me, the mountain range of Greenland's east coast slipped silently past.

That was when I reduced power, lowered the nose and retrimmed the Beaver for descent. Had to get down, my injured arm was becoming useless. I took my right hand from the controls and wiped the thin film of sweat from my forehead. Jesus, it hurt. And that was all it needed; suspension of concentration through pain. Suspension of everything, except perhaps the will to remain conscious.

The next moment all hell broke loose. He came out of nowhere. Lying in wait, perhaps down in the glacier. And I had known he'd be back. What the hell was I doing? The machine-gun fire raking down the Beaver's fuselage told me that whatever it was, it was wrong.

A two-second burst and the Cessna rocketed past the front of the nose before pulling up into a long climbing turn. I snatched the controls back and slammed the throttle fully open. Another few miles and we would be directly over the Kulusuk airstrip ... out in the open ... vulnerable. The wrong place to be. Then I was diving for the deck, wringing every knot out of the tired old airframe. Left a bit ... left. Maintain the dive and head for Teardrop Glacier. Okay you bastard, let's see how good you really are.

'Any sign of him?' I shouted to Hannah.

She was already twisted around in her seat, scanning as much sky as was possible. 'Nothing.'

I racked the Beaver over on to her left wing tip, at the same time kicking in top rudder. 'Anything now?'

A pause, then, 'Got him ... four o'clock high.'

I snapped the wings level. 'What sort of range?'

'Perhaps half a mile ... close ... he was starting to dive.'

I looked up ahead to the glacier. Maybe a mile. Too far this time. I yanked back the throttle and, keeping the nose down, counted to ten; then swung hard right. Into and underneath him, forcing him to tighten and steepen his descending turn before he could bring his gun to bear.

I had a momentary glimpse of him as I fed the power back on; his wings swinging to the vertical as he tried to make it.

Suddenly his wings snapped level and he overshot, pulling up to start again from scratch. Too late pal, too late. Next time I'll have you. I hauled the Beaver round, on course for the pass up through Teardrop Glacier.

Hannah twisted around, scanning the sky. 'What are you going to do?'

'See how good he really is ... so far I'm not impressed.' I eased the Beaver into a fast climb up the glacier. 'See him?' I rolled the wings and stamped in some rudder.

'Coming up behind ... fast.'

I levelled up and jerked the controls forward, down, down, down, until we were skimming over the ice. Either side the jagged mountains rose menacingly. Now he would be on our tail. But he didn't have those sort of guns. His were strictly sideways shooting. I snatched the plane up and gained a rapid 200 feet. Directly ahead the ice canyon was closing in. Of course with an F-4 Phantom I could have lit the afterburners and gone straight up like a homesick angel ... but then with a Phantom he would have been dead a long time ago.

The walls of ice were closing rapidly as I stuffed the nose down and went for maximum speed. With my anti-glare goggles in place I could just about make it out – where the glare stopped becoming glare and became something more permanent. The sweat was trickling into my eyes as I snapped the control column back. Throttle all the way home. The Beaver leapt up at the sky as the walls of the pass pressed tightly against each wing tip. Then the propeller was clawing towards the blueness of space. My eyes flashed out to the left wing tip, trying to judge the vertical ... now! ... I snapped the column forward and held it ... speed Spence ... the bloody speed! I caught it rushing back through fifty ... the point of stall. I stamped in full left rudder and the old Beaver cart-wheeled gracefully through 180 degrees.

Now, engine screaming, we were going vertically down. I pulled off a handful of throttle as I tried to judge the last possible second we could commence pulling out. Then, imagining rivets popping, I hauled the controls back and sent the Beaver hurtling back down the floor of the pass at practically zero feet. I eased the power back and worked the aircraft over to the right side. 'Hannah!'

She was looking, head low. 'He's still there … he's still there!'

'Not the next time,' I yelled.

I firewalled the throttle and started to climb. Up the side of the mountain pass as it led back down the icefall at the end of Teardrop Glacier. We must have been at 400 feet above the ice. The pass was wider there, opening out to at least five or six wingspans. I kept hard in to the right side, reducing power and speed, willing him to pull up alongside and start shooting.

I banked gently, through a slight dogleg in the pass, and suddenly the sun was streaming into the cockpit. White and blinding. I eased a little more power off. 'Where is he now?'

'Closing … about a couple hundred yards … no more.'

He'd bitten the bullet. He was coming up. Slower this time. This time he wasn't going to overshoot. This time he was going to get it right.

'Fifty yards …' Hannah shouted. 'Thirty … twenty … I can see flashes … he's shooting.'

That was it. His mind was split. His head full of the stench of cordite. His eyes full of watching me and the ice wall on the other side of the pass. I went hard left then right, at the same time dropping full flap. We hit an invisible cushion of air, but I'd already anticipated that by pushing hard forward on the controls. The effect was similar to heavy braking in a car; the guy on your tail never has a chance. The Cessna was on top of us in an instant. Pulling up to avoid a midair collision. Pulling up and going for the power. Pulling up and up and not seeing his airspeed until it was too late … and for him it was too late. He appeared over the top of the Beaver, hanging at an almost impossible angle. Even then I imagined I saw orange tracer curving through the morning … only I wasn't imagining it, it was really happening. I felt the bullets thudding into the engine cowling even as the Cessna's left wing stalled and flicked it into a spin.

Not that Cessnas spin very well, they tend to develop a spiral dive. But either way once you're in, you can use as much as a thousand feet to pull out. When he went in I doubted he had much more than five hundred.

I rammed the Beaver's nose down and pushed the throttle open, retracting the flap in stages. Below, in a final flurry of activity the Cessna's wings levelled as he began to pull out. Pulling and pulling ... and almost making it. Almost but not quite. He hit the ice once, almost level, then the aircraft was slewing around, breaking up. It came to rest near the top of the glacier. There was no fire.

The Beaver's engine faltered and died about two heartbeats later. There wasn't time to check the cause. We were too low and too slow. I instinctively closed the throttle; if the engine caught again at the point of touchdown it would do more harm than good. For one fleeting moment I caught a glimpse of Hannah's face, a glimpse of what could have been a prefiguration of death, then I was pulling the Beaver through a gentle wing-over, lowering the flaps and heading back up the narrow pass of the glacier. The surface looked impossibly rough as I selected the skis down – something like the sastrugi up on the snowfield but worse. The only sound was the hiss of airflow over the cockpit. I reached down and switched off the fuel, screamed for everyone to hold tight, and started to flare. We hit hard, bouncing over the rough ice. The left ski went first, screwing the aircraft round to face the opposite way. The way to Kulusuk. The way towards the crashed Cessna. Then we were lifting in slow motion – the Beaver threatening to go over on her back. But she didn't, she reached the near vertical before crashing noisily down. Right way up. Suddenly it was silent. Impossibly silent.

The scream on Hannah's lips never came. Instead she shivered, cleared her throat, and said nervously, 'What happened?'

'Lucky shot, at a guess.' I screwed my body round, wincing as my left arm banged against the controls. 'Akalise ...' She sat motionless. Eyes staring, unseeing. 'You okay?'

'I am all right ...'

I turned to the Eskimo. 'Che?'

208

He put his hand to his mouth. 'Okay,' he mumbled.

Akalise said in a frightened voice, 'Where are we ... what happened?'

'On Teardrop Glacier. Looks like whoever was doing the hunting in Narsarsuaq finally caught up with us.'

'That was the shooting?'

'Was. Their plane just crashed.'

'Crashed ... they are dead?'

'Perhaps ... I'll go and look.' I turned to Hannah. 'Stay with them, I won't be long.' I pulled on my mittens, took the shotgun from her lap and opened the cabin door.

'Then what?'

'I'll see if I can fix this pile of scrap metal.'

She looked out through the Perspex at the drunken angle of ice. 'You're not proposing to try flying out of here!'

'Well I'm sure as hell not going to leave it. I own it, remember.' I lowered myself down on to the glacier. 'Back in ten minutes.' Hannah nodded uncertainly as I turned and picked my way over the uneven surface. Perhaps she was right, I thought. Perhaps it was crazy to even contemplate taking off from this. Perhaps the damage was too much. I glanced back. One quick possessive glance, hoping to see her as she had been at Gander. Squat, serviceable and shining in the morning sun. All I saw was a crooked, damaged hulk. Someone else who might not have a future.

I approached the wrecked Cessna with caution, fanning the spread of broken wings and fuselage with the shotgun. It looked non-survivable, but then I had seen a few of those in Nam, and drunk a beer with the pilot an hour later. My foot scuttled a bent aileron noisily over the ice. I flinched at the sudden noise, silently swore at my carelessness, and slowed to a near standstill. Nothing moved, nothing jumped up. I saw the bodies as I approached the twisted cockpit. Or at least what was left of bodies, unrecognizable, brains spilling out over the smashed dials. My eyes went down to the twisted controls that were embedded in what had been a man's stomach. Entrails crawled like frozen worms down the black metal tubing. That was when I realized the black metal

209

tubing wasn't a part of the aircraft but the mangled remains of an M-60 sub-machine gun … and that was when I also realized that the mangled mess of broken bones and torn flesh was only one man. Only one … the other …

My thinking never got any further. The heavy click of a rifle bolt echoed down the glacier, turning my feet to lead and my heart to stone. Somewhere in the back of my head was a sick, uncomfortable feeling. A premonition of death.

A voice suddenly barked, 'Drop the gun, Spence!'

The shotgun fell instantly from my hands and clattered noisily to my feet. But it hadn't been the command. It had been the voice which had issued the command. The Canadian-accented voice I had known for seven years. I turned slowly and looked across the crumpled fuselage. O'Shaughnessy moved silently forward from a hollow at the side of the glacier.

'You look surprised,' he said, inching his way towards the wreck. When I didn't answer, he snapped, 'Get away from the gun.' I shuffled slowly back and watched him move in and pick it up. He hurled it the dozen yards or so over the edge of the glacier.

I said, 'So it was you flying this thing?'

'It was me.'

I half smiled. 'You know how long you'd have lasted in Nam with those kind of battle tactics …'

He sneered. 'Still good enough to get you.'

'Lucky shot.'

O'Shaughnessy gave an ironical little laugh. 'They all count, I'd say … like the one in your shoulder.' He looked quickly to his right. Towards the Beaver. 'Who else is in the plane?'

'One male, two females.'

'Any guns?'

I remembered the Browning Hi-power, its clip empty. I'd stowed it in the door pocket earlier that morning. 'Only the shotgun, the one you just threw over the edge.'

'We'll see,' he said disbelievingly.

'So how did you find out about this?'

'The gold, you mean?'

'The missing planes.'

'Long-time legend. Heard about it some time after the war ... a lot of pilots used to talk about it in those days.'

'But no one ever bothered to come and look for them?'

'In this place? Impossible.'

'So why now?'

'Scarth. The guy who bailed you out in Frobisher ... then I was talking to Pete LeFrance and found out Scarth had bought off your job. Bit more checking and I discovered you were in Gander preparing to come up here ... had to be the gold, didn't it? And I figured any man who was going to that kind of trouble must have found out where it was.'

'But how did you know the exact location?'

O'Shaughnessy waved the rifle barrel towards the Cessna's cockpit. 'I employed some help. That's what's left of him.'

'From Narsarsuaq?'

'Bluie West One as it was called in the war.'

'Kolb ... the police sergeant?"

O'Shaughnessy gave a mean laugh. 'A Husky ... you gotta be kidding. No, I employed somebody with brains, name of Thiessen. He was an inspector over at Bluie.'

'Thiessen?' I said incredulously. 'Why would he want to get involved with you?'

'No money, and shortly no job. How does that sound for starters?'

I shrugged my shoulders heavily. 'Yeah ... it figures. So how did you come across him?'

'The trip you did for me to Narsarsuaq, remember?'

'So?'

'So, Jack Lovatt mentioned the missing planes to me. Course I thought nothing of it at the time ... but once Scarth appeared on the scene and then hearing you were down in Gander I reckoned there had to be more to it all than just the old story.'

'And after that?'

211

'I flew over to Narsarsuaq, and as luck would have it bumped into Thiessen. He didn't tell you he was being kicked out, I guess.'

'Not directly, but I had the feeling the Greenlanders didn't want the Danes any more ... not after Independence.'

'Scraelings,' O'Shaughnessy remarked. 'They're not called Greenlanders ... Scraelings.'

I laughed. 'Since when did you call them anything but Huskies, you one-eyed bastard ... or does the promise of a fortune in gold change things?'

O'Shaughnessy said meanly, 'Don't push it, Spence ... I'm the one with the gun, just remember that.'

'I'll remember,' I said quietly. 'And while I'm doing that you remember what I said to you back in Frobisher ...'

'You'll be singing a different tune when I'm through with you,' he said vehemently. 'Now move.'

'Where to?'

'To your plane; where else?' Then as an afterthought he added, 'How bad is it ... flyable?'

'Haven't had time to check.'

O'Shaughnessy laughed drily. 'You got the time now, Spence ... let's go.'

We were halfway towards the Beaver when he said, 'You found the gold, I take it?'

I kept shuffling forward at the same pace. 'No, can't say we did.'

'Still up at the camp on the snowfield then?'

'There's nothing there either ... except the crashed planes and, if you believe in it, a few Greenland ghosts.'

'Stop!' he screamed. I stopped.

O'Shaughnessy came nearer; I could hear his rough breathing rattling in his throat. 'You're telling me you found the planes and not the gold, is that it?'

'Something along those lines, yes.'

'You're lying, Spence.' The voice was sharper now. 'I'll talk to Scarth about it.'

'You'll have a job,' I said quietly. 'He's back there on the ice desert. Dead.'

There was a short, uncertain silence. 'So who's in the plane with you?'

'Scarth's secretary, Hannah Dawson. An old Eskimo who took the supplies up to the snowfield by sled, and Akalise Palmarsson.'

'Palmarsson ... the wife of the guy from Narsarsuaq, you mean?'

And that was the link. Then I knew how Palmarsson had been killed. 'The guy you murdered, you mean?'

'Thiessen, not me,' O'Shaughnessy said harshly.

'Same difference. Don't tell me how it happened, let me see if I can guess. You go to Narsarsuaq, find Thiessen is out for revenge against a country to which he had given most of his working life. You then find the man with the information is none other than Palmarsson the weather man. So between you, you cook up a plan, to get the information and then get rid of him. Only thing is, you need a suspect. You leave that to Thiessen, of course. Leave him to do the dirty work ... except neither of you were expecting me to go back to Narsarsuaq, were you? And that almost spoiled everything ...'

'Almost, but didn't, Spence. Thiessen was on the radio to me that day. He'd got to Palmarsson before you, got the information you were supposed to get. After that we just brought everything forward, that's all.'

'And put the blame on some innocent old Eskimo guy

Another dry laugh. 'From what I heard they were about to pin it on you.'

'But you wanted everyone, didn't you? So you arranged for someone to fix the ferry system on the Beaver.'

'Yeah, we figured you found out. Checked up with the US Air Force at Sondrestromfjord, they said a Beaver had gone down with a fuel problem, but then he'd sorted it out and continued to Kulusuk.'

'I'm surprised you didn't come out earlier.'

'No rush ... it's been around for forty years, another few days wasn't going to hurt. And why the hell would we want to do all the legwork?'

'There's still no gold,' I said.

'How many planes did you find?'

'Three ... all empty.'

'You're lying.'

'That's what Scarth said.'

'And you killed him?'

'Yes.'

'Why?'

'AkalisePalmarsson. She's blind ... he was responsible.'

'What is she, Dane?'

'Half Eskimo.'

O'Shaughnessy laughed long and hard. 'What is it with you, Spence ... you flipped out or something? I mean what did these people ever do for you?' He laughed again. 'Jesus, I just don't believe it ...'

The laughter died after a while and he prodded me sharply with the rifle. 'Move, you crazy bastard ... let's get over to that plane.'

Two hours later I was ready to start the engine. Hannah was at the back of the right wing strut and Che-mang-nek on the opposite side. Ahead of the nose O'Shaughnessy held the muzzle of the rifle at Akalise's head. The only serious damage the sub-machine gun had inflicted was a shattered fuel pipe, and all that had taken was a bit of salvage work on the crashed Cessna to find a suitable replacement. With that complete I had set to work and removed the right ski; the left had detached itself on landing. After that O'Shaughnessy had made a thorough search of the aircraft and found the Browning. After finding it was unloaded he had thrown it as far as he could back up the glacier. Now, if I could get the engine started, I was going to taxi down to the end of the glacier. The last fifty yards were reasonably smooth. Smooth enough, but never long enough to afford even a short-field take-off. The only way was to hope to pick up sufficient speed to launch the Beaver out from the icefall. The 2,000-foot drop would hopefully be enough to pick up flying speed and therefore control. There would be no second chance.

The engine caught at the second attempt, and settled into a lumpy tick-over. I advanced the throttle until the wheels broke from the ice, then jabbed the brakes to arrest the sudden acceleration. Ten minutes later the aircraft was in position. That was when O'Shaughnessy signalled me to cut the engine.

'What now?' I said, ducking under the strut.

O'Shaughnessy pondered the question for a moment. 'Now I want the truth about the gold.'

'I already told you.'

'And this Husky here told me the same story.' He jerked Akalise around savagely. I took a step forward. 'Don't try it, Spence ... one more move and she's dead.' He turned towards Hannah. 'You,' he snapped. 'What do you know about the gold?'

Hannah gave him a black look. 'Spence has told you the truth ... perhaps it doesn't exist.'

'Oh it exists all right ... it exists.' He turned back to me. 'You said earlier that the sack of bone and rags over there brought your supplies up to the snowfield.' His one good eye glared fleetingly at Che-mang-nek.

'His name's Che-mang-nek.'

'His name's animal, now just shut up and listen. You said he took the supplies to the snowfield, yes or no.'

'Yes.'

'How did you find the exact location of the crashed planes?'

'We searched.'

'Garbage you searched. Without knowing the exact area you'd have been there until the fires of hell had frozen over ... did he lead you to them?'

'I told you we searched ... Erik Palmarsson gave us a rough location and we took it from there.'

O'Shaughnessy's one good eye looked crazed. He placed the muzzle of the rifle beneath Akalise's chin and gently lifted it, until her head was pushed back as far as it would go. 'Erik Palmarsson gave you nothing, you lying bastard, we got to him first, remember. And even if he did, you would have known that rough location was about the size of downtown Montreal. So we try again. Did he lead you to them ... yes or no.'

215

'Yes ... he led us there.'

O'Shaughnessy eased the rifle back down. 'So he knows where the gold is,' he said simply.

'The planes were empty, I've already told you that.'

'I'm not talking about the planes, Spence, I'm talking about the gold. How did he know where to locate the planes?'

'There were Eskimos here at the end of the war. They saw it happen. I imagine the location is known to most.'

'Was he here at the end of the war?'

'How the hell should I know?'

'Ask him.'

I turned to Che-mang-nek. 'How long,' I said. 'How long have you been at Big Gunn?'

He gave me a thousand-yard stare. The kind of look I had seen in the eyes of fatigued pilots after the battle. I repeated the question. 'Long time ... many years,' he said, as his eyes refocused on mine.

'The crashed planes ... did you see them go down?'

For a moment he seemed to be considering the question, then the eyes went totally blank and moved away to some fixed point in space. 'You're wasting your time,' I said, turning back to O'Shaughnessy. 'He's an old man. I doubt he even remembers half of what happened last week.'

'He remembers all right. You said the planes were empty. No pilots either?'

'No.'

'So. The Eskimos saw the planes go down and went up to find them. How long would that take?'

'Three days providing the weather was okay.'

'And there's your answer. By the time they got to the pilots they would have found a bunch of frozen corpses. And Huskies being Huskies and not wanting to be plagued by the spirits of the dead they would have taken them away and buried them.'

'It's possible,' I conceded.

'Of course it's possible. And if they did that what about the gold?'

'Buried it with them, you mean?'

'If they figured it would speed the souls off to their happy hunting ground, why not?'

Hannah, who had been listening intently, said suddenly, 'You mean they're buried up on the snowfield ... near the planes?'

O'Shaughnessy looked at her for a moment. 'No. Bears and foxes can dig up snow. Have to be rocks ... a tomb.' He turned to me. 'Ask him again. This time tell him the woman here walks off the edge of the icefall if I don't get the right answer.'

I moved over to Che-mang-nek. In his eyes there was a look of uncertainty.

Speaking with slow precision I said, 'Where did you bury the dead pilots? It is important ... Akalise will die if you do not tell me.'

He thought the question over carefully, as if torn between two loyalties: one to his fear, the other to his people. In his eyes the pieces of memory slipped silently into place. 'They are not far,' he said hesitantly.

I said, 'How far?'

The Eskimo lifted a hand and pointed towards the steep trail that descended to the rolling tundra thousands of feet below. The trail he and Akalise would have fought their way up to take the supplies to the snowfield.

'All of them?' I said in disbelief.

'All of them.'

I turned to O'Shaughnessy. 'He says the pilots are buried down that pass somewhere.'

'Tell him if he's lying I will shoot the Eskimo woman. Make sure he understands.' There was a cold, controlled anger in his voice.

I turned to Che-mang-nek, 'You understand?'

His watery eyes smiled sadly. 'Yes ... I understand. They are there.'

'He's telling the truth,'i said to O'Shaughnessy.

'Good. In that case you can tell him to take us there. Both of you and the Dawson woman will lead the way. I'll follow with the Husky.'

Che-mang-nek said quietly, 'It is not good ... the *tarneqs* ... the spirits ...' His eyes were pleading when he added, 'You understand!'

I understood all right. Enough to know the reason for the cold sweat shining on his face. Enough to know his smell was more than body odour. It was fear. Fear of disturbing the dead.

'We leave Che-mang-nek here,' I said, facing O'Shaughnessy.

'Like hell we do.'

'He won't go. Eskimo taboo. Start disturbing the resting place of the dead and you join them a lot sooner than you intended.'

'I know all about that, Spence. Look, I'll give you two minutes to convince him otherwise, then your Mrs Palmarsson goes over the end of the glacier.'

Two minutes wasn't enough to persuade Che-mang-nek to break with a few thousand years of tradition, but it was enough to quietly convince him that by starting the journey we would at least have bought the time to try to turn the tables on the man with the red hair. We started the descent sixty seconds later.

It was, at first glance, an impossible journey. A rough granite path covered with ice, its width no more than that of a sled. Initially it dropped steeply; a narrow funnel between the mountain's Pre-Cambrian granite and the awe-inspiring curve of ice – a mammoth frozen waterfall caught in full flood. Then, further on, the path began to curve gently left; the incline became less formidable. But then it needed to be, because now the right edge of the trail fell sharply away. One slip and you would fall as much as two thousand feet before hitting the bottom. And I had thought Che-mang-nek was responsible for losing the supplies on his journey to the snowfield. Now I knew that the journey itself held more danger than anything I had ever experienced in the air.

I glanced back towards O'Shaughnessy and Akalise. They were a good twenty yards behind. 'Where is the place?' I whispered urgently to Che-mang-nek.

He stopped and without turning said, 'It is ahead on the left ... the opening.'

'Can we go in?'

'I cannot go in!'

218

'You've got to … it's our only chance.'

He shuffled on. 'The place is fifty paces into cave,' he pointed down and back under the path. 'You understand?'

'Fifty paces. Got it.'

The opening was almost the size of a normal doorway, and it led back under the icebound pathway to a cave beneath the glacier. We were now juggling to keep our feet on the smooth ice. One slip was all it needed.

A sudden gust of wind forced me to press hard against the icy granite, before it whistled eerily through the funnel. I stopped and turned back. 'This is the place,' I shouted.

O'Shaughnessy called back, 'Where? I can't see anything.'

'Entrance to a cave!'

'Wait there,' he ordered, easing Akalise ahead of him down the icy path.

'Be careful,' I yelled, 'it's slippery.'

O'Shaughnessy said something I didn't catch, and Akalise pressed her back against the mountain wall; left hand clawing, feet shuffling, inching her way slowly towards us.

I was crouched in the doorway, waiting. Watching for an opportunity to grab the gun. It didn't come. O'Shaughnessy was too canny for that. He stopped a couple of arm's lengths away.

'How far inside?' he asked.

'About fifty paces according to Che-mang-nek.'

'What about light … have you got a torch?'

'No.'

Che-mang-nek turned to me and said, 'It is light… there is no problem … many windows.'

'There's your answer,' I said. 'Natural light.'

'Okay, you and the Eskimo and the Dawson woman go in slowly. No tricks, Spence, remember I've got Mrs Palmarsson.'

'No tricks … but Che-mang-nek waits here at the entrance.'

'Like hell he does. He goes with us.'

'He won't, it's against his beliefs. The only way you'll get him to go is to shoot him and you might only get off one shot.'

O'Shaughnessy sneered. 'I doubt that, Spence ... you know what kinda gun this is?' He held the rifle out to one side of Akalise. Black barrel, varnished stock and a long curved banana clip.

'Probably know more about them than you do. Our guys had them in Nam. M14 automatic.'

'Exactly,' O'Shaughnessy said with some satisfaction. 'An automatic. Which means the second shot won't be too far behind the first.'

'He still won't go.'

'That's up to you, Spence. Either you take him with you or we have a few dead bodies around here.'

There was a momentary pause as the wind moaned coldly through the funnel and I weighed up the pros and cons and found they were all working for O'Shaughnessy. I explained it all to Che-mang-nek. That he was dead either way. The gun or the spirits, and at least this way he might get back to see his son before the *tarneqs* wreaked their revenge. In those fleeting seconds of explanation he became the oldest and saddest man I have ever seen in my life. There were tears in the yellowed eyes as he nodded mute acceptance and we moved through the doorway of ice.

It was unbelievable, heart-stopping, breathtaking, a vast underground cathedral carved from ice. But it was more than that. More than magnificent pillars reaching up to the latticed dome; it was carefully spaced Norman window arches spilling light in criss-crossing searchlights, blue and green and amber reflections, a thousand stalactites hanging with the majesty of jewelled chandeliers. It also had that chilling feeling of not belonging. To the living at least.

'Which way?' O'Shaughnessy's voice echoed harshly.

I looked at Che-mang-nek. He pointed, powerless to speak. I started walking, Hannah by my side, counting off the paces; passing through the borrowed light of a thousand suns as it bounced through a million prisms of clear white ice.

It took forty of my paces, but then I figured Che-mang-nek, being a smaller man, would have made it fifty. And there it was. A twenty-foot-high pyramid of granite.

'Move ten paces further, Spence, and don't turn around.'

'You'll never pull that down by yourself. It's frozen solid.'

'I'll manage ... just do as I say.'

I moved ten yards further and stopped. 'I think you can forget that, O'Shaughnessy.'

I heard the footsteps scraping slowly across the ice. Then the gasps.

'What are they?' Hannah said in a small voice.

'At a guess I'd say Patterson's Volunteers.' We all moved as if of one mind. Slowly, disbelievingly, towards the neat row of roughly made wooden coffins. The top of each was weighed down with enough large rocks to fulfil the old Eskimo belief that the ghosts should be kept quiet. Kept bound to their burial place. I passed quietly down the line, feeling the same strange reverence that churches and funerals bring. I counted as I went. Fifteen coffins. Fifteen men who had once belonged in the war-torn skies of Europe. Fifteen coffins that should have been sixteen.

'There's only fifteen,' I said to Che-mang-nek. 'Where is the other?'

He didn't answer. The spirits had his tongue. Or was it just *the* spirit? The spirit of the sixteenth pilot. The one they had never found, and boxed, and weighted. The one of which they were all afraid.

'How about under the granite?' Hannah said in a hushed whisper.

I looked back at the pyramid. 'The American of fifteen summers,' I said.

'How do you know?'

'Just guessing ... more evil in a body taken over by the *tarneqs*, therefore more rocks to keep the evil imprisoned.'

O'Shaughnessy said cynically, 'Quite the authority, eh Spence?' Then to Hannah, 'To listen to him, Miss Dawson, you'd think that the North is one big romantic legend.'

Hannah said cuttingly, 'And you know differently, right?'

'I've got nearly forty years of knowing differently,' he spat. 'And believe me there's no romance. Just a pagan hell full of pagan savages.' His good eye ran quickly over the line of coffins before he snapped, 'Now move over to the right ... all of you.'

I moved and almost fell over the crates. I looked down in disbelief before I heard Hannah's startled voice say, 'The gold ... that's it ... it's got to be!'

O'Shaughnessy moved in, his mouth falling open. 'Get back,' he shouted suddenly. 'All of you get back.'

We all moved away, as he pushed Akalise roughly ahead of him.

O'Shaughnessy dropped down to one knee and reached out for the first crate. He tugged one-handedly for a while, then gave up. 'Okay Spence, I want you to come slowly forward and open this box. The other two don't move or they're dead.'

I looked down at Hannah. 'Keep Che by your side, don't for Christ's sake let him start wandering off.'

Her face twitched nervously as she placed a restraining hand on the old man's shoulder.

I moved forward as O'Shaughnessy pulled Akalise ten paces back.

'They're frozen solid,' I said, looking up from the first crate.

'Of course they're frozen solid. What do you expect after practically forty years?'

'So how the hell do you expect me to open them without a lever of some kind?'

'Quit stalling, Spence, and get on with it.'

'Impossible.'

'Try, for Christ's sake; you won't know until you do.'

It took me about five minutes of kicking, before I knew I was wasting my time. 'No good,' I said breathlessly. 'Need to get the tools down from the aircraft.'

'Damn the tools, Spence, you're almost there.'

'I'm almost nowhere,' I snorted. 'Why don't you use the butt of the rifle on it?'

'Sure ... sure,' O'Shaughnessy said mockingly. 'And while I'm sweating my guts out you jump me.' He laughed, before adding menacingly, 'Keep trying or I'll use the rifle ... on her.' He jabbed the barrel into Akalise's body and she let out a startled cry of pain.

'Try that once more and I'll ...'

'You'll what? You'll damn well do as I say ... now open that bloody box.'

Another ten minutes of kicking, of loud ringing echoes, had moved the lid marginally. Then pausing to get my breath I spread my arms in a final gesture and stab-kicked at the narrow opening. Then again and again. At the third kick the lid came loose.

'That's enough,' O'Shaughnessy said. 'Now back off.' I retreated slowly, until I bumped into Hannah. Her eyes were transfixed on the box. As if they could already see the gold gleaming dull yellow in the light of a thousand suns.

Using Akalise as a shield O'Shaughnessy moved forward and dropped to one knee, then with his left hand he slowly lifted the lid. It creaked noisily back, the groan of metal being amplified twenty times in the tall cathedral. The noise continued for a short while after the lid had stopped moving. And out of the new-found silence I watched O'Shaughnessy's left hand lifting the ingot. Saw the grin spread across his unhealthy, colourless face.

'God Almighty!' he whispered. 'Will you look at that!'

Hannah, eyes still wide and staring, moved involuntarily forward, as if drawn by some great invisible magnet.

O'Shaughnessy, startled by the sudden noise, dropped the ingot and swung the rifle towards her. 'Keep her back, Spence ... I'm warning you. One false move.'

I reached out and grabbed Hannah's arm. Her body resisted for a moment as if it had no control over the magnetic attraction. 'For God's sake, Hannah!'

She stopped pulling then, her arm going quite limp. 'Rollo was right, then!' she said. 'How much did he say ... fifteen million?'

O'Shaughnessy stared at me in disbelief. 'Fifteen million? ... fifteen million dollars?'

I said, 'That's what he reckoned.'

'How did he arrive at that?'

'Said something about each aircraft carrying fifteen ingots; which made a total of two hundred and forty in all. So if there's two hundred and forty there and his current gold prices were correct ...'

O'Shaughnessy glanced briefly down, before pulling first one ingot out and then another. 'Fifteen!' he said at last. His sweat-glistening face turned quickly to the crates. 'And sixteen of these.' More disbelief. 'Now how in hell did he know that?'

'He was in England during the war ... at a place called Debden. He was there when the planes left.'

'That figures ... he didn't seem the kind of guy who would go off on a wild-goose chase.'

'Of course,' I said, 'have you ever considered it might be government property?'

O'Shaughnessy laughed. 'No ... and I'm not about to. More important matters to consider, the first of which is how fast we can get this lot up to the plane.'

'How do you propose to do that?' I said.

'Drag them.'

'They're frozen into the ice. You'd need a pickaxe to free them.'

'Or a blowlamp,' O'Shaughnessy offered. 'And I saw one of those in the back of the Beaver, didn't I?'

And he had. The one I had used that morning to try to force a little heat into the cylinders before starting. What was perhaps more ironic, was that it had been O'Shaughnessy who years ago had showed me all the ways to get engines started in the arctic. Now without realizing it he could be offering me a way out.

'Well?' he said impatiently.

I nodded. 'Yes.'

'So what the hell you waiting for?' he snapped. 'You've got ten minutes.'

'Me? You want me to go? How do you know I won't take the plane?'

He fixed me with his one good eye. Still big, round and staring. Still unusually green. Still colder than an arctic winter. 'You won't take any plane, Spence. I've known you for too long. Too many years. You'll be back ... the one-man crusade of the North out to save the Eskimo race.' He laughed. The old familiar, cynical laugh. 'Now get going. As I said before you've got ten minutes ... after that you're going to be down on your head count.'

'Ten minutes isn't long enough. It took us practically that long to get down.'

'Fifteen then ... and don't go getting any ideas about fixing the plane. You're flying it out.'

I reached the Beaver in a little over five minutes. I didn't doubt O'Shaughnessy's threat but I still had to try. I wouldn't get a second chance. I started to run, slipping and skidding over the rough ice, jolting my injured arm until the pain became practically unbearable. I gritted my teeth and kept going. Running back to where the plane had been after landing. Running, gasping for breath, trying desperately to remember in which direction O'Shaughnessy had thrown the empty Browning. Four minutes later, in a cold sweat, I was scouring the ice. No good, no damn good. I couldn't see it. I had to get back. Swearing violently I turned towards the distant Beaver and broke into a run – and kicked the Browning on the second step. Relief flooded through me as I scooped it up with my right hand and made a headlong dash for the aircraft.

Two minutes left. I took the 'last man's bullet' from my trouser pocket and fumbled it into the breech. Safety – checked off. Then thrusting it into my parka pocket I snatched up the blowtorch and ran towards the funnel. I almost came to grief in those last seconds, losing my footing completely and sliding uncontrollably down the steep pass. Ten feet further there would have been no supporting wall on my right. Nothing but a sheer drop. My right wrist saved me, wrapping itself around a sharp protrusion of ice, jerking me to a wrenching halt. Then I was shuffling, back pressed against the mountain, wind blowing hard and cold straining to lift me off my feet. Dizziness was sweeping over me as I fell into the cave entrance and literally crawled around the semi-circular path which led back to the underground cathedral. I swore at the new-found pain in my right arm. The one I needed to use the Browning with any chance of accuracy.

O'Shaughnessy's voice boomed out, 'Is that you Spence?'

I dragged myself up from my knees, fighting to get my breath, fighting the pain which seemed to be engulfing my very body. 'It's me,' I said exhaustedly.

'Spence?'

'It's me,' I shouted, making my way unsteadily towards the voice.

'What the hell took you so long?' O'Shaughnessy said as I reached the gathering.

'Couldn't find this damn thing.'

He grunted disapprovingly. 'Let's move it then ... lot of work to do before dark.'

An hour later we had succeeded in getting one crate to the top of the glacier. Hannah was now using the blowtorch to free the second one, for which Che-mang-nek and I would again provide the sweated labour. Only problem was it wasn't going to work. On two counts. The two I put to O'Shaughnessy as I collapsed exhausted against the row of coffins. First we were going to run out of daylight before we could man-handle the total consignment up to the plane. And secondly and more importantly I had estimated the weight of the gold at something like one and a half tons. The Beaver might take a third of that under normal conditions. But not with fifty yards of rough ice the only runway.

'Figured that out for myself,' O'Shaughnessy remarked. 'We make four runs. Four crates a run.'

'Four runs ... four runs? You're crazy. There's about fifty yards of usable runway on that ice. On take-off you fall off the edge and hope a violent updraught doesn't smash you into the icefall before you've picked up sufficient flying speed to clear it. Okay, so assuming you can pull that off; how the hell do you propose to get back in?'

'Fly up to the lip of the glacier and stall it on to the end ... it should stop in fifty yards.'

'Not with a bloody tailwind it won't.'

O'Shaughnessy thought about that for a moment. 'Is that ferry tank full?'

'Yes.'

'How much ... fifty-five gallons?'

'More or less.'

226

'Okay, that should do the trick. We drain it off, then after you're airborne I'll spread the gas down the rough ice and fire it. That should smooth out another fifty yards.'

'After I'm airborne ... and where the hell am I going exactly?'

'Unload the gold down at the Kulusuk strip.'

'It won't work. What about the crates? We need floor spreaders to prevent them dropping out the bottom of the fuselage; not forgetting high-breaking-strain nylon rope for tying down ... and we don't have either.'

'Thought of that too. There's some stuff on the crashed Cessna we can salvage.'

'Okay. Supposing and I mean supposing, that all of that works out; we're still going to run out of daylight before we even get all these crates to the top. And if somebody doesn't do an engine run pretty shortly no one goes anywhere ... and without supplies of any description how long do you think we'll last?'

O'Shaughnessy lowered the rifle fractionally, as if suddenly realizing that without his help, it wasn't going to work, at least not the way he had planned it. The barrel of the M14 dropped another inch and another, as I worked the mitten off my right hand and reached slowly for my pocket. Reached the Browning, gripped it tight and slipped my finger over the trigger. O'Shaughnessy's rifle dropped another two inches. Akalise was still close but to one side. At ten feet I couldn't miss. I gave myself a count of three, one ... two ... three ... and summoned all my strength.

The blow lamp spluttered and died on three. The soft roaring background, which I'd somehow forgotten existed, was now an oppressive ear-tingling silence. One that had caught everyone unawares. O'Shaughnessy included. The M14 dropped completely away from Akalise. And then the gun was out of my pocket swinging two-handedly on to its target. The long yellowish flame spitting out of the barrel added the final touch of drama to the ear-shattering explosion as the Browning kicked violently in my hands, sending a searing pain through my shoulders. O'Shaughnessy seemed to lift off the ground in slow motion, the result of a high-velocity 9-mm bullet slamming into his body. He fell back still gripping the M14. Fell, finger closing on the trigger, sending one long fearful burst into the high ceiling of ice.

By the time I had Akalise safely in my arms the bullets had stopped; the criss-crossing searchlights of arctic sun were filled now with hanging smoke and the unmistakable smell of cordite. My ears were still ringing as, arm around Akalise's shoulder, I turned to Hannah. Hannah who was pressed tightly to the floor, arms over her head. A little way beyond her Che-mang-nek had fallen back against the pyramid of granite. I took a step forward, and stopped. Stopped and listened – and heard the deep, far-away rumbling.

The sound you hear at a subway station when a train's approaching. A sound growing steadily louder. A sound that sends shockwaves through the soles of your feet. I looked up at where the bullets from O'Shaughnessy's rifle had impacted. The stalactites seemed to be swinging, catching and turning the borrowed light in long sweeping movements. The rumbling sound grew louder. Now the entire floor was rolling; pitching and rolling and breaking up.

'It's going,' I screamed at Hannah. 'Move ... move.'

She dragged herself drunkenly to her feet. 'What about the gold ...' her eyes searched past me to the crates. 'We can't leave it here.'

'Forget it... take Che ... up to the plane.'

'Like hell,' she screamed. 'Leave all this ... you've got to be crazy.'

'There's nothing we can do,' I reasoned, 'besides there's still the crate up by the aircraft.'

She looked at me with uncertainty in her eyes. 'You'll take it then ... what about the floor spreaders ... you said it would go through the floor without those!'

'We'll unpack the crate ... lay the ingots over the cabin floor.'

'And that will be all right?'

'Maybe ... maybe not. We'll take a chance.' It was a lie, of course. For a start there was no way I was going to attempt to haul that much extra weight off the end of the glacier, especially unsecured. Unsecured loads can shift. And if that one shifted back towards the tail we would all be dead. But it was the only way she would leave this place. And if she didn't leave now she would be buried alive.

The noise grew painfully louder as Hannah's expression slowly changed to one of resignation, then turning reluctantly she pushed the old man towards the cave entrance. All around was the thunderous groan and grind of breaking ice.

By the time I emerged with Akalise, Hannah and Che had already made the funnel; the old Eskimo dragging his injured leg, Hannah pushing him ahead of her. The seconds dragged agonizingly on as I eased Akalise along the ledge. Up ahead the narrow pass was bowing and bending, rising and falling, threatening with every move to disintegrate. Far below, in the bowels of the glacier, the thunder rumbled angrily on. We slipped and skidded to the top a long time later. Too long for me. The last fifty yards leading to the icefall would already have started to break away, taking the Beaver with them.

But they hadn't; by some miracle they were still intact, the aircraft rocking slightly as the ice began breaking up in fast-snaking fissures. Che-mang-nek was standing under the wing hanging on to the strut; Hannah struggling with the crate of gold – trying unsuccessfully to pull about two hundred and fifty pounds of dead weight towards the cockpit.

'Leave it, Hannah,' I yelled, 'for Christ's sake leave it.' I rushed past her and pushed Che towards the step. Once he was inside the doorway I thrust Akalise up towards him, waited until they were both safely inside the cabin, and went back to Hannah. 'It's too late ... we've got to go.'

She looked up at me, face glistening with sweat. 'You promised,' she cried. 'You bastard ... you promised ...'

'There's no time ... if we don't get off now we never will.'

'I'm not leaving it,' she shouted defiantly. 'Not after all this ... not after all we've been through.'

'You'll have to ... we haven't the time. Look at the ice for Christ's sake, it's breaking up.'

'Help me then,' she pleaded, 'help me ... I'm not going without it.'

I grabbed her by the shoulders and started pulling her towards the cockpit. 'It's too heavy ... we'll never make it.'

229

Her eyes came round and met mine, and perhaps for the first time I saw the real Hannah Dawson. The one who had once been beautiful and vibrant and young. The one who was now wrinkled and dirty and old. The Hannah Dawson who had been with Scarth too long. The Hannah Dawson whose life could only be gauged by an endless supply of American dollars. 'Just a few bars then,' she whimpered. 'Something ... anything!'

I was on the point of giving in, of helping her to grab a few ingots, when the fifty-yard stretch of ice, our makeshift runway, dropped violently. A sickening explosion of splintering ice. Ice swallowing ice. A sudden frightening jolt which knocked us both off our feet. I scrambled up and grabbed the Beaver's left wing strut as it lurched forward. When I looked back I saw Hannah fighting to hold the crate as it slid down the section of ice that was still falling. 'Leave it ... leave it ... Hannah ...' I watched as the crevasse paralleling the wing tip opened even further, watched as two feet became three, and three became four ... and four become one final running chance. Watched and shouted and shouted, until I knew my words were wasted. I doubt she even heard.

The last thing I saw of Hannah Dawson was a wild-eyed frenzy as she tried to push almost twice her own weight in gold uphill towards the Beaver. Uphill on slippery ice. Uphill without a hope in hell of ever succeeding. Then, mouth opened wide in shocked disbelief, she and the heavy metal crate plunged over the edge of the icefall. If there was a scream I never heard it.

I turned and pulled myself one-handedly up to the cockpit. Then I was knocking on switches and pressing the starter button down. Don't fail me now ... for God's sake not now. The propeller jerked as the engine belched, fired, missed, and fired again. It caught on the final turn, adding its own roar to that of the breaking ice. Holding it on the brakes, I slammed the throttle fully open. The Pratt and Whitney coughed and backfired, protesting at going to full power from cold – after two or three seconds it got the idea and caught on all seven cylinders.

The Beaver snatched forward and dropped again, further this time. The glacier was going! I released the brakes and felt the wheels free themselves from the ice. Then we were running. Slowly bumping our way over what had been the last fifty yards of relatively smooth surface. Only now it was ridged and pitted, tearing itself apart even as we began our take-off run. Come on, you ugly bitch ... more speed ... more speed. The ASI flickered idly through thirty miles an hour as the tail lifted off. Hold it down Spence, hold it down. Don't try to pull it off, you'll never make it. Not enough speed. Ahead of me the glacier suddenly disappeared beneath the Pratt and Whitney's cowling. All that was left was the open sky, blue and cold and cloudless. I pushed the throttle harder forward, seeking something which didn't exist – more power – we were already on the stops. Thirty-five ... thirty-eight ... forty ... the speed inched agonizingly on. It was the stuff of which bad dreams are made: trying to outrun the darkly cloaked figure – the ultimate evil – and finding your feet have turned to lead.

The Beaver lurched dramatically as we rolled off the top of the icefall and hit the violent updraught. Stall ... stall ... stall ... we were stalling. And I was too late. Before I realized, the left wing snapped viciously down and flicked the aircraft into a fully developed spin. I sat dumbfounded, watching the world cartwheeling beyond the windshield. Sun and shadows rushing across the instrument panel with a mesmerizing strobe effect. Everything was white ... a thousand shades of white.

Spinning ... you're spinning, Spence. Instruments ... go to instruments! My eyes refocused on the blind-flying panel, isolating the turn and slip indicator. We were spinning to the left. To the left! Get it out... get it out. My brain struggled with the recovery action. Full opposite rudder; my right foot kicked the pedal to the stops. Pause. Control column forward until spin stops; my hands pushed forward ... now centralize controls ... wings level ... pull out of dive. Pull out, damn you! The airspeed was winding up to the red line – the never-exceed speed. My ears were filled with the scream of airflow as I began to pull; the sweat streaming into my eyes; the pain in my left shoulder transferring itself throughout my entire body. That was when the sweat in my eyes turned to a wavering mist, taking away the unbearable hurt. Taking it away for ever. And in the wavering mist there was peace. A place without pain. Jesus God! Not that ... not again ... not that.

I slammed my left shoulder into the door frame with all the strength I could muster, opening up the wound, opening the floodgates of pain once again. The pain that was exploding inside my head. A hurt that reached out to my hands and pulled the control column back, and back, and back.

We levelled off at about three hundred feet. Somewhere ahead, not too far through wispy veils of blowing snow, the Kulusuk airstrip. I don't remember the landing. I don't even remember seeing the runway. But somewhere deep inside there was a faded memory of opening the cabin door, and missing the step completely. I ended up face down in the snow, as the mists rolled welcomingly in. In the distance I imagined I heard a pack of huskies whining to be fed.

Weak sunlight was filtering through a window somewhere. I tried to move to see exactly where that window was and found I couldn't. Couldn't bend my back. I lay still and waited for my eyes to focus on the ceiling above. White wooden planks, yellowing with age, plugged with moss to keep the arctic out and the warmth in. Roughly hewn cross beams. There was also a fireplace. Not that I could see it; but I could hear the flames crackling; feel the comfortable warmth. But it still didn't tell me where I was. I couldn't remember. Nothing, but the memory of dogs whining in the distance.

The dogs! And before that the plane. The pictures came slowly back. The unbelievable cathedral of ice under Teardrop Glacier; the coffins of a group of happy warriors, ones who had belonged to that other war – a war they had won; the shattering explosions of O'Shaughnessy's rifle, the prelude to an icequake which had destroyed a million years of natural beauty. Hannah Dawson, with her own brand of beauty. A beauty which had been ravaged by the cold, jealous winds of the north. A beauty, which in the end had been nothing but a veneer. And beneath that veneer a Scarth disciple believing that wealth was the only answer in a crumbling, decadent world. And now it was gone for ever. Fifteen million dollars, trapped for all time beneath the ice.

Then the take-off. Falling off a glass mountain, spinning, somehow pulling out. Somehow reaching the airstrip at Kulusuk ... and the dogs. What came after the dogs?

As if in answer a door creaked open, letting in a flurry of snow and wind. I listened as it gently closed. A moment of silence, then soft, shuffling footsteps. Stopping and starting again. Akalise suddenly appeared, feeling her way down the side of the bed. 'Spence ...' Her voice was barely a whisper. 'Are you awake?'

I reached out, burning pain running across my back, and took her hand. 'Yes ... I'm awake.' I pulled her gently down until she was sitting on the bed beside me. 'Where am I?'

'Big Gunn ... you collapsed yesterday, after we landed at Kulusuk.'

'Yesterday! I've slept since yesterday?'

'Exhaustion. And the old woman who cleaned your wound said it was very bad. She said it would take a long time to heal.'

'The way it feels at this moment, I think she's got it about right. Anyway, how did we get here?'

'Che-mang-nek's son ... his sled.'

I squeezed her hand. 'Thank God for fathers who have sons,' I said. 'And Che-mang-nek, he is all right?'

'I am afraid,' she said sadly, 'he is dying.'

'Dying ...'

'He is an old man, Spence. I think it was all too much for him ... the body can only take so much.'

'Yes ... I suppose so,' I replied, thinking of the spirits, and an old man's acceptance of the inevitable.

'He wants to see you,' she said suddenly.

'To see me ... now?'

'No. Not today. When you are better I will take you to him.'

'What was the reason? Did he say?'

233

'He said Patterson, that is all.'

'I thought that was finished with ... after all the gold *has* gone now, hasn't it?'

She smiled. 'Yes ... it has gone now. I am glad for that.' She paused. 'But you will see him ...'

'Yes ... I will see him.'

We were silent for a while then. Holding hands, dreaming dreams, remembering how we had hoped it would be, and now finding it had all somehow changed. It seemed a long time later when I said, 'Your eyes ... they are still the same?'

She turned her face towards me. Towards the voice. 'Yes. They are still the same.'

'It might not be permanent,' I said. 'There could be a cure ... surgery ...'

She stiffened slightly, then said hesitantly, ' You think so?'

'I'll take you to the States ... when I'm better. We'll find a way.'

'And if there is no cure. If I am to stay always blind. What then?'

I stared at the ceiling. At and beyond. A long way beyond. What then indeed? She was telling me that my world was not her world. That arctic flowers do not bloom without snow. But I was all she had now; me and an aging father who would be unable to support her. And my world was the sky; hunting and trapping might work for a while but then the withdrawal pains would start in earnest, the need to return to the jealous mistress who had controlled my life for all of my adult years. 'You know something,' I said, stumbling to find the words. 'When I first saw you ... and ever since, I wanted to tell you ... wanted to tell you something I'm not very good at ...'

She reached out and put her hand to my face, working the fingers gently down to my lips. 'Not now, Spence ... not now.'

'Why? Why not now?'

A small sad smile touched her lips. 'I think it would hurt too much.'

'But if you know ... how can it hurt any more?'

She lowered her head to the pillow and lay beside me. 'Now we are two worlds apart,' she said gently. 'First the world of the Eskimo and now this place of darkness ... I thought we might overcome the first ...

234

but now ...' The words trailed away, as quietly as a distant breeze dusting snow across the ice.

I turned my head painfully towards her and saw the tears on her cheeks. 'If you think you can get rid of me that easily,' I said, 'you're very much mistaken.'

She said, 'And what does that mean?'

'It means you're coming back with me. We'll find a way ... I promise you that.'

Later, when the tears had dried and the short arctic day had faded from the window, I told her about O'Shaughnessy. How he had known of the Greenland legend. How he had recruited Thiessen. How Thiessen, under O'Shaughnessy's radio instructions, had sabotaged the ferry-tank system on the Beaver. How they had later found out from the USAF at Sondrestromfjord that we had survived and continued to Kulusuk.

'And Erik?' she had said quietly.

'Thiessen again.'

She had been silent then, remembering a husband. A drunk perhaps, but still a husband.

After the silence, the afterthought. 'What about Kavavouk ... they said he was the one?'

'If they hadn't caught him before Thiessen disappeared, they may think differently.'

'And if they had?'

'I don't know ... I just don't know.'

It was the next morning when she came to take me to Che-mang-nek. Dressing proved to be the problem. One which I finally solved by rolling off the side of the bed and dropping to the floor; there, trying to bend my back as little as possible, I struggled into my trousers. Pulling on my stockings was even harder, even more painful; so that when I was done I was soaked in sweat. I lay back on the wooden floor and let my heart rate return to something like normal before dragging myself to my feet and tugging the thick sweater over my head.

Akalise found my boots and helped me into them. Then wrapping the parka around my shoulders I followed her slowly to the door.

We found Che-mang-nek in the third cabin, the one that lay on the rough icy track of road. I counted five buildings in all, scattered in no apparent order. All had rooftops heavy with settled snow, and chimneys pluming grey smoke in long unbroken lines through a windless morning. I breathed deeply of the cold dry air. It was good to be up and about, even though I would probably regret it later when I would pay in pain for a few minutes' premature exercise. The third cabin, the one which Akalise had directed me to, had two kayaks near the doorway. Elsewhere, a number of scattered oil drums, empty cans and bottles – a sign in the Eskimo world that the owner of this house was prosperous.

Che-mang-neks's son was sitting at his father's bedside as I steered Akalise into the small untidy room. It was darkly lit with the flickering flame of a little stone lamp. In this uncertain light the ceiling and the walls of the cabin became vague forms, dissolving the confines of the room as if the darkness of night had already entered. The two windows were cloaked with what seemed to be patched-up sail cloth. A smell of rancid sweat, rotting grease and bad alcohol hit me as I went through the doorway. But it wasn't that smell which halted me in my tracks. It was the other unmistakable stench; the sickening, slightly sweet smell of rotting flesh. Gangrene!

Che said something to the boy who stood up stiffly, nodded brief acknowledgement at me, and hurried out of the door. The old man then beckoned me to the chairs beside the bed. I sat Akalise in one and lowered myself painfully to the other.

'The leg,' I said at length. 'It gives you much pain?'

He shook his head. 'It burns badly ... but soon no more.' He lifted his left hand feebly as if waving the matter aside. 'The planes ... I wanted to tell you about the man Patterson.'

'You did know him, then?'

The partially hooded eyes glittered for a moment. Two wine-yellow topaz stones set in a dried-up, weather beaten face which had known the arctic for too many years. His mouth for once was clearly visible;

236

thin lips turned down at the corners. I imagined I saw the teeth move as he went to speak. Imagined, but in the semi-darkness, couldn't be sure. The first time I had met this man I had sensed he was different, unlike any other Eskimo I had ever known. And then I had it. The anomaly. Something which Jack Davidson had told me back in Frobisher many years ago. 'In a way,' Che was saying, 'in a way ... I knew him ... he was I think a good man ... if not ... if not ... mistaken ...' He thought about the last word, face screwed up in concentration.

I said, 'Mistaken, or misguided?'

'Misguided ... that is the word. Yes, he was a misguided man ... at first, but not afterwards. Afterwards I think he ... knew ... yes, he did know.'

'Was he the sixteenth man?' I asked. 'The one for whom there was no burial place?'

'Yes ... he was the one.'

'So what happened to him, where did he go ... or was he the American who came back after the war? The one who searched for the planes for fifteen years?'

'No ... no. The man who came ... that man was a stranger ... we know not who that man was.'

'So where is Patterson? Did he go back home ... to America?'

The yellowed eyes smiled sadly. 'America ... no he would not go back there. He said after what had happened he would never go back. No ... he went away one night... here at Big Gunn ... he was never seen again.'

I rubbed my face tiredly and moved my body to ease the crippling pain. 'Why?' I said. 'Why didn't he go back?'

'Why? The gold ... the gold killed them all. It came from Füssen in Germany ... the American zone ...'

'Patterson told you this?' I said with some surprise.

The old man's head rolled towards me. 'End of the war ... there was place called ... called ... Neun ... Neunschwantstein castle ... on border of Liechtenstein ...'

I stopped him. 'You're telling me the gold came from there?'

He nodded weakly. 'That was what I heard.'

'You're wrong,' I said. 'My father was in the American sector at the end of the war. Neunschwantstein was Goering's hiding place for looted art treasures ... not gold.'

'And ... Jewish gold,' Che-mang-nek whispered.

'Jewish gold?' I said disbelievingly. 'Jewish gold ... he told you that?'

'The Dachau gold, Patterson said ... you know of that place?'

'Yes, I know of it. It was a concentration camp, a place where Jews were murdered in tens of thousands.'

'Then that was the place ... I think there were others ... others of these camps ... there were more?'

'Yes,' I tried to think. 'Auschwitz was one ... Belsen was another. There were more.'

'It ... they ... they had gold teeth ... the Jewish?'

'Gold fillings ... yes, perhaps.'

'He was right then ... he said all the gold ... rings ... other things like that... and the gold from teeth were also in the boxes ... not much he said ... only a part of all of it...'

'Did he tell you how he got the gold?'

'Yes ... he told me ... but it is long years ... some names I forget. He was in Germany when war finished ... they were sent to airfield at Füssen ... before American soldiers came they had found the gold ...'

'And decided to take it?' I said.

Che-mang-nek's head rolled back, his eyes, caught in sudden pain, stared unseeingly at the moss-plugged ceiling. He didn't answer. But I could see the logic in what he was saying. An American squadron in Germany at the end of the war. Around them everything in a state of total confusion. Traditional government broken down and as yet not replaced by a system from the occupying armies. Indeed if he was right, Patterson and his men had arrived before the main force, Patterson being a colonel, and finding out that Neunschwantstein castle had been the headquarters of Hitler's chief of air staff, Goering, would have made a beeline for the place. Air Force types on both sides had a similar passion for comfortable messing facilities. Perhaps a castle was a touch ostentatious, but it was there. The best rooming house in town. And if

238

they didn't grab it first, the Army sure as hell would when they arrived.

And when they arrived at that castle, and started poking around, checking for snipers or booby traps – or pretty fräuleins the enemy had left behind – they stumbled across the treasure. The treasure my father had often told me about when he had returned from Germany.

But Patterson would have looked at the hoard in amazement: jewellery, porcelain, paintings, pistols ... and gold bullion. The easiest to move and sell had to be the gold. And faced with a fortune so immense, with no one looking on, they had to be tempted, had to move it down to the airstrip. The rear cockpit fuel-tank area would have provided the perfect place to store the gold. Reinforced flooring to take the weight of the fuel ... or gold. And who was going to find out? No one at first. Then perhaps when they flew to Debden, England on the long haul home, one of the pilots, overtaken by the euphoria of being a rich man, said a few words too many in a heavy drinking session one night. Perhaps a mechanic even took a look, and thinking it was some type of official secret operation didn't say a word. Except to a corporal in Supply. A corporal named Rollo Scarth.

I looked down at Che-mang-nek. 'What happened after they got to Greenland ... what went wrong?'

His head turned slowly towards me, the lines of pain around his mouth deepening into crevices. 'They had winter in the sky ... you understand this?'

I nodded. 'Go on.'

'The winter in the sky was very bad ... they found difficulty in finding way ... he said ... he said compasses ... you know of these?'

'Yes, I know of them.' He didn't have to say any more. Now I knew. Had heard the story what could have been a thousand times from a thousand different pilots. The story of the heavy iron-ore deposits in an undefined area of southern Greenland. An area which plays havoc with your compass system should you fly over it. And flying in bad weather the squadron would have been following a leader who was unwittingly following an ever-changing compass heading. How long that lasted would be hard to say; certainly as long as the flight to

Narsarsuaq should have taken. And then, still out of radio range, and with no beacon indications, Patterson would have begun to realize he had a major problem. Some time after that the squadron would have popped out into a patch of relatively clearer sky and observed the sun in a place it should never have been. A rough fix in time and space telling them they were hopelessly and irretrievably lost. Because by then it was too late. By then their fuel state had gone to critical. By then they had to find a place to land.

A deceptively cruel hand was dealt a short while later. A flat snowfield and enough visibility to pull off the impossible; and after that a hopeless task ... the long walk to civilization. Except all points of the compass would have offered only one unknown chance – the Eskimo settlement at Big Gunn. With odds of 360 to one and without local knowledge and arctic survival gear they were never even offered a fair crack of the whip. Except for Patterson. Patterson who somehow survived long enough to be picked up by the Eskimo search party. Then, having been nursed back to health, the sickening realization, the voices in his head, waking from feverish sleep with shaking hands, watching the planes crash as though it had happened only a few minutes earlier. The sick return of panic as he witnessed the unrelenting arctic still for all time, and the brief laughter of survival. Witnessed his men slipping, one by one, into that semi-comatose state – that deep unnatural sleep from which they would never wake. They were all dead now, all gone. The flock he had shepherded for so long through the bitter conflict of war. The flock which had relied on his judgement, his leadership. The flock he had destroyed.

Perhaps after that he found God, the God who lives in all deserts, the God who had entered his mind. The God who offered to absolve him of his sins. Thus, against a backdrop of darkening skies and icy winds sweeping down from the convulsive folds of Archaean mountains, Patterson realized he could never go back to his own country. That would mean a court of enquiry, a court which could uncover the hidden truth. Could persecute fifteen men even in death. And they must never be branded as criminals. They must always be remembered as heroes – every last one.

Then came the night he decided to take the long walk – accept the alternative offered by his new-found God. And that was what happened. The sixteenth pilot. The *tarneq* who haunted the snowfields beyond the mountains. Patterson.

I looked down at Che-mang-nek. 'I think I understand now,' I said. 'Perhaps in the end he did the right thing.'

The old man reached out and touched my hand. 'You ... you think so?'

'He didn't desert his men. did he? Yes I think so.'

Che-mang-nek smiled briefly. 'A safe journey to your world ... Captain.'

I struggled to my feet and felt strangely sad. I had no words to offer him on the journey to his.

Two nights later Che-mang-nek died. It was the night of the storm. The night he left his son sleeping peacefully and dragged his wretched body out into the snow. Perhaps by then the pain had become too much. Perhaps he still wanted to feel he had some control over his destiny. Or perhaps the ghosts had beckoned once too often from their dark underworld.

His son found him the following morning, sitting half a dozen paces from the cabin door, frozen to death. His hands were clasped together as if in silent prayer. O'Shaughnessy would have had a few ironical words to say over that final act. Something about a pagan soul not being worth the saving. They buried him that same day, on a piece of unconsecrated ground high above the village. His final resting place was beneath a cairn of rocks. With him they buried the last chance I had of finding out who he really was. The way he had spoken through almost closed lips, the unconscious act of lifting his hand to his mouth when he did speak. And what, in that ill-lit, wretched little room, I had imagined to be a set of loosely fitting false teeth. And as Jack Davidson had told me a long time ago, no true Eskimo wears false teeth, for the simple reason of bad spirits entering the head.

Akalise came to the cabin after the burial, the new-found happiness we seemed to have discovered suddenly gone. I put it down to Che's death and tried to cheer her up with talk of our journey to America.

It was when the small talk had eventually dried up that she said, 'I am bad company for you, I think.'

'You're never that,' I said. 'We've had a rough time. It gets better from here on. I promise.'

'Yes. Perhaps you are right.' She reached for my hand. 'The arm is not so painful today?'

'No, not so painful.'

'So soon it will be time to go?'

'Soon, yes. Providing of course I can get the plane started.'

'Agaguk told me he has covered the engine. Also the battery ... I explained how you always took it out when we were on the snowfield.'

'Agaguk?'

'Che-mang-nek's son.'

'Ah ... and he knows that much about aircraft?'

'Yes. His father always took him to Kulusuk; every time a plane came he would show the boy as much as he could. Or ask the pilot to.'

'What will happen to him now?' I said. 'Now he has no father.'

'You know of that ... yes I suppose you do.'

I knew all right. Knew that a boy of about fourteen would have to fend for himself. Hunt for his own food. Survive a lot of hard winters. And if he beat the odds he would eventually take a wife and have children, and the familiar pattern would begin all over again. 'Will he be all right? Is he a good enough hunter?'

Akalise shrugged. 'I don't know. Perhaps he will continue to run the airstrip, if the officials in Godthaab approve it. We will know this summer, when the ship comes, we will use their radio.'

'And if not?'

'If not, he must do like all men.'

'I hope he gets the planes,' I said. 'I think he would be all right with that job.'

'Yes ... and now I go to see ...' She checked herself. 'To talk to my father and then I will see the old woman about your food. You have not eaten since this morning.'

'You said yesterday your father would come and see me ... when?'

Akalise lowered her head. 'I only said that because you kept asking about him. I am afraid he is not happy for me. He wants me to stay ... especially now.'

'Because of the eyes, you mean?'

'Yes.'

'But you're not staying ...'

The head stayed down. 'I don't know, Spence. Everything is so different now.'

'Different ... since when different?'

'Che-mang-nek ... he asked me yesterday to look after his son. To make sure he was all right ... to take care of him.'

'Didn't you say you were going away?'

'How could I ... he was dying. It is a very hard thing to do. Then of course there is my father.'

'But haven't you told him it is possible to perhaps have an operation to restore your sight?'

'He is an old man, Spence ... much like Che-mang-nek was. Their ways are the old ways. They do not like change ... they do not understand it. For them the loss of eyes is punishment forgoing against the *tarneqs*. If there is to be a cure it will be foreseen by the shaman.'

'I appreciate that, but couldn't you explain to your father that our magic is just as strong as his? Besides, it is *your* life.'

'And it was he who gave me life ... I think I owe him something; especially now, when his life is nearly over.'

I think I knew at that moment. Realized she would never leave this place; not even for the one chance of restoring her sight. Here she had always belonged; here she would always stay. There, in a new world, she would slowly wither and die.

That was when I said, 'I will stay also.'

Her head jerked up. 'Stay ... here?'

'Yes, here.'

Her hand drifted up, searching for my face. Then the fingers were tracing the outline of forehead, nose and lips. Stopping at the lips. 'It is not your land, Luke Spence. You understand many ways of the North, more than any white man I have ever known, but your roots are somewhere else ...'

'Roots can be transplanted.'

Her unseeing eyes touched momentarily on mine. 'In your land, Spence ... only in your land. Here they would not survive.'

'You're asking me to go?'

Her fingers pressed my lips to silence. 'A few weeks ... perhaps a month. A month that some people never find.'

I was nearly halfway. Halfway it seemed to everywhere. To Iceland. To civilization. To the seaplane company in Key West. Halfway nearer the old ending, and halfway further away from what had seemed a new beginning. Halfway, when the battered Pratt and Whitney surged and almost died, and then for some unknown miraculous reason picked up again. There was a moment of heightened perception, of gut reaction when you know you're going in, and then normality. The ferry pilot's normality of noisy engines, empty skies and no one to talk to. Except yourself. And then you're trying to think back, trying to remember every item you checked. Trying to find the one you may have forgotten. The one that is going to catch you out ... to kill you. After ten minutes of nursing a broken old lady, of sweet-talking her into giving you another two hours of her valuable time, you have convinced yourself it was all in the mind. After ten more minutes you have convinced yourself it never happened.

It was after that ten minutes that I wound the h.f. aerial out and called Iceland Radio. They passed me the weather; the same sort of stuff I was running into now at 3,000 feet, dirty frontal clouds that ran all the way down to the unloved waters of the Denmark Strait. It wasn't going to get much better, the controller said, but the Loftleider guys were still getting in and out. I said something like they would, wouldn't they, being the pro's they were. There was a touch of Icelandic pride in his voice when he asked me to give a call at X-Ray 120 – a small black triangle on a NAT-1 radio navigation chart – a reporting point 120 miles northwest of Keflavik. I said I would and left the aerial trailing. And sat and ran my eyes back and forth across the instruments. Crystal balls staring into the past, the womb of past that was my future. Watched the crystal balls until I saw a face. The face of Lieutenant Anderson, the fresh-faced young man who was acting as my defence counsel.

He gave me a nervous smile. 'Of course if it hadn't been for those war correspondents picking it up, the generals would have dropped the entire matter.'

'But they haven't,' I replied. 'So why not get on with it?'

He cleared his throat as if to hide some embarrassment. 'Colonel Marlin was your flight commander, correct?'

'You know damn well he was ...'

A pained expression filled Anderson's eyes. 'Just yes or no will suffice, Captain.'

'Yes.'

'Good. So, we must be explicit on his orders.' He consulted a sheaf of papers on his desk. 'You said that you took down the coordinates for the strike from the FAC, the Forward Air Controller, that is, because Colonel Marlin was experiencing radio problems at that time.' Anderson read silently for a moment before adding, 'And that was when Colonel Marlin signalled to you to take over as leader ... you are absolutely sure that is what happened?'

'Yes,' I said, edging my chair around to get more of the fan's cooling air, 'I'm sure.'

Lieutenant Anderson's eyes went back to the papers. 'But you stated at your debriefing that the colonel was in two-way radio contact with you on your return to base. Don't you find that odd, Captain?'

'Odd? In what way odd?'

Anderson smiled thinly. 'Well, if his radio was functioning normally on your return, why not on the way out?'

'Ask the technicians, that's their department ... perhaps it was after he got hit by the ground fire over Thud Ridge ... the sudden jolt could have remade a faulty contact.'

Anderson clasped his hands together in prayer-like posture and stared briefly towards the ceiling, searching perhaps for divine guidance. 'Perhaps ... perhaps. But surely the colonel should have aborted the mission at the first indication of problems?'

'Aborted the mission,' I said, almost laughing at the thought. 'Over some partially unserviceable radio gear ... tell that to the generals and see how far you get.' Anderson took a handkerchief from his pocket and dabbed in gentlemanly fashion at the sweat on his face. 'I see what you're getting at,' I continued. 'All I've got to do is say Harry was the leader on the strike, that he ordered me in on the wrong target, that he was responsible, and I'm off the hook ... better still he zapped the village ... nothing to do with me. Is that about it?'

Anderson looked crestfallen. Anderson of two months service in Vietnam. Anderson the Bostonian gentleman sent off to some dirty little war, full of dirty little people, hoping he was going to wake up amidst silk sheets and find it was all a bad dream. But bad dream or not, Anderson wasn't asking me to perjure myself, he was simply trying to get at the truth. 'It's a very serious matter, Captain ... do you realize how serious?'

'Yes ... I realize.' I also realize that I failed to check Harry's wheels were down and locked. I also realize Harry saved my neck on at least three occasions. I also realize that Harry had a devoted wife back home in the States. I also bloody realize that Harry isn't going back to her ... ever. And because of that she must never know. She must always believe that Harry was a hero ... because in the end his memory is all she has left.

'So you still wish to plead guilty?'

I looked at the young Lieutenant Anderson. Shirt still somehow immaculate in the oppressive, sticky heat; no sweat stains, everything around him neat and orderly. He couldn't have been that far behind me in age, but in years lived he was as much as a lifetime. 'Y'know something Lieutenant,' I said sadly, 'this time I have the feeling we're on the losing team ...'

246

It had been after the thirty days Akalise had given me, that I found myself at the Kulusuk airstrip. Thirty days of healing a wounded shoulder. Thirty long winter nights of lying with her, holding her, making love to her, grabbing a handful of wishes. Wishes for a new ice age. One which would freeze time – would lock it, like the glaciers, into a million-year-old time capsule. Then towards the end the realization ... slowly unclenching the fingers, opening the hand, and finding it had been empty all along.

Now a month later I was working on the damaged Beaver, finding more problems than I had thought possible, the worst of which was the heavy wrinkling of skin on the engine firewall. The result of the heavy landing on the glacier. The heavy landing which meant I now had a slightly out of line engine. As Reykjavik was the nearest engineering base I would have to try for there. Perhaps I could even rent some hangar space and do most of the work myself. I still had Scarth's six-thousand-dollar bankroll, but when it comes to unbending bent aeroplanes six thousand dollars doesn't go very far.

Satisfied that structurally she might last for a four-hour flight, I went to work constructing a hot box over the Beaver's engine. Forty-eight hours of thawing frozen metal and I was ready to install the battery. The battery that Agaguk had thoughtfully removed and kept wrapped in furs.

And then the moment of swinging myself up to the cockpit and running through the pre-start checks. The old familiar seat, the old familiar switches and levers and instruments. The old familiar prayers as I hit the starter button and saw the prop turn and kick. And again ... and again. At the fourth try she caught, the Pratt and Whitney rumbling noisily into life. I ran it for a good thirty minutes, making sure the temperatures and pressures remained stable, then I put the boy Agaguk into the pilot's seat, and went off to find Akalise.

She was by the cabin, face turned towards the lumpy tick-over sound of the radial engine. 'It is all right?' she said.

I took her hands in mine. 'Yes ... it is all right.'

'Now ... now is the time?'

I pulled her gently towards me. 'Yes. Now is the time.'

'You will be all right... the plane will be safe?'

I looked down at the strained but beautiful face. 'It will be safe.'

She flung herself hard against me then, pressing her face beyond mine, hiding the tears. The tears, which drowned the words I wanted to hear. The words she never said.

It was a long time later that the parting was over and she pulled away from me. 'There is something, something I forgot,' she reached into her pocket. 'Che-mang-nek, he left this for you before he died. It was with a note for his son. The note said you would understand.' She handed me a small rectangular piece of metal. It was old and worn, corroded with the passage of time. I turned it to the sunlight and tried to read what was left of the faint inscription.

Akalise said, 'What is it?'

'A military dog tag ... something you wear around your neck. It carries your name and number.'

'There is a name?'

My eyes went back to the tag, and then across to the Beaver with the smiling Eskimo boy at the controls. 'No ... no name. Worn away. Perhaps it was from one of the dead pilots, the ones who were buried up at Teardrop Glacier ... Che might have thought it was of some importance.'

'And it is not?'

'No,' I said quietly. 'Not any more.'

Young Lieutenant Anderson's face had long since faded, the crystal balls becoming a junk-shop assortment of instruments once more. Instruments that all pointed the way to some far-off beacon. The first landfall on the long journey back. Behind me, lost behind thickening cloud, seven years or a lifetime of something no one would understand. I took the dog tag from my pocket. The dog tag with the indecipherable serial number, but which still carried the name *Patterson George*. My thinking being to open the storm window and consign the truth, whatever it may have been, to the unloved waters of the Denmark Strait.

Instead I found myself thinking of the beautiful, gentle Akalise, the woman I loved. A woman facing a hard almost impossible life by herself. And what was waiting for me in Florida that I didn't have in Greenland? A different family of ghosts to accompany me down the remaining years, nothing more.

I checked the instruments and the fuel gauge, and slowly commenced a gentle right turn. Once established on track I put out a radio call to Iceland Radio advising of my return to Kulusuk.

Naturally, they requested a reason for the diversion, but I already had that covered. I reported an area of thicker cloud and severe icing conditions. Given the majority of light aircraft are not equipped with wing de-icing systems, my decision would be seen as good airmanship.

Somewhere ahead, in a hopefully still sunny morning lay my final landfall, and if she would have me, a wife. I glanced once more at the dog tag in my hand, before slipping it back into my pocket, realising the colonel and his ghosts of Greenland, who had; as a code of honour, adopted the motto of the legendary USMC – *Semper Fidelis*; known me better than I knew myself.

Glossary

Anabatic wind: A warm wind which blows up a steep slope or mountain side, driven by heating of the slope through insolation. It is also known as an upslope flow. These winds typically occur during the daytime in calm sunny weather.

ASI: air speed indicator.

Aurora: Aurora Borealis.

B-17: The Boeing B-17 Flying Fortress was a four-engined heavy bomber developed in the 1930's for the United States Army Air Corps (USAAC).

Compass swing: The process of swinging and compensating an aircraft compass by determining and reducing the deviation coefficients and recording the residual deviations; resulting in a small deviation correction card being attached to the compass showing corrections to be applied to specific compass headings, *e.g. For East (090 degrees) – fly 092 degrees.*

DEW Line: The Distant Early Warning Line was a series of 63 radar stations across the arctic, from Alaska through Canada over Greenland to Iceland; installed in the 1950's. The Americans conceived that the DEW line could detect enemy bombers coming over the North Pole that could threaten North American cities.

FAA: Federal Aviation Administration, a governmental body of the United States with powers to regulate all aspects of civil aviation in that nation as well as over its surrounding international waters.

F-4: United States McDonnell Douglas F-4 Phantom is a tandem two-seat, twin-engine, all- weather, long-range supersonic jet interceptor and fighter-bomber. It was used, amongst other conflicts, in the Viet Nam War.

HF radio: High Frequency radio used for long-range communications.

Kentucky painkiller: Military Slang for 'Kentucky Bourbon'.

Katabatic wind: Katabatic winds are downslope winds created when the mountain surface is colder than the surrounding air, usually at night. A katabatic wind is a drainage wind, a wind that carries high density air from a higher elevation down a slope under the force of gravity. Such winds are sometimes called fall winds; the spelling catabatic winds is also used.

Labatt: Canadian beer.

Medevac: Medical Evacuation.

MiG: Russian Aircraft Corporation jet fighter, commonly known as Mikoyan and MiG – as used by the North Vietnamese in the Vietnam War.

Notams: Notice to Airmen is a notice filed with an aviation authority to alert aircraft pilots of potential hazards along a route of flight or at a location that could affect the safety of the flight.

P-51: The North American P-51 Mustang was a long range, single seat fighter and fighter-bomber used during WWII and the Korean war.

Rationeringsark: Ration cards were issued in Greenland in an attempt to restrict the use of alcohol by the Greenland Inuits from the early 1950's to the 1980's, which was at that time twice the consumption rate of Denmark. In the 1980's the ration cards were withdrawn as consumption rates declined.

RCMP: Royal Canadian Mounted Police, colloquially known as the 'Mounties'.

Semper Fidelius: Latin Motto of the legendary USMC (United States Marine Corps), which translates as: 'Always Faithful'.

Synoptic chart: A map that summarises atmospheric conditions (temperature, wind speed and direction, atmospheric pressure and cloud coverage) over a wide area at a given time.

Shaman: A person regarded as having access to, and influence in, the world of good and evil spirits, especially among some people of Northern Asia and North America and Arctic regions.

Tarneq: In Inuit culture, the supernatural soul which leaves the body at death to travel to the Land of the Dead.

USMC: United States Marine Corps.

Acknowledgements

To the people of Greenland, for their kindness and generosity of spirit, and for once saving my life and that of my co-pilot, following a crash in a white-out near Narsarsuaq.

In a long flying career, the latter years being spent mainly as a ferry pilot – generally found operating the north Atlantic route, eastbound from Goose Bay to Narsarsuaq and Reykjavik and onward to Europe. Westbound, the opposite way. My log books record 183 trips east and west, usually solo, over those years. Those operations afforded me some of the most spectacular and magical vistas as well as truly memorable moments in a long and fortunate life.

Apart from the Inuits of Greenland, the Danish pilots and engineers and meteorologists working for Greenland Air, also became friends. Those who shared their stories of the real Greenland, when I was weathered-in at Narsarsuaq from time to time. It is those stories, those handed down tales of historical record of this vast frozen wilderness, that were used to weave the fabric of this ghost story. Naturally there was more to recount than can be covered in this volume; not least walking down to the local harbour on a day of gale force winds when flying was cancelled for the day and listening to the wind-song from the mountains; symphonic in its majesty – oft times reminiscent of stanzas from Sibelius' tone poems. So much so, that I was always surprised not to find a classical composer from civilisation, secretly recording nature's hauntingly beautiful music!

My grateful thanks to the nurse I have named Akalise in this story who patiently and skilfully stitched up my wounds following my crash and having no anaesthetic provided me with a bottle of scotch to ease the post-operative pain. To that dear lady, I hope your life continues long and happy.

As for the characters in this story, they *all* existed in one way or another in those far off days and in those latitudes, including (in my imagination) the ghosts.

John Templeton Smith
Gibraltar

Made in the USA
Coppell, TX
05 June 2021